TROUT FISHING FOR BODIES

BOOK TWO

THE BOB ROOSEVELT MYSTERY SERIES

by

Robert K. Swisher Jr.

OPEN TALON PRESS

OTHER PUBLISHED NOVELS BY ROBERT K. SWISHER JR.

Historical Fiction: Trade and E-book
Published by Sunstone Press
The Land
Fatal Destiny

Contemporary Western Fiction: Trade and E-book
PUBLISHED BY SUNSTONE PRESS
How Far the Mountain
The Last Narrow Gauge Train Robbery
The Last Day in Paradise
Love Lies Bleeding
The Man From the Mountain

Literary: Out of Print
Published by Samisdat Press - Canada
American Love Story

Young Adult: Trade Only
Published by Echo Press California
The Weaver
Published by Sunstone Press
Only Magic

Humor: E-book only
Conversations With the Golf God

Mystery Series: E-book and Trade
Bob Roosevelt Mystery Series – 4 novels

Contemporary Fiction: E-book only
Hope
A Circle Around Forever

Trade and E-book
Published by Open Talon Press
Vent
Grammar Nazis Are Not Always Rite, Right, Write
Vent Revisited
The Lonely Cowboy
How Bridge McCoy Learned to Say I Love you

Short stories and poetry in literary journals, articles in outdoor magazines. Reviews by Publishers Weekly, Best Sellers, Library Journal, and many others.

PUBLISHED BY
OPEN TALON PRESS

EDITORS: Sheila Awalt

COVER DESIGNER: Samantha Fury...Mike Nguyen
PRINT FORMAT: Samantha Fury

Library of Congress - In Publication Date

Swisher, Robert K, 1947 -
TROUT FISHING FOR BODIES: A novel / by Robert K. Swisher Jr.
Summary: mystery, humor, satire
ISBN is 978-0-9979096-6-1
LCN is 2020920312

DEDICATION

POOR LITTLE TROUT FISH
BRING ON THE BUTTER AND SKILLET

BUT PLEASE DEVELOPERS
LEAVE THE RIVER ALONE

TROUT FISHING FOR BODIES

BOOK TWO

TABLE OF CONTENTS

CHAPTER ONE
THIS AIN'T NO TROUT

I sighed deeply and felt the tension drain from my body like a highly overdue oil change. I was finally leaving the modern world behind, no petty crime, no murder, no private investigating. Matilda, my black 1966 Volkswagen bug, the only lady in my life I have been able to hang on to, putted contentedly south on Colorado Highway 285. There was not a house in sight. For the first time in many years I was not on a quest to find myself and a soul mate. I was on a quest to catch a trout - finding myself and a soul mate could come later. I had stopped in Denver and deposited $3,000 of the $5,000 I had made for solving a kidnapping and murder case in Iowa. After buying fishing and camping gear I still have $1,000 big ones in my pocket.

My Guardian Angel was in the back seat pretending he was sleeping. I know he was pretending because guardian angels don't sleep, but, he was doing a good job of it as he started snoring like a gorilla with adenoids. I looked at him through the rearview mirror and frowned.

My Guardian Angel was assigned to me when I was in Vietnam and saved my life many times both during and after the war. But my Guardian Angel is not a normal guardian angel. He is snide, sarcastic, and lecherous. He told me that by going against the grain of what most people think a guardian angel should be makes him an individual. He also thinks I am boring because I am moral and have made a vow to myself I will not sleep with a women unless I love her. If it was up to my Guardian Angel it would be against the law for women to wear clothes and be nothing more than sex objects. I am also the only person who can hear my Guardian Angel, besides talking way too much, he normally talks in a dull, bored, monotone with about as much emotion as a dead fish. When I do talk to him it is normally through my mind, which is a good thing, if not, people would think I talk to myself all the time. And, thank God, I am the only person who can see him - he is not a pleasing sight. He is a 14th century monk with a shaved head. He is 5'2" tall, in his early 60's and his body looks like an over inflated basketball. His eyes are tiny brown slits that show he is not to be trusted. His eyebrows are so bushy birds could nest in them. He has a splotchy, uneven beard, and his complexion is close to watery flour paste. He wears sandals with no socks and a knee length, stained, brown wool robe that exposes mats of black curly hair on his bowed legs. For many years he would not tell me his name saying it was none of my mortal business, but then in a weak moment, which we all seem to go through, he informed me his name was Wright, which is completely out of character, so I nicknamed him Pea Brain. A name he does not really like, but what the hell, I am his boss, and how many people in life like their boss? But, in an effort to be nice, I only call him Pea Brain when he peeves me off. I have also discovered he used to take money to forgive sins and slept with as many women as he could informing them he was a blessing from God. In a lame excuse he told me the Bishop made him do it.

“Pea Brain, wake up," I ordered him. The snoring was starting to bother me.

My Guardian Angel grunted a few times, scratched his belly, scratched a hairy leg, and climbed into the front seat like having to move hurt him. “Roosevelt, lost one who considers himself a private investigator, are you sure you want to go trout fishing?" my Guardian Angel asked in between fake yawns and giving me a look like I am dumber than a puffer fish.

"I didn't buy all this camping and fishing gear in Denver to play baseball," I said, giving him back his dumber than a puffer fish look.

"If you go fishing I have a strong feeling you are going to fish yourself right smack dab into a murder, more adultery than you can count, and a pornography ring that has no qualms about killing people," he warned me moving his bushy eyebrows up and down like exclamation marks.

"That's impossible," I said. "Trout don't murder each other, or commit adultery, they don't even get married, and they for sure don't need dirty movies to fight loneliness."

"I also think more than one person is going to try and kill you. I don't give you more than a five percent chance of surviving," my Guardian Angel said, but with very little foreboding in his voice.

My Guardian Angel has the tendency to lie so I do not always heed his advice and I ignored him.

"You remember my warnings and don't blame me when God asks you if I did a good job?" he said, then added with a big grin, "But looking on the bright side, if you get killed, God in all is wisdom might assign me to a female rock star."

"I hope he assigns you to a Tibetan Monk who doesn't smoke hash," I replied.

"Not funny," he said, but I could tell he was thinking over the possibility.

Rolling down the window I let the cool, early September air, blow through my long white hair and gazed at the distant mountains on the horizon that for some strange reason reminded me of the bellies of fat elephants. The mountains brought back memories of when I was a hippie and spent a lot of time walking, or riding horses, all around Platoro, Colorado while trying to find myself by inhaling anything that would burn - sadly, the only thing I discovered was disorientation. I no longer do anything that will alter my mind except beer.

"You should have never left the mountains," my Guardian Angel said longingly. "You were so much fun then, the little girls with no bras, free love, the parties, all the 'wows' and 'I can dig it' and 'groovy man' - those were the days. Now look at you, a long white haired sixty two-year-old private detective who is alone and lost."

"And if that isn't bad enough," I said. "I am saddled with a Guardian Angel who talks too much."

"You need me, oh ungrateful and non-advice taking one," he replied giving me the finger.

"Pea Brain, friends like you I don't need," I said and gave him the finger back.

“I am not a Pea Brain,” he said and looked away from me like his feelings were hurt.

What feelings? He might have been able to fool God into making him a guardian angel but I am not God and I have a feeling the only reason he protects me is because he has to.

Occasionally I passed a rutted dirt road that cut through the rolling, sagebrush-dotted grasslands. The only evidence that there was a house at the end of each road was the rusty mailbox nailed to the top of weathered cedar post. The mailboxes looked alone and reminded me of old people who had been abandoned by society and have lost all hope.

There were a few scattered cattle that seemed confused and were debating if they wanted to be turned into Big Mac's or Wendy's. In one field was a single Llama that was as out of place as a jackrabbit in New York City.

I went through the sleepy town of Antonito, Colorado, population 271 counting dogs. It was a mixture of beat up trailers that wanted to be someplace else, crumbling brown adobe houses with rusted tin roofs, a grocery store, a gas station, one stop sign, and a sign proclaiming they have a jail. Without jails towns aren't considered real towns anymore.

I turned west on Highway 17 and headed for the mountains, the vision of trout frying over an open fire in my mind. Within twenty minutes I had left the sagebrush and grassland behind and I was on a narrow and curving mountain road surrounded by pine and spruce trees. Rounding a bend in the road there was a Ranger Station with two new green trucks parked in front. It wasn't there the last time I visited the area.

"You still have time to change your mind," my Guardian Angel said. "I've heard there are some great bars in Durango and hundreds of rich single women who are aching to meet over the hill men like you."

“All you want to do is for me to get a woman in bed so you can watch,” I said.

“We all have our vices,” he replied with a twinkle in his eyes.

I passed a sign dotted with bullet holes, stating, '20 miles to Platoro'. I take it many modern hunters don't know what deer look like. I turned west off the pavement onto a dirt road. Surprisingly, just as I turned, a Sheriff's car stopped at the stop sign where the dirt road ran into the pavement. The Sheriff glanced at me, but seemed to be nervous and in a hurry, and turned towards Antonito. I figure the Sheriff was in his late 50's or early 60's. He was wearing a large black cowboy hat and had a matching handle bar moustache that was at least 4 inches long on each side.

"A modern Wild Bill Hickok," my Guardian Angel said disdainfully. He doesn't like any form of police officer. When he was alive he had a run in with one of the King's constables and it left a sour taste in his mouth. "I wonder if he plays a lot of poker on city time and plans on getting bushwhacked," he added, thumbing his nose at the Sheriff's car.

The Chama River paralleled the road. It was only about 30 feet across at its widest spot and in most places only a few feet deep, but, there are a few pools that are close to six feet deep. The water was crystal clear and has always put a picture in my mind of what liquid diamonds would look like. I thought about all the mayhem that had happened in my life and how the river had gone on its merry way filled with no cares or wants or needs. The thought made me feel old - old and insignificant - and yearn for a simple life.

"You are old and stupid, insignificant has nothing to do with it," my Guardian Angel said with as much sympathy as a chipmunk has for a sunflower seed. "And not living a simple life is your own fault, not anyone else's."

"Pea Brain, be nice. I'm on a vacation," I said firmly, the truth making me angry. I know my anger should have been directed at me not Pea Brain, but we all love our excuses in life.

"It won't be much of a vacation if you get killed," he said.

"Why is it most people look on the dark side of life?" I asked.

"I'm not people. I'm an angel," he said, like people shouldn't even be a word.

"You're not much of an angel," I said.

"Nothing is perfect, Roosevelt, and besides, I like the way I am," he said and winked at me.

A man winking at me has never been my cup of tea but I let it slide.

I drove by two log cabins about 500 yards from each other. Tall stacks of cut firewood were in the front yards and laundry was flapping happily in the wind outside both cabins. The second cabin had a satellite dish. I suppose the people were tired of looking at the stars at night. There was a wooden bridge that went over the river to get to the cabins.

About two miles further down the road, I drove by four new looking log cabins that were about 50 yards apart. I figured a rancher needed money and sold some of his land to a developer. I felt sorry for the rancher, but the cabins didn't disturb me. The cabin furthest from the road had a corral next to it. Two horses were contentedly chomping on hay.

"We could rent a cabin and then we wouldn't have to camp out," my Guardian Angel said giving me a pretty please look.

"What does it matter to you?" I said. "You don't have to sleep on the ground anyway?"

"Communing with nature to me would be a room with shag carpet that overlooked the mountains," he said.

A mile after the community of cabins, there was a small sign stating 'Rio Grande National Forest', from here on there would be no more vestiges of man, except forest service camping areas.

I relaxed more. I am a pilgrim returning to the woods. I am a lost and disillusioned member of society who is searching for a refuge and the truth.

"You're an idiot looking for yourself in all the wrong places, who does not know when to listen to his Guardian Angel, knowing I am God-driven to try and protect you," my Guardian Angel said with a pompous air like he was the Dean of Harvard whose mistress was an undergrad at Vassar.

"You truly think I should turn around?" I asked feeling slightly apprehensive.

"I don't talk like most of your kind merely to run my head and inflate my own ego," he said.

The ego bit I knew was a lie. My Guardian Angel is an ego freak - the hell with apprehension.

I drove on, pulled by the vision of trout and sleeping under the stars. I passed two unused camping areas, hoping nobody was using the one I wanted to camp at. The last time I was in the Platoro area there were only ten designated camping areas between the highway and Platoro. The camping areas are set at the beginning of trails that head back into the wilderness area.

To my relief the camping area was empty. The main reason I've always liked this camping area is that it is next to a stand of aspens.

The forest service had added a cinder block fire pit with a grill over the top. There was a level area to pitch a tent and an outhouse. Close to the outhouse was a green garbage can with its lid secured to it by a chain. I have never had the desire to steal a garbage can lid, but I suppose it takes all kinds. Not far away was a wooden corral hunters or campers used to keep their horses in before they trek into the wilderness. About thirty yards away was a footbridge over the river. It also marked the beginning of the wilderness area. There was no concrete anywhere. Maybe I should write the forest service a letter and tell them they should lay a small circle of concrete in all their remote camping areas so people from town would not go into shock and sue them for mental distress.

When I turned Matilda off I was awash in the sound of the river and the wind dancing through the leaves. In the distance a raven called. I got out of the car and looked at the swaying tops of the trees, the river, the clouds moving without purpose over the tops of the mountains, and I knew why the city is only good for politicians and private detectives. My Guardian Angel had a look on his face like this was the ugliest place he had ever seen either alive or dead.

It didn't take more than an hour to pitch my pop up tent, lay out my sleeping bag, set up my Coleman stove and lantern, put my canned goods, potatoes and onions, bacon and eggs, cooking utensils, cookies, candy bars and all the other necessary stuff into the tent. Modern man needs this much stuff when he is communing with nature. I took two cases of beer to the river and put them in the water - with a big rock on top of each case to make sure the current didn't carry them away. As well as I know trout don't like beer. They like all types of weird stuff but not beer.

I dragged dead aspen branches close to the fire pit. Camping without a fire is like a movie with no popcorn.

Overflowing with excitement, I put on my waders, fishing hat, light wool shirt, and hung my net from my side.

I had the fly rod ready to go and I was trying to decide what fly I wanted to use from the two dozen I'd bought. My flies normally hit the water with as much grace as a football player trying to dance on toe, and since it doesn't take any skill to cast one, I put on a small black Wooly Worm.

I was ready to catch a trout - but, bowing to my primitive side, I am not going to release it. I am going to fry him in bacon grease, heat a can of corn, and wash it all down with two or three or maybe six cold beers. I headed toward the river with no thought of being a famous private eye who had been on TV for fifteen minutes for solving a kidnapping in Florida. I felt better than I had in months. I have always been able to handle non-responsibility without burdening myself with guilt feelings.

"Roosevelt, please," my Guardian Angel pleaded, putting his hands together like he was praying. "Let me warn you one more time. I don't feel good about this. I have no doubt trout fishing is going to cause you nothing but grief."

For a brief moment I hesitated, my Guardian Angel pleading was completely out of character, but warning or no warning I am going fishing.

My Guardian Angel followed behind me shaking his head and muttering. The only words I could pick out were ‘stupid’ and ‘brain dead’.

At the head of the trail that runs beside the stream I stopped. Beside the trail were four freshly cut pine boughs stacked on top of each other - each was about three feet long. Seeing them puzzled me and for an instant made me feel paranoid.

"It is really getting bad when tree branches start bothering you," my Guardian Angel said. "You old hippies didn't inhale pine needles did you?"

I have had a few paranoid attacks in my life, but this one was ridiculous.

About fifty yards downstream from my camp I was about to make my first cast to a ripple behind a large moss covered boulder when I had a great realization - I hadn't bothered to buy a fishing license. Even in the boondocks I can't escape the ever-lengthening long arm of the law. I looked at the river. I looked at my wooly worm. I thought about how much the fine would be. With a flick of my wrist the fly pole arched and shot the wooly worm into the water. The wooly worm hit the water like a rock and any trout for two miles would high tale it for Kansas. I took my time and steadily fished downstream, but didn't have one strike. It was beginning to look like I was going to have corn with no fish but, I was so relaxed, it really didn't matter. It is the fishing that matters, not the catching.

"That is a feeble excuse for failure," my Guardian Angel frowned. "If fishermen really didn't care if they caught fish then they would take up hiking and not waste all that money on fishing equipment."

Why is it that the truth hurts more than lies?

I came around a small bend in the river and there was a pool over ten feet wide and twenty feet long. The water was so deep I couldn't see the bottom of the stream. A thick stand of red alders grew on the far side of the pool. There was no way there wasn't a trout waiting anxiously for my wooly worm in the deep swirling water. A skittish water spider darted away from me as I cast my wooly worm. My Guardian Angel leaned back against a tree with a worried look on his face - either that or he had an attack of gas.

Cast after cast invaded the pool with no trout. I decided to add weight to my line to sink the wooly worm deeper into the water. I attached two small lead split shots to the leader and plunked the wooly worm back into the water. It hadn't drifted more than two feet when suddenly my line stopped. I pulled back with enough force I could have set the hook in a shark's jaw.

The rod bowed fiercely, but there was no thrashing on the end of the line, disappointedly, only the steady pull of a snag. I don't think fried snag would taste good unless I was a vegetarian and into soggy tree bark. Although, in some places, soggy tree bark might cost $18.95 for a lunch special - especially if the soggy tree bark was soaked in high mountain, sparkling, stream water, and served by a girl who didn't shave her legs.

I waded carefully out to where the line entered the water. The water was almost to the top of my waders. Holding my rod in my left hand, with my right hand I followed the line into the cold murky water. My fingers touched something the fly was embedded in - it was soft and gave to my touch. It didn't feel like a stick, but more like firm rubber. I grabbed the wooly worm and tried to free it, but I couldn't pull the hook from the snag.

"Cut the line and let's get out of here," my Guardian Angel yelled and took several quick steps toward camp.

For some reason, the cheap fly that had been made in India was important to me, and instead of breaking the line, I put my hand around the snag and pulled with all my might. If I could get the snag up and out of the water I could see what I would have to do to get my fly. The first thing I saw coming out of the gloom of the water sent shivers down my spine. It was not a tree limb, but a hand, a woman's hand, with long slim fingers, painted red nails, a diamond ring, and a gold and diamond tennis bracelet. The naked body bobbed inches below the surface as I held onto the arm, my wooly worm was embedded in the crook of her left elbow. The face, opened eyed, gazed vacantly at me in bewilderment, as the long blond hair curled around her head like golden seaweed. I know the lady did not drown. There was a small hole in her temple - the type of hole caused by a bullet. Around her slender hips was a gold chain.

"Oh Roosevelt," my Guardian Angel moaned, burying his face in his hands. "I tried to warn you. But no, will you listen to me, what am I, just another pretty face?"

I felt empty and devoid of life. The woman was young, mid-thirties, pretty, who would never have to worry about getting crow's feet. I tried to pull the body toward the shore, but could only make it bob to the surface and then partially straighten out. Something which I could not see was attached to her left leg securing her to the bottom of the pool. I tried several more times to pull the body to the bank but to no avail. I pulled the wooly worm from her arm, released the hand and watched the pale body disappear back into the darkness. The last I saw were her two breasts disappearing like two moons behind a cloud. I took a deep breath. I was not mortified, Vietnam cured that, but I did feel sad.

It was strange, here, surrounded by the mountains, the rushing song of the river, and the distant calls of birds - somebody had killed and dumped the body of the woman.

As I started back to camp, I wondered what I've done in my life to mess up my karma so bad that every time I turn around, I stumble into a crime.

"For one thing you don't take advice," my Guardian Angel said.

"Old friend, I should have listened to you," I said, apologetically.

"Let's not take the friend bit too far," he said and gave me a disgusted look.

Although feeling lost and disillusioned, my private detective side of me kicked in and I looked closely at the ground for anything out of the ordinary. My Guardian Angel, who enjoys investigating, scurried around like a blood hound that couldn't smell. There was nothing but my own footprints along the shore back to camp - no clothes, no drag marks. Back at camp, I went over the bridge and walked twenty or thirty yards on the other side of the steam but did not see any foot prints or drag marks. I will explore further tomorrow.

Heading back to camp the sun was going down. The sky above the mountains was a blood red and the clouds were crimson. It was like the sky was bidding farewell to the murdered lady.

"I told you, you should have gone to Durango," my Guardian Angel said.

"Everything in life has a reason. I was supposed to find the woman," I said. "I was supposed to find her and now I am supposed to find out who killed her."

"You poor mixed up idiot," my Guardian Angel said sadly while holding his arms up to the sky. "Don't you know that nothing in life has a reason? It is all random."

"Why didn't I listen to you," I pleaded, more to the sky than my Guardian Angel. "I don't want to find a killer. All I want to do is fish and be left alone for a little while."

"Well listen to me now, get into Matilda and let's head out of here. You can buy a trout at the grocery store and fry it."

"Even though it would be the smart thing to do I can't," I said dejectedly, accepting my fate.

"Oh, Roosevelt, your morals and sense of justice are going to get you killed. What am I going to do with you?" my Guardian Angel lamented.

"Pray for me," I replied, feeling a sense of doom settling around me as thick and green as the Rocky Mountain air in Denver.

“I’d rather take you to a topless bar,” he said but without a smile.

CHAPTER TWO
IN OVER MY HEAD

The sun was down by the time I got back to camp. I decided there was no need to go to town and report the body until in the morning. I don't think the lady will be going anywhere. I would lie to the authorities and tell them I had discovered the body in the morning and drove to town as fast as Matilda would go - which isn't much faster than a turtle on espresso.

I lit my lantern and broke up some of the aspen to start a fire. As I stacked the aspen in the fire pit I disturbed several hot embers. Somebody had made a fire at the camp earlier in the day. With one of the aspen sticks I pushed through the layer of ashes and found several burnt bottle caps that were still slightly warm. I put the bottle caps in my shirt pocket.

"Bottle caps won't solve this murder," my Guardian Angel said, giving me a look like the only person dumber than me had not been born yet.

"You never can tell," I told him. "Even the smallest thing can have a large impact."

With a fire burning, I went to the stream and brought back three beers. It seemed like a three-beer night. I opened a beer and looked up at the stars, but I really didn't see them. I could only see the woman's bewildered face coming up out of the water at me. The face was saying, "Bob Roosevelt, you were sent here to catch me with a wooly worm and to find out who did this to me."

"If you believe that bunk, Roosevelt," my Guardian Angel scoffed, "You should become a fantasy writer or better yet become a mystic and you can bilk people out of their hard earned money."

I gulped the beer down in three swallows and opened another one. Already my mind was churning. There is no perfect crime. Everybody makes a mistake.

"Your mistake is staying here," my Guardian Angel said wishing he was not an angel and could have a beer.

I have always thought life is predestined, and we go through life on a treadmill we can't stop, until the treadmill makes our heart burst like a rotten apple hitting a car. I finished the second beer and opened the last one I'd brought up from the stream. It wasn't going to be a three beer night. It was going to be a no count them night.

"Lady," I said to the fire, "I'll find who made you fish bait. I'll find them because they really messed up my vacation and because Buddha, Allah, God or Confucius, made me hook you with a wooly worm."

"It might have been the beer god, or the money god, or the golf god," my Guardian Angel said.

"That's ridiculous," I said.

"Exactly my point, you staying here is ridiculous. Pack up all this gear and get out of here," my Guardian Angel ordered. "I really don't feel like protecting you, especially after you won't listen to me. All these years assigned to you have about worn me out."

"Pea Brain, it's not my fault that you were on God's black list and got assigned to me," I snapped back, adding. "And don't you order me to do anything. I am the boss around here."

I hate being told what to do.

My Guardian Angel made a face at me, spun around, and stomped into the trees where I could not see him.

I headed to the river for more beer. As I put my hand in the water I had a disturbing thought - the water going over my hand would soon caress the body of the lady. Although it has been over thirty years since I abused drugs in the name of trying to find my inner self, my mind still at times is filled with strange thoughts.

I went to Matilda and rummaged through my suitcase and found my spiral notebook and a pencil. Back by the fire I jotted down my first two clues. I do not own a laptop or a cell phone. Laptops need batteries and I have a weird thing about batteries. Cell phones are considered open airways by law which means they can be recorded without a warrant or a phone tap - so - I make all my phone calls from a pay phone. Even to this day pay phones can be found at hospitals, airports, bus stations, and a few random gas stations.

I drank two more beers before I decided to turn in for the night. The Coleman lantern turned off and the fire fading, I pulled my sleeping bag out of the tent and lay down with nothing but the stars as my ceiling. Gazing at the stars I pondered life's mysteries - life, love, war, pollution. Why did Simon and Garfunkel split up? I felt small, insignificant, worthless, and lost. Nothing that unusual, but the stars seemed to personify the feelings, although I slept like a half-drunk rock.

I woke up in the morning before the sun rose. My Guardian Angel gave me a distant look but said nothing. I hoped being in the mountains had made him speechless. A bird, obviously happy, was singing to the pre-dawn. I made some coffee and waited for the sun. I couldn't think of the last time I had seen the sunrise without watching it through the multi-layered zones of car exhaust, factory gas, pesticides, or other industrial waste residue we breathe and store in our livers. I had the strange idea I should start Matilda and stick my nose in her tail pipe so I could get a shot of real air. I wondered if my system could make it through the day breathing clean air and I really don't want to get the shakes while talking to the police in Antonito.

As I finished my second cup of coffee the sun cleared the mountains. Murder has a way of dampening a glorious sunrise. I put my waders on and retraced my steps to the deadly pool. My Guardian Angel was on the other side of the river. I still found nothing. Instead of heading back, I walked further down from the pool. Although the river runs close to the road, there aren’t many points I could access the river from the road, due to thick vegetation or deep ravines. I walked over 1/4 of a mile and found no access to the river except from where I had camped other than from the wilderness side of the river.

I crossed the river and followed it back toward the pool and my camp. To my left was a large meadow fanning out between pine-covered mountains. The waving wild grasses in the meadow were over two feet tall. I could see several trails worn into the vegetation. I know the trail to the right side of the meadow leads to Red Lake - I had taken it years earlier. From Red Lake, a trail circled around and came out in the town of Platoro itself. All in all it was about a 10 mile journey, which does not take long on a horse. Where the other trail leads I don't know.

I came to a small stream that emptied into the Chama River and crossed it. My Guardian Angel was about thirty yards from me and looking at something on the ground, he waved excitedly for me to hurry over and look. There was a stack of neatly folded clothes. There was a black lace bra, non-supportive, one of those a Victoria Secret model looks ravishing in and fits other women like a sack. There were matching black panties, a pair of white cotton socks, a pair of women's Levi's and a gray sweatshirt. Next to the clothes was a pair of hiking boots. A few feet away a large bath towel was spread out on the grass, and I could see the indentations where a person had laid on the towel.

In my mind I could see the lady sunbathing in the nude. It was a warm day, bees buzzed, the wind gently moved the grass, and no one could see her from the other side of the river because of the alders. She felt young and happy as she took off her clothes. The wind touched her bare breasts, her thighs, she was alone, she was free. My Guardian Angel nodded his head sadly.

I didn't touch anything, nor did I see any footprints or fresh horse tracks in the area, but the ground was dry and hard. Not more than fifteen yards from the clothes was the pool the lady now resides in, but from this side of the river I can hardly see the water because of the thick alder branches. I walked around the alders and looked closely at the bank of the river. In the sediment, pointing into the river was a bare footprint. Looking closer, there was another one. The lady had walked into the river and waded into the pool. There were no footprints coming out of the river. She was brave as she stepped into the cold water and felt every nerve tingle and come to life. I carefully searched the area one more time, but I didn't find any blood.

On the way back to camp I found nothing else. I couldn't find any other vehicle tracks except Matilda's around the camp. I checked the corral for fresh signs of horses, but the corral hadn't been used in weeks.

I lit my Coleman stove to warm up some coffee and made a few entries in my notebook. I now have eight clues.

Finished with my coffee I put all my gear in the tent. To this day I've never had anything stolen from a camp. Most petty thieves only want car stereos and tires. I can't see a thief fishing for relaxation. I can see them sitting in front of a TV all day or playing pool, but fishing isn't in the picture.

Matilda was her same old reliable self and started with one turn of the key - in all our years together she has never failed to start. As I was about to turn right out of the campground toward Antonito, a glint caught my eye. Getting out of the car I picked up a pack of Lucky Strikes that had only two cigarettes out of it.

"People who smoke non-filtered cigarettes have a death wish," my Guardian Angel said.

"Maybe somebody tossed them out the window because they are quitting," I said.

"With the price of smokes they would have sold them," my Guardian Angel said.

I started to drive to Antonito, but changed my mind, stopped, backed into the camping area and turned towards Platoro. "What are you doing?" my Guardian Angel asked with a bewildered look on his face.

"I don't know."

"Normal," he stated. "But it is also called obstructing justice."

From my camping area I passed two more primitive camping areas that were not being used. The forest service was building a new cinder block fire pit in the second one - it only needed a few blocks to be completed. When I got to Platoro I had driven close to ten miles.

Platoro, in the late 1800's was a small mining town, but it went defunct quickly. It is now an ugly scar on the face of the earth - gray slag piles surround rusted out mining equipment and dilapidated old wood buildings. In the 1960's an old cowboy renovated one of the buildings and started a bar and a restaurant that is only open in the summer.

Nothing had changed, but I was surprised that there were two pickup trucks and a new blue Ford Explorer parked in front of the bar and restaurant. The trucks didn’t belong to campers - they were all beaten up, had hay bales, pieces of old rotten wire, rusty bits of chain, assorted rocks, rotted out fence posts, beat up saddles, beer cans, empty oil cans, and other junk in the back.

Across from the bar was a large corral with a dozen or so horses in it. Several wilderness outfitters guide in the area and I imagined the horses belonged to them.

Cowboys still trying to be cowboys, and not truck drivers, can eke out a living guiding people into the mountains on fishing and photography trips in the summer, and elk and deer hunts in the fall.

I went inside. The restaurant walls, unpainted planking, were covered with old, dried up chaps, rusty spurs, old cowboy boots with the toes curled up, and various tools miners used in their futile search of wealth. Interlaced between the relics were framed photographs of when the mine was in operation - men smoking pipes stood around wagons filled with ore, prostitutes brazenly showed off knees and bare shoulders. Nobody was smiling, men didn't work in a mine because they had a choice and women didn't become prostitutes because their life was full of possibilities.

The restaurant had four tables with red-checkered tablecloths and small kerosene lanterns in the center. The menu, all cold sandwiches, was painted on a plank that hung on the wall. Nobody was in the restaurant. To the left was a swinging door, like those seen in cowboy movies, with a sign painted over the top - WATERING HOLE.

When I pushed the doors open and walked into the bar, the four cowboys sitting at the bar glanced at me for a moment then went back to their drinks like I really didn't exist. The days of cowboys being offended by people with long hair went out the window when cowboy singers started wearing braids.

The men were real cowboys. Their dirty cowboy hats were pushed back on their heads, revealing suntan lines that cut across the center of their foreheads. Their boots, pants, and shirts were worn from work, and their hands were rough and calloused.

The bar itself looked like it had fallen asleep in the 1860's and had forgotten to wake up. I stood at the bar, one stool down from the four elbow to elbow cowboys and got my first sight of the bartender. My world stopped for an instant, butterflies started flying around in my head, soft music filtered into my heart.

"Be careful, Roosevelt, believe me, she is not your soul mate," my Guardian Angel warned but his eyes were bulging out and he danced a little jig, "but I would really like to see her naked."

The lady was beautiful, in a cowgirl way, early 40's at most. She was tall with mid-length black hair pulled into a ponytail. She was wearing a sleeveless white western shirt with two buttons open at the neck - nothing was exposed, but the hint was seductive in a nice way. She had dark eyebrows that accented the blackness of her eyes - gypsy eyes - free - almost haughty, and a tad naughty. Her lipstick was as red as blood and she was wearing large, gold loop earrings which added to her gypsy air. She could spin a spell on me anytime she wanted. I sat at the bar and she smiled at me so genuinely she reminded me of a naive young girl - only this young girl was wearing Levi's that were so tight she had to melt her body from the waist down and pour herself into them. Her arms and face were deeply tanned.

I'm Ann," she said, in the most perfect voice I have ever heard. "What suits you?"

As she waited for me to answer her eyes darted over my faded Levi's, worn brown cowboy boots, my green eyes, and I could tell she liked my close kept white beard and shoulder length white hair. The fact I am six foot tall, 190 pounds, in good shape, with a 34 inch waist and with no beer gut might have helped also.

I felt my heartstrings twang. I wanted to tell her I loved her and would take her anyplace in the world she wanted to go. I wanted to tell her I was an investment banker who was going to buy a ranch and she could run it for me. I was smitten.

My Guardian Angel was trying his best to look down her cleavage while at the same time rubbing her fanny.

"I'll have a Coors," I said to Ann, my voice, to me, sounded about ten thousand miles away. When Ann turned to get the beer I motioned for Pea Brain to get away from her. He sat down beside me looking like a little boy who had lost his pet frog.

Ann brought me a Coors. "While you're at it," I told Ann. "Get these men a round."

The four cowboys smiled like I was the best thing that happened since zippers on Levi's.

Of course, the cowboys weren't drinking the cheap stuff - they were drinking whiskey chased with beer.

Thanks," they all said in unison, after they'd been served and had their shots of whiskey halfway to their mouths.

They drank the whiskey like it was water.

"You fishing?" the cowboy sitting closest to me asked. He wasn't tall, but was about as wide as a door. I couldn’t really tell what his face looked like because it was covered with a bushy, black beard, and his eyebrows are so long they could have been curled with a curling iron. He had black hair that was a mat of curls. He reminded me of a bear on a bad hair day.

"I've been trying," I replied, "but no luck."

"Fishing ain't been no good less you go up high," he said.

"These boys should know," Ann said with a smile. "They guide in the high country and have a fishing camp set up at Red Lake.”

Her smile could melt snow. I smiled back and wondered if this was the love I have been searching endlessly for.

"You want some good fishing we can take you up to the high lakes, and you can catch so many trout you'll never want to see another one for at least a year," the cowboy at the end of the bar said.

He was tall, thin, red-headed, clean-shaven and had a happy face.

I noticed all four of the cowboys were young, at the most, in their late twenties. The two in the middle had to be brothers, both had sandy hair, the same facial features and light brown moustaches.

After our initial conversation, Ann started washing glasses like she was expecting a large happy hour crowd to emerge out of the forest. The four cowboys looked at Ann and dreamed about her doing a table dance.

I was about to finish my beer when the four men slid away from the bar to leave. I wasn't paying much attention, lost in my thoughts about Ann, until the bear took a pack of Lucky Strikes from his pocket, thumped one out of the pack and lit it with a stick match he expertly struck with his thumb nail.

"Here we go now," my Guardian Angel said rolling his eyes back in his head.

"What are your names, if I decide to hire a guide?" I asked Bear.

"I'm Willie Hood, these two guys here in the middle are Frank and Ray Colbert, the man at the end is Jesse Killton."

"How do I get hold of any of you?"

"Just call up here and talk to Ann, she'll know where we are."

"Thanks for the drink mister," Jesse said, as all four of the men nodded at me and left.

"They just got back out of the mountains. They set up some camps for the early deer hunt. It's easier to cut the wood and get everything ready ahead of time. Then all they have to do is take in the food," Ann told me.

"Where do they live?" I asked as I pushed the empty beer can toward her.

Ann brought me another beer. I noticed she did not have a wedding ring. "The two brothers work for their father on the Forked Lightning Ranch, one of the biggest ranches in the Antonito Valley. Jesse lives in a cabin down the road. When he isn't guiding he drives a logging truck. And Willie lives in a trailer in Antonito."

I barely heard her words I was so mesmerized by her eyes. My Guardian Angel wasn't looking at her eyes.

I wished I had all afternoon to sit and talk, but I still had to go to town and report a dead lady. That's how opportunity is for me, when it knocks, I don't have the time.

"Opportunity in your life is something you mess up on purpose," my Guardian Angel said.

I finished the beer and stood. "Thanks," I said.

"You have to go," Ann said, her voice made my heartstrings twang again. "There can be some long, lonely days here."

"How about I come back tomorrow," I said. "I plan on fishing for at least a week."

She didn't answer me but smiled, the smile could have meant yes, or could have meant, now or never. Now or never would have been more my luck.

As I neared the door, I turned. "You wouldn't happen to know a woman who lives around here that's in her mid-thirties, has long blond hair, is pretty, and wears a diamond tennis bracelet?" I asked.

There was a slight hesitation before she answered, as if my question had frightened her. "Know her, yes I know her, she and I live together, we have the second cabin...."

I cut her off. "Those new cabins close to the main road?"

"They're nice," she said, and then gave me a quizzical look. "Why do you want to know about Barbara?"

I looked at her like an idiot really not knowing what to say. I couldn't tell her it was a great possibility I had found her friend in the river and she had been murdered before I notified the police.

Ann started to laugh, "Forget it," she told me, "she could be your daughter. I'm more your age and I like the longhaired scruffy look."

"You can't trust a woman who likes over the hill old hippies," my Guardian Angel said.

Ann didn't seem to be offended by what she thought I had been thinking.

I smiled like I'd been a bad little boy and would do anything to get back in her good graces.

"What is your name?" Ann asked.

For some reason I felt like I should lie to her, but I didn't. "Bob Roosevelt."

"You should have lied," my Guardian Angel said seemingly truly concerned.

Ann looked puzzled, like there was something about me she knew and it bothered her, but she couldn't put her finger on what it was, she shrugged her shoulders, gave me her gypsy smile and said. "You come back tomorrow," like it was an order and not a request.

I smiled and nodded.

I started to push open the swinging doors, but turned around. "Did the Sheriff come up here yesterday?" I asked.

"Nobody came up here yesterday except a ranger. It was his day off and he was going fishing."

"What's the ranger's name?" I asked.

"Brad Fisher, he drives an old rusted out jeep Cherokee when he's not in the government truck."

"See you tomorrow," I told her knowing it was no idle promise.

"I think she likes me," I told my Guardian Angel.

"You could really cheer up my camping trip if you could get her naked," my Guardian Angel said and licked his lips.

"How did you ever get to heaven?" I asked him.

"Connections," he smiled.

The only vehicle remaining in front of the bar was the Ford Explorer - it had to be Ann's.

"It doesn't take a 'famous for fifteen minutes detective' to figure that one out," my Guardian Angel said.

Driving away from Platoro my Guardian Angel warned me, "You're getting in over your head."

"But I've met a good-looking woman that has moved me," I said.

"I don't know why, but I think you had better be careful with Ann," he said.

I thought about Ann. I hadn't met a woman in ages, which with one glance, made me feel like a giddy little boy. But even enraptured, I did note that it was 11 miles from my camp to the new cabins.

"You had better take note about Lucky Strikes, too," my Guardian Angel said.

He thinks I miss more things than I really do.

CHAPTER THREE
SMALL TOWN COPS

As I drove past the forest service station on the way to Antonito I was tempted to stop and report finding the body. I figured they would have radio contact with the police, but I decided it would only lead to more hassle by bringing in another government agency. I also wanted to meet the ranger, Brad Fisher, but now wasn't the time.

In Antonito, I turned left at the small sign that stated 'JAIL', and drove past two crumbling adobe houses that had wooden front porches attached to them. A dog lounged on one of the porches. He looked like the last time he had eaten was when a congressman took a pay cut. The jail, to my surprise, was made out of brick and had a paved parking lot and a fancy wooden sign. Crime must be booming in Antonito. The small grass yard was mowed and there was a sidewalk from the parking lot to the front door. On the left side of the jail was a basketball court surrounded by a 10-foot high fence with barbwire on the top. I could see six small windows with bars across them so I figured there were 12 cells in the jail - enough to hold about half the male population of Antonito.

When I went into the jail, a buzzer went off that sounded like a recess bell at an elementary school, only it was broadcast through a boom box. I only had to take two steps to be at a wooden counter that ran the entire length of the room. It was about elbow high. Behind the counter was a desk with a computer and the wall was covered with wanted posters. The counter was hinged on one side to swing up and let a person go through. There was a metal door in the wall behind the counter. The buzzer continued to sound as I

waited. There wasn't a chair in the room or any magazines to pass away the time, but, I suppose, most people being admitted to jail really don't want to read Outdoor Life or True Romance.

The metal door swung open, and the Sheriff who had waved at me on my way to go fishing walked out, closed the door, and locked it with one of the keys on a monster key ring that had a special clip so it snapped back onto his pistol belt. The pistol he wore was a 357 magnum. He was wearing his black cowboy hat, which in most cowboy circles is a big no no to wear one's hat indoors, but I really did not feel in the position to sound him for his breach of etiquette. He sat down behind the desk and pushed a button that stopped the buzzer. "What do you need?" he asked me as he twisted both sides of his four inch handle bar moustache.

Anytime anybody asks me what I need I always want to say. "I need $300,000, a Learjet, a new house, a woman who loves me, and I would like to know my purpose in life."

But, it's not wise to joke with any form of policeman, they normally aren't funny people.

"I found a dead body," I said. I could see no need to beat around the bush.

The Sheriff stood up as fast as a cork coming off a cheap bottle of champagne. "A body, where?" he demanded.

"There's a lady in the Chama River and I don't think she drowned," I said.

I noticed the Sheriff's nametag, Rogers. All I could think of was the late Mr. Rogers, the kid's show host, but this Mr. Rogers didn't look like he would sing you songs and say "hello boys and girls." This Mr. Rogers, even if he was pushing 60, looked like he would have no problem breaking both of my legs, dislocating my arms, and ripping off my nose before he tossed me into his new jail with a warning if I caused him any grief he would take away more than my TV privileges. Sheriff Rogers was big, strong, shaved his head, and had deep green penetrating eyes that would make the devil tap dance. He had no eyebrows and furrows in his forehead that resembled a freshly plowed field. The effect made his black handlebar moustache seem that much longer. He reminded me of a Texas Longhorn bull with his horns in the wrong place. Although he had on a long-sleeved shirt I know he has tattoos on his forearms. A body like his without a tattoo would be like Betty Crocker without a cake mix. His tattoos would not be roses, but, BORN TO DIE, or, LIFE IS DEATH, written beneath a skull with a dagger stuck in it.

"Why don't you think she drowned?" Sheriff Rogers asked me, his eyes boring into mine trying to see if I had any trace of guilt written on my face.

I have enough guilt in me for ten people but not from killing young women.

"She has a bullet hole in her head. And there's something holding her underwater."

"You tried to pull her out?" he asked menacingly, which I thought was a useless question. How else would I know something was holding her underwater?

"I tried, but couldn't get her out easily so I felt it best not to disturb the area. As it is, my wader marks are there now."

"Good thinking," Sheriff Rogers conceded his voice not as menacing.

He probably thought the only things I know about crime scenes are from what I've seen on cop shows.

I hadn't noticed the phone on the desk until the Sheriff picked it up and made a call. "This is Sheriff Rogers. You'd better send a couple of your boys down here pronto - we might have a murder," he said, looking at me like I was a suspect.

After he hung up, he flipped the counter top up and held it open for me. "Let's you and me go drink some coffee and maybe eat a sandwich," he said.

"I don't like this guy," my Guardian Angel said. "Plus, I've heard jail food is terrible."

"You have been quiet for a long time, about time you joined in," I said to my guardian angel.

"At times it is better to listen and observe than talk," he said.

The Sheriff opened the metal door and held it open for me. He locked the door behind us and led the way down a hall to a small mess hall. There were two steel tables bolted to the floor, a coffee machine, and a serving counter in front of a kitchen. He poured us each a cup of coffee and set it on the table without asking if I wanted one.

"Now," he said, sitting, and pouring enough sugar in his coffee to make a diabetic do back flips. "Tell me about this body."

"Sheriff Rogers is a small town cop, but don't think he is stupid," my Guardian Angel told me.

I told the Sheriff about hooking the body with a wooly worm and about finding the clothes. I didn't tell him the lady was young, blond, and had on jewelry, and I didn't tell him about going to Platoro, or the fact I waited a day to report the body.

When I finished my story, the Sheriff took a pack Lucky Strikes out of his pocket, offered me one, I refused, and then he lit one with a Zippo lighter with a marine insignia on it.

"Lucky Strikes are popular around here," my Guardian Angel said

"Too popular," I said.

"You in Nam?" I asked the Sheriff.

"Wouldn't have missed it," he told me, inhaling deeply.

"Me too," I said. "Infantry."

He nodded in understanding.

Zippo made a fortune on us. Every unit in the military had a Zippo with its crest on it. Who gave a hoot at the time about cancer compared to bullets and booby traps?

The Sheriff took another drag on his Lucky Strike but said nothing else about Vietnam, which suited me fine - the past is the past - I only hope one day we stop repeating it, which, as of now, we have not.

"What's your name?" the Sheriff asked. A question I figured he should have asked me first.

"Bob Roosevelt, I used to live close to here only in New Mexico. But since then I've been about everywhere in this country there is to be."

The Sheriff looked closely at me, and then a grin spread across his face like he had just busted two Mexicans who had a suitcase full of money, and he was going to keep the money and tell the Mexicans to get their 'no green card' rears back to Mexico. "I seen you on a TV show a while back, you're the private detective who solved that kidnapping case in Florida."

"That's me," I said, smiling and trying not to show too much pride.

"Fame isn't everything it is made out to be," my Guardian Angel said giving me a 'you should know better' look.

"I'll be," Sheriff Rogers said, smiling. "Let me shake your hand."

"Save me," my Guardian Angel said touching his forehead like he was about to faint.

Sheriff Rogers grip would have made Hercules take notice.

"There used to be a commune not far from here back in the late 60's and early 70's," Sheriff Rogers said eyeing me suspiciously. "A lot of hippies would come over here, eat mushrooms and peyote, and run around naked thinking they were rocks or trees. When I picked them up they always told me they were looking for their center."

"I heard about that place," I replied casually.

I used to live there and I'd been one of those rocks. But, about the only center of the universe I ever found is called confusion.

"You know, hippies are coming back, I seen some kids with peace signs on their car the other day," the Sheriff said.

"Hippies are better than bikers," I said.

The Sheriff made a sour face. I don't think he liked my statement. In his mind, at least, bikers fight back when they get arrested. Hippies don't give the police an excuse to give them a couple of good swats with their nightsticks.

Sheriff Rogers was about to say something when the front buzzer went off. When he came back two Colorado Highway Patrolmen were with him. "Boys, this here is Bob Roosevelt. He was on TV a while back. He's the private detective that solved the kidnapping when that rich kid got herself abducted down in Florida."

"What are you doing here," one of them asked as I stood to shake hands.

"I've been trout fishing for bodies," I replied.

My Guardian Angel, true to his not liking police, mooned them, which is easy to do for a monk from the 14th century because they did not wear underwear, but, which in all reality was a worthless gesture as I am the only one who can see him.

The two Highway Patrol officers' names were George Hoffman and Gary Hayworth. I couldn't tell them apart and figured

Colorado must clone their cops. They were both well-built men, over six feet tall, 200 pounds, had short hair - almost on the verge of being skin heads in uniform - and were wearing sunglasses with reflective silver tint on the outside of the lenses - the kind that Colombian hit men prefer - only Colombian hit men make more money and do stronger drugs than caffeine.

Sheriff Rogers told them my story and they seemed to perk up, like it gave them something to do besides sit in their cars and give speeding tickets all day. I figured they were based out of Alamosa. Alamosa is the only town of any size in the area and about sixty miles north.

Within five minutes we were blasting down the highway, sirens blaring, red and blue lights flashing. I was in the Sheriff's car with the Highway Patrol car not more than twenty yards behind us. I didn't know why we were in a hurry. The lady in the river, as far as I know, isn't going to be serving tea.

"This is kind of exciting," Sheriff Rogers told me puffing on another Lucky Strike and screeching around a corner. "We haven't had a murder around here in over 20 years."

"I wish it would have waited until I was done fishing," I told him.

We didn't see another vehicle as we drove. The sirens were as necessary as Israel telling the United Nations they have enemies.

After we skidded to a halt at my camp the sirens were turned off. It seemed so quiet I felt uneasy. Standing by the fire pit Officer Hayworth asked me in a sly tone. "How long you been camping here?"

I am a suspect. "Yesterday afternoon. The Sheriff saw me driving in."

"Sure did," the Sheriff verified my story. "I thought he was some old hippie driving that ugly Volkswagen."

My Guardian Angel laughed.

I was glad Matilda was in town and not here. Her feelings get hurt easily.

Hayworth looked disappointed, but he gave me a dirty look like, 'you're not out of hot water yet.' I could tell Hayworth doesn't like me. Some private detective had probably been hired by his ex-wife and caught him sleeping with her sister.

"I'll put on my waders," I told the three police officers.

Hayworth and Hoffman followed me to my tent. As I pulled my waders out of the tent, they looked inside like I might have a stash of Hustler Magazines.

"Leave him alone," Sheriff Rogers told them. "He didn't do it. There isn't a murderer in this world who would report his own crime."

Hayworth and Hoffman looked at each other feeling stupid. I wondered if two people wearing reflective sunglasses, when they look at each other, can see themselves reflected back or if the reflections wipe each other out.

"That's a good question," my Guardian Angel said trying to pretend that he could think.

I had my waders on and started toward the stream. As I got to the edge of camp I saw a set of cowboy boot prints that hadn't been there when I left for Platoro.

I looked closely at the boot prints. They could have belonged to a small man or a woman. The Sheriff was wearing cowboy boots, but too big. The highway patrolmen were wearing black, round-toed Wellingtons. I said nothing about my discovery.

None of us talked as we walked to the pool. I didn't see any more boot prints. Standing by the pool, I wondered if either the Sheriff or the highway patrolmen were going to go into the river in their freshly starched uniforms.

When they didn't move I said, "I'll get her."

I waded out into the pool and reached down into the cold water where I had snagged the body. I felt nothing. I moved down a foot and reached back into the water - nothing.

I felt the three sets of eyeballs watching me that were not amused. I moved down even further and reached into the water - nothing. I kept doing this until I was at the end of the pool - still nothing. Sheriff Rogers coughed. I looked over my shoulder at him and knew by his look, if there wasn't a body, he would find some reason for me to take up jail basketball.

"If there is no body then we can get out of here," my Guardian Angel said.

I moved back to the center of the pool and stepped deeper into the pool, when I reached in, I felt her. I hooked both of my hands

under her armpits and tugged. She came to the surface and I pulled as hard as I could and started to walk backwards. When I got to the shallow water, Sheriff Rogers stepped into the water, grabbed my belt and helped pull. In tandem, we dragged the body, with a chain attached to her leg, and circled through two cinder blocks, out of the water. I lay the body down. The chain was padlocked to her leg, looped through the two cinder blocks and padlocked back to itself. I looked closely at the bullet wound in her temple. There was no exit wound so I gathered it had been a 22 or a 32 caliber.

"It's Barbara Maiden," Hoffman, Hayworth, and Rogers said at the same time, in voices somewhere between a gasp, surprise, and fear.

There is nothing nice about looking at a nude, beautiful young woman, who is dead, unless you are an undertaker and can only see your fee.

"You two take her back to Roosevelt's camp and cover her up," Sheriff Rogers ordered and then turned to me. "Where are those clothes?"

He and I splashed across the river and I led him to the clothes. I saw a single boot print in the trail and I could see where the person had walked in the grass. Before I could say anything, Rogers stepped on the boot print with his number 14 wet boot. The smaller print would be gone like it was a mouse after a rhino had stepped on it.

Sheriff Rogers quickly picked up the clothes. "We had better get out of here and not step on anything. The homicide boys will have to come in from Denver and take a look," he said.

"Do you think he stepped on that track on purpose?" my Guardian Angel asked me.

I was going to show the Sheriff where the lady walked into the river, but since he was in such a hurry I decided to wait.

When we got back to camp, Barbara lay on the ground, wrapped in two survival blankets Hayworth and Hoffman must have had in their vehicle. The chain and cinder blocks were outside of the blanket. "You two had better take her to the morgue in Alamosa, but don't let them do anything to her until the state boys come in," Sheriff Rogers said.

Hayworth and Hoffman looked shaken and nervous. They didn't say anything as they picked up Barbara and put her in the squad car. They turned on the siren as they drove away.

"You can help me," Rogers said to me.

He didn't look shaken at all, but was all business. He got a roll of yellow plastic crime scene ribbon out of his car and we went back downstream and taped off the area where the body was found. He was careful not to damage the area any more than he had to. We said nothing during the process.

Back in camp I went to get two beers out of the river. As I bent down to get the beers, I noticed a used stick match lying on top of the grass. I picked it up and saw the heel print of a cowboy boot, but there was no indentation in the dirt from an emblem on the heel of the boot. Before I put the match in my shirt pocket I examined it closely - the end had been chewed on.

When I gave Sheriff Rogers a beer he looked relieved and after taking a long swallow he said. "It's weird."

"No, it's murder," my Guardian Angel chastised him.

I took my waders off and put my boots back on.

When we finished the beers we headed back to town.

"Are you going to be here long?" Rogers asked me as he drove. There seemed to be a strange undertone to the Sheriff's voice, almost fear, or apprehension.

"I'm going to do some fishing."

"The state boys are going to want to talk to you."

"You know where my camp is," I said, adding, "You all knew the lady."

"Barbara Maiden," he said. "Her father is a big shot Texan who owns the bar at Platoro now. She came out for the summer."

"She cause any trouble?" I asked.

The Sheriff blew air through his nose and half-laughed. "The only trouble she caused was trying to dodge every cowboy in this area who wanted to get her naked."

I had a feeling the autopsy would show that somebody did more than get her naked.

Back in town I didn't go into the jail, but started to walk toward Matilda. "You going to be doing some fishing around here, you'd better buy a license," the Sheriff called to me.

How he knew I don't have a license I don't know. Maybe the same way I know he has tattoos.

"You are in for it now, Roosevelt," my Guardian Angel said. “Your fate is sealed. There is no way you can leave here."

"Pea Brain, can guardian angels be bad luck?" I asked him.

He didn't answer.

I bought a fishing license at a small grocery store and another case of beer. The Mexican man who ran the store didn't say a word and didn't seem to care if I bought anything or not. Down the street, I filled up Matilda at a gas station. An older Mexican man ran the station. Like the man at the grocery store he didn’t believe in speaking.

“White people could screw up the neighborhood,” my Guardian Angel said, giving me a wry grin.

There was a small cafe on the edge of town with a hand painted sign over the door - BEER FOR SALE, DRINK IN OR TAKE OUT. Since it was getting late and all I had had to eat all day was beer and coffee, I stopped.

There were no other customers in the cafe. A Mexican lady, about 250 pounds of laughter and hot peppers, waddled up to the table and smiled at me so genuinely I wanted to hug her and thank her for letting me know there is some good in the world. "Don't look at the menu," she told me. "I make the best enchiladas you have ever eaten, put an egg on the top, a side of beans, and you'll be the happiest guy in the world."

"I believe you," I smiled back at her.

“You’ll also get gas,” my Guardian Angel said.

While she was making my dinner I got out my notebook and writing. When the steaming plate was set in front of me, with more smiles, I had 26 clues in my book. Some of them had to be good ones.

"Most of them aren't worth a hoot," my Guardian Angel said.

Eating, I was bothered; there was something about the two police officers I didn’t like.

"That’s different,” my Guardian Angel said, slightly taken back. “We agree on something.”

The food was delicious and I tipped the lady five dollars, two dollars for the food and three dollars for the happy smiles.

When I got back to my camp it was almost dark. I built a fire and sat looking into the flames. I had a strange thought. Someday somebody will invent a fire you can change the channels on.

"You can be funny," my Guardian Angel grinned.

"I don't feel funny," I told him. "Most of the time life only confuses me."

"Most of the time death confuses me," he said. “Especially since I am dead.”

CHAPTER 4
ANN OH ANN

The fire was blazing and the flickering shadows on the trees seemed to keep beat with the tumbling stream. I was holding the things I had found - the pack of Lucky Strikes, the chewed on stick match, and the bottle caps. I didn't expect vibrations to jump out of them and tell me the name or names of the killer, but I had hopes a few ideas would enter my brain. I know there is always some deeper meaning in the most trivial of things, one merely has to find it, usually in my case, by luck.

"Well, tell me what you know, oh wise and lucky one," my Guardian Angel said, in a tone like I don't know the difference between wet and dry.

I know Sheriff Rogers had been in the area when Barbara was murdered. If Ann is telling the truth I know he didn't go to Platoro. I also know he smokes Lucky Strikes.

Willie Hood, alias the Bear, smokes Lucky Strikes and lights them with a stick match.

I know somebody had been in my camp by the boot print I discovered, but nothing looked disturbed in my tent.

There was also the boot print by Barbara's clothes that had been wiped out by Sheriff Rogers.

"I still think he stepped on it on purpose," my Guardian Angel said.

A ranger, Brad Fisher, had been fishing the day I found Barbara, and had stopped at the bar in Platoro. To get to the bar he had to drive by the camping area.

I know it is 10 miles from my camp to the bar at Platoro and 11 miles from my camp to the cabins where Barbara lived with Ann. How did Barbara get here? I doubt if she walked.

Whoever killed Barbara had surprised her while she was in the pool and not sunbathing. Her footprints only pointed going into the river. If she would have been shot before she got to the pool I would have found blood traces. But, also, whoever killed her, happened to have a chain, a padlock, and a couple of cinder blocks - padlocks, chain and cinder blocks are not something one finds in the wilderness. And, whoever it was hadn't left a trace of their coming or going.

I know Barbara Maiden would have dated a few of the cowboys in the area. Her last name, Maiden, rang a bell with me. I had heard about her father, but I couldn't remember in what context.

Even with the murder, I know one thing for certain. I want to get to know Ann better. There is something about her that warms me.

"Warm or not warm, I want to see Ann naked, even though I don't trust her," my Guardian Angel said with a lecherous grin.

You amaze me," I told him.

"I amaze myself," he said.

The fact Barbara had been shot with a small caliber pistol didn't seem to fit. Most cowboys own a pistol big enough to blow holes in things I could drive a truck through. They are not into prissy little guns.

I put the cigarettes, match, and bottle caps in my shirt pocket.

"You know a lot more than I thought you did," my Guardian Angel said. "But I have no doubt you will muck it all up."

"I have surprised you before," I answered, trying to sound confident.

"I have an eerie feeling you should be careful tonight," he said. "Something is out to get you and I don't think it's a bear trying to steal your beer."

Even though my Guardian Angel is snide, sarcastic, lecherous, and not always reliable, he has saved my life more than once, and since he had been right about my ill-fated fishing trip, I got my 9 m.m. out of the car and loaded it. I took my sleeping bag out of the

tent and after dousing the fire, went to the stand of aspens, and only removing my boots and socks, got into the sleeping bag. The stars twinkled between the tree branches, I tried not to think about anything and let the night, the breeze, the stars, and the sound of the river flow through me - make me one with the universe.

"You becoming one with the universe would be like trying to tell an Arab Extremist his true calling is to be a Jewish Rabbi in the Bronx," my Guardian Angel said but strangely not in a cutting way.

I thought about a young lady I was in love with years ago. I met her while passing out leaflets in front of a grocery store telling people why not to eat grapes. She was only a few years younger than me, but since I was a veteran, our minds were about twenty years a part. She believed all problems could be fixed, humanity really wanted to be good, evil was only a product of abuse, and capitalism was the cause of most problems. She had a child's smile and dancing blue eyes. The last I heard of her she was a nurse.

"I was in love once," my Guardian Angel said in a faraway tone. "It was before I was a monk." The statement surprised me. "She was 16 years old and prettier than spring. The first time I saw her it was like I had known her my complete life. We went on picnics. We danced and sang. I thought I would always be with her."

"What happened," I asked, noticing his eyes were tearing.

"She married a knight," he said simply and walked away into the trees.

I felt sad for him. Whoever said to have loved and lost is better than to have never loved at all is full of diarrhea.

I was half-asleep when my Guardian Angel whispered in my ear, "On your toes soldier boy."

Sound in the mountains travels a great distance. The thin air, the absence of outside noise, even a snapping twig rings like a fender bender in L.A.

I didn't jump up, but lay quietly, listening. The river sounded like Niagara Falls, but in the background, I heard footsteps. They were so faint it was as though I felt them more than I heard them. I raised my head slowly and tried to pick out forms in the dark. I could see the dark shell of my tent. I could see Matilda. I heard movement that could have been ten yards from me or a hundred. Slowly, I put my hand around my 9 m.m. and inched off the safety. I heard the footsteps again. Each foot placed down carefully, slowly, as if the ground was covered with ice and the intruder was afraid of slipping. I was unable to see the form of a human. But there was no mistaking the four shotgun blasts that erupted from the side of the road, or my pup tent evaporating into black mist, and my Guardian Angel hot-footing deeper into the trees. I saw a red flash from the muzzle blast of another shot and I exited out of my sleeping bag as fast as a rat terrier comes out of a raccoon hole with a skunk on his heels. I fired at the blast. One shot, two, three, four, five. I pulled the trigger seven times. I heard running, but I was not fool enough to run directly after the person. I was not going to chase after a person in the dark who was armed with a shotgun and wanted my body to look like Swiss cheese.

I darted to the edge of the aspen stand, which was close to the river, cut away from camp and then raced back toward the road. Branches snapped in my face, while unseen obstacles grabbed at my bare feet. As I neared the road I heard a vehicle start, the grinding of gears as it was put in gear, and the sound of spinning tires as it screeched off. Running to the road I couldn't make out the vehicle. Whoever it was had kept the lights off.

What had been a mad barefoot dash was now a slow painful walk back to camp. After putting my boots on, I lit the lantern, went to Matilda and got another clip for my pistol, and enough bullets to reload my half used clip. My tent was destroyed. The shotgun blasts had blown up all the canned goods and riddled my waders. I carried the lantern and searching beside the road I found five spent shotgun shells. I didn't pick them up. They were from a twelve gauge and had been loaded with buckshot. Somebody doesn't shoot buckshot at a person in hopes of only scaring them. I did not see any footprints. Finding a small stick I picked up the shotgun shells by putting the stick in the blown out end and dropped them into my handkerchief. I didn't think there would be any fingerprints, but it was worth a try. I know the police will be out to see me in the morning so there was no need to drive to town. I put the shells in Matilda.

My coffeepot would hold enough water to make a few cups and I started a fire. I didn't feel like sleeping, and don't think whoever my not so brave assailant had been would be back. But, I also had a strange feeling that whoever had tried to kill me wasn't the person who had killed Barbara. Whoever had killed Barbara shot her point blank in the head. The same person would have been smart enough to shoot me while I was sitting by my fire, or waiting for a time when he or she knew they couldn't miss.

While drinking a cup of coffee out of a tin cup that would now only hold two swallows before hitting the level where it had been shot, my Guardian Angel came back and in his normal dull, monotone voice, said. "I saved you once again. See what a good guy I am." Guns and violence do not usually phase my Guardian Angel. I think it is because he can't get hurt.

"Pea Brain, where did you run off to?" I grumbled. Besides not being the happiest person without my eight hours of sleep, getting shot at makes me grumpy.

"I thought maybe I could circle around behind whoever it was and get a glimpse of them. But it didn't work."

"Thanks for trying," I replied.

He shrugged his shoulders like, 'what are guardian angels for'?

After another cup of coffee, I went back to the aspen stand and lay back down, only this time I kept my boots on. I didn't really sleep, but tossed and turned, not all of it because of the coffee.

The sun had been up for several hours when Sheriff Rogers, followed by a white Ford sedan, drove in. Two men got out of the car, dressed like they had been to the Eddie Bauer store and bought all new outdoor outfits - all except the shoulder holsters - and the cameras hanging around their necks that would have made a Japanese man envious. They looked like they fit in the woods about as much as most people who sing in a country western band have ridden a horse - riding horses is not good for starched Levi's or blown dry hair.

"What happened to your tent? It looks like an ambush in Nam that backfired," Sheriff Rogers said.

"Somebody last night riddled it with shotgun blasts. They must have thought it was a raccoon," I said.

Sheriff Rogers didn't say a word but looked at the tent, scowled at me, and then looked back at the two Eddie Bauer guys, who were looking around like there were a lot more places they would rather be than in the woods.

"This is Homicide Detective Rich DeLong and Detective Andy Chavez. Their home office is in Denver," Sheriff Rogers said.

"Glad to meet you," I said to each man as I shook hands.

They both mumbled something that was a greeting. I imagine they had been driving most of the night, and back in Denver they don't have to be at the office until 9 in the morning, which is when most crooks are going to bed.

Pea Brain was walking back and forth between them pretending he was peeing on their shoes with a smile on his face like he was having an affair with the president's wife and not even the C.I.A. knew.

"You found the body?" Chavez asked me, now all business.

I nodded.

"Somebody shot up his tent last night," Sheriff Rogers said to Chavez.

Chavez didn't show any surprise.

"Rogers here says you're some kind of famous private eye?" DeLong said, his voice sounding like he was talking to a guy who liked to fondle sheep.

"Famous is a strange word," I told him.

"Good answer," my Guardian Angel said and kicked DeLong in the shin.

"Do you have any idea who might want to shoot you?" Chavez asked me. "Make any enemies, bar fights, grab somebody's girlfriend?"

"I haven't been anywhere," I lied, not knowing why I lied, but it has always been hard for me to tell the truth to the police, even detectives who I have great respect for. Always remember the legal system is not based on justice. It is based on lies and deceit - may the best liar win - and, if you do get into trouble, it helps a lot if you are an athlete or a politician, but not good if you are brown, black, or any combination of the two.

"The way your tent is riddled how did you manage to not get hit?" Chavez asked.

I pointed to the aspen trees and my sleeping bag. "I was sleeping over there. I shot back seven times," I told him.

Chavez and Delong didn't say anything, but I could read their minds. They thought I was a lousy shot, but, they didn't bother to ask why I bought a tent and then slept in the trees, which suited me fine as I didn't want to get into a lengthy conversation about my Guardian Angel. Trying to tell somebody about an entity that nobody can hear or talk to except me is tough.

"A bad thing about my job is no recognition," my Guardian Angel pouted.

"It builds character," I told him.

"I don't need character. I'm dead," he replied sullenly.

Delong and Chavez started taking pictures of everything, leaving Sheriff Rogers and I standing by the fire. "These guys won't be in town more than a few hours. They came down to make a report and head back to Denver. They don't give a barn owl's hoot what happens down here in the boonies. There are two or three murders a day in Denver to keep them busy," Sheriff Rogers said.

"The joy of city living," I said.

Chavez walked over to us. "Are these the casings from your pistol?" he asked me, holding out a baggy with seven spent cartridges.

"9 m.m.," I said. "Browning."

"Mind if I keep them."

He could keep them and melt them down and pound them into ashtrays for all I cared. The Vietnamese made a fortune on shell casings making everything from ashtrays to lamps. I don't see anything wrong with a detective making a little honest money on the side. Before I could answer, Chavez was already walking away looking for something else to take a picture of.

After another few minutes of snooping around both detectives came over - a crime scene two days old is not exactly a hot bed of information. I started walking toward the river before they could say. "Ok, show us where you found her."

Sheriff Rogers and I stood by the pool while the detectives did their detective thing. I'll say one thing, they weren't afraid to get wet as they trudged back and forth across the river, scrutinized everything carefully and snapped photograph after photograph. They only asked two questions. "All of these tracks are from you guys when you recovered the body?"

The area around the pool looked like a wallow for cattle it was so tracked up. Sheriff Rogers answered, "Yes."

Their second question was directed to Sheriff Rogers specifically. "Why didn't you take photographs of the crime scene before and after you removed the body?"

I also wanted to hear his answer.

Rogers squirmed around like an 18-year-old private in the army who had just been told he had K.P. for the weekend. Needless to say he didn't have an answer.

Chavez and DeLong frowned at Rogers like he was as dumb as a defense attorney. When they were finished, they took the yellow ribbon down and we crossed the river. I showed them where Barbara's clothes had been. They didn't say a word.

When we got back to the camp, we all fidgeted around like a bunch of men at a family reunion who hadn't seen each other in years. There really wasn't much to say and we were trying to show how good we were by not telling dirty jokes, getting drunk, or looking at each other's wives.

Finally, Detective Chavez said to Rogers, "When you get a copy of the autopsy report, send us one."

DeLong gave me a hard long look. "Whoever shot at you was probably the person who killed the girl."

"Well, duh," my Guardian Angel said.

They then drove off without saying goodbye.

"I hate detectives," Rogers muttered.

Sheriffs, Highway Patrol officers and street cops, all hate detectives. The same way a guy working the floor in a factory hates his shift boss.

"You want some coffee?" I asked him.

He shook his head.

"You'll probably want to clear out of here after last night," Rogers said.

I went over to Matilda and got the handkerchief with the shotgun shells and gave it to Rogers. "I found these on the road, check them for prints. There's a long shot the person didn't wear gloves when he loaded his shotgun. "And no," I added, "I'm not leaving yet, the killing of my tent made this thing kind of personal."

"If I was you I'd at least move my camp," Rogers told me, then held up the shotgun shells. "You should have given these to the homicide boys."

"I don't like detectives either," I said, adding, "But I will move my camp."

As Rogers walked to his car he was smiling, but he had seemed bummed out I was staying. I called to him. "I'll come by soon. I want to see the autopsy report and find out about those shells."

He was gone before I could ask him if the news was out yet about the murder. But I figured it was - news in small towns travels faster than the speed of light.

Most of my gear I pitched in the garbage can. The Coleman lantern and stove were ok, as was my fishing pole, my little packet of flies made in India, and, thank God, the beer had been in the river. Everything else lost the battle with the buckshot. I put the remaining gear in Matilda and was about to get in when I stopped. I've always been a stubborn man and I don't give up easily. I locked Matilda. I needed to search the area one more time. What the hay, there is no boss waiting for me to punch the time clock.

The boot print by my camp had been destroyed by the detectives. I searched the road one more time for any footprints left by my shotgun shooting assailant, but struck out again.

"Maybe they don't have feet," my Guardian Angel said.

Any tire marks left by his vehicle were destroyed by either the detectives or Sheriff Rogers' vehicles.

I wondered what I would do if I was going to kill somebody, who I knew was by the river, but I didn't want to leave any trace.

I sure wouldn't walk down the trail running beside the river. About ten yards from the trail went off the trail and walked through trees and small bushes. All the way to the pool I found nothing. I crossed above the pool, where the water wasn't over a foot deep, and cut back to where the clothes had been neatly stacked. I came to the small stream that emptied into the Chama River from the meadow. It wasn't deep or wide, but I figured farther into the meadow there are places it could hold fish, and would probably have a few scattered beaver ponds along its banks. Turning back, I didn't follow the trail, but went off it about ten yards and walked in the tall, clumpy grass. I hadn't gone more than ten yards from where the clothes had been when I saw a glint in the grass. I picked up a wrapped stick of Wrigley's Spearmint gum. It hadn't been there long as the paper was still bright, although the gum itself felt brittle. I put the gum in my pocket, searched the area where the folded clothes had been and the edge of the pool, but found nothing. I discovered nothing else on my way back to camp. I crossed over the footbridge and looked back up the meadow into the wilderness area before going to Matilda.

"That was a lot of searching for only one lousy stick of gum," my Guardian Angel said.

Matilda started right up, reliable lady that she is, and while she warmed up, I wrote in my notebook. I now have 33 clues. Driving off, I wondered if Ann makes decent coffee.

"A lady as pretty as Ann doesn't have to know how to cook," my Guardian Angel said elbowing me in the side.

I was driving into the community with the four new cabins as Sheriff Rogers was driving out. He didn't smile or wave.

Ann's blue Ford Explorer was parked beside the second cabin. There was a stack of firewood as tall as a man and as long as the cabin. I admired the log cabin. It wasn't large, two or three bedrooms at the most, natural logs giving it a cozy look. It had a large picture window with the curtains closed. There was no TV antenna on the roof or satellite dish in the front yard. There was a wooden porch by the front door with three steps up, leaving space underneath for storage or where a dog could sleep. I went to the front door. There was a barbecue grill in the corner of the porch. I knocked on the door three times.

Ann opened the door, clutching a brown bathrobe tightly around her. She was barefoot. The tears running down her face would have put a rain forest to shame. I wanted to hug her. Pig that he is Pea Brain fell to his knees and started kissing her feet. "Come in Roosevelt," she sobbed, rubbing her face with the sleeve of her bathrobe. "I must look a mess."

"No, even crying you are beautiful," I said.

She gave me a fleeting smile.

The door opened directly into the living room, which connected to a small dining room with an open kitchen. The floors were stained wood, with colorful Indian rugs scattered around, and all the furniture was pine. One wall was a massive rock fireplace. Prints of western scenes were hanging on the other walls. There was a small hall that must lead to the bedrooms and I presumed the bathroom.

Ann sat in a chair and curled her feet underneath her. She reminded me of a sad little kitten. Pea Brain stood behind her rubbing her shoulders. I sat on a small sofa with a low table in front of it. On the table was a large wooden bowl filled with odds and ends. "It's so terrible," Ann sobbed. "My poor sister, murdered."

I felt her pain, her anguish, her loss. I felt like I had known her my entire life. I didn't know if I should get up and hold her, give her my handkerchief, or be polite and tell her I could come back later. I was trying to think of something to say, when several objects in the wooden bowl caught my eye. There were four packages of Wrigley's Spearmint gum, each opened, with sticks of gum out of each one. Ann oh Ann.

"Alert, run, dive, escape," my Guardian Angel warned running over to me.

Ann started to sob and buried her face in her hands. She was wearing large gold loop earrings and they seemed like haloes on either side of her head.

"Either that or links of chain," my Guardian Angel said.

CHAPTER FIVE
COWBOY SOUP

Sitting in Ann's living room her last name, Maiden, suddenly rang a bell in my head that put Big Ben to shame. Ann's and Barbara's father, Big Abe Maiden, as he is called in Houston, owns more topless bars across Texas than there are oil wells. His topless bars are called gentlemen's clubs, have valet parking, four star meals, young ladies with no tattoos, and are always located as close to the downtown government complexes and main police stations as possible. He is also reputed to be in every other racket except drugs. It is said he thinks drugs are the root-of-all-evil while gambling, prostitution and extortion have honor. There are rumors that his girls have slept with every politician in the Lone Star State and every football player who played for the Dallas Cowboys. He lives in a house in Houston that is so big, people driving into town for the first time think it is a hotel.

"Sheriff Rogers told me all about you, Mr. Roosevelt," Ann said. "He also informed me you were thinking about trying to find out who did this awful thing."

I started to speak, but Ann cut me off. "I'll pay you to find out who murdered my sister."

I have learned that money is not a detriment to being an old hippie.

"Is $7,500 in cash enough?" Ann asked.

Hearing the amount I went weak at the knees. "Yes, I....." Ann cut me off again. "I'd also like you to stay here with me. There are no hotels close by and it would give you a place to work from. I was going to drive up to your camp and ask you, but you happened to stop by."

"I don't know," I said, “It is not always a good idea to get to close to ones work.”

"Please?" Ann half begged. "It would make me feel safer. Whoever killed my sister might also want to kill me."

"Staying in a house with a good looking, single, distraught woman has many tantalizing possibilities,” my Guardian Angel said, “Even if I don’t trust her.”

Even with my feelings for Ann I wondered if Ann was a Black Widow who chewed Wrigley's Spearmint gum. But, at the same time, it was true somebody might want to kill her. "Ok," I said, throwing any apprehension to the wind.

My Guardian Angel smiled so big I thought his cheeks might crack.

Ann smiled at me in relief and for a reason I could not understand she reminded me of a Cocker Spaniel who was about to get a chewy bone. "Get your things and I'll show you your room," she said.

I got my suitcase and briefcase out of Matilda and went back into the house. Ann led me to my room. The door to Ann's bedroom was open as we passed and I noticed her clothes were folded neatly on a chair.

Another bedroom door was closed and I figured it was Barbara's old room. My room had a single bed, a small divan, and a closet. "We have to share a bathroom," Ann told me.

"I wonder if in her grief she would like to share her bed?" my Guardian Angel asked and rubbed his hands together so fast I thought they might catch on fire.

"Pea Brain, you can really be sorry at times," I told him.

"Opportunistic is the word," my Guardian Angel said with a sly grin.

"No crude," I said.

"You hang your things up while I get dressed and then I'll rustle up some breakfast. I imagine you have some questions?" Ann said.

She closed my door as she left.

Pea Brain started to follow her to her room but I stopped him.

"You are about as much fun as mud," he pouted flopping down on the floor like a spoiled kid about to throw a tantrum.

It didn't take me long to hang my few pair of Levi's and shirts in the closet and set my shaving kit and towel in the bathroom. Looking in the mirror, which I hadn't done in a few days, I noticed how dirty I was.

Vanity was a big question to me when I was a hippie. How can a person not condone ego and be a non-conformist when the act of wearing long hair and beads was in fact vanity and conforming to other hippies?

"Everyone has their own uniform," my Guardian Angel said, "and in truth most of you old hippies were just stupid."

Ann's bedroom door was closed and I figured I had time to take a shower. A few days in the boondocks are a great reminder of how great indoor plumbing and hot showers are. I think the thing that really killed the hippie movement, besides the police and people had to get jobs, was people found out what a bummer outdoor outhouses and lice are.

After my shower, trimming my beard, and all that other pampering stuff, I put on clean Levi's and a blue western shirt. I even put on my good pair of cowboy boots. I was ready to two-step across Texas with a big old gal from Dalhart, Texas who could drink more beer than Willie Nelson, while he was trying to figure out how the I.R.S. had caught him, and how many more gigs he had to do to pay at least half of his alimony.

Smelling bacon and coffee I headed for the kitchen. Ann was wearing a pair of black pants that were painted on, a white western shirt with no sleeves and red boots. She had two buttons open at the neck of her shirt. Her hair wasn't pulled back into a pony tail but fell down her back in black waves. She had on red lipstick. She was wearing a dangling pair of earrings made from beads that resembled multi-colored feathers. My heart fluttered as I looked at her.

"Your mom would not approve," my Guardian Angel said, "but who cares."

Within a few minutes we were eating scrambled eggs, bacon, toast, and drinking coffee. I was ready to ask her if she would marry me. "What time do you have to go to work?" I asked her instead.

"A lady in town is going to run the place for me for a few days," Ann said. "But truthfully, I don't know why my father even keeps it open. It doesn't make enough money to gas up a Volkswagen."

"From what I understand, your father doesn't need money," I said, trying to be tactful and ignore the snide remark about Volkswagens.

She smiled. She had a gorgeous easygoing smile that really didn't match her dark eyes. "My daddy doesn't need anything," she said, with an undercurrent of bitterness, or sadness, or a little bit of both.

"Have you called him yet and told him about Barbara?" I asked, sounding like a concerned big brother.

"I called his office and left a message. They don't know where he is. He can disappear for weeks at a time. He'll call as soon as he hears. I doubt he'll come out here. He'll arrange for the body to be shipped back to Houston and buried by her mother," Ann said matter-of-factly, with no trace of her earlier sadness.

Maybe she was one of those people that when grief hits, they have a good cry and then go on with their lives. I don't want to get into her personal life with her father, or Barbara's. I want to solve a murder and I knew I would hear all the sordid details in time.

Ann started to clear the table. Watching her walk to the sink was enough to take my breath away. If she was working in a country bar in Texas she would need a suitcase to carry her tips home every night.

She refilled our coffee cups after she put the dishes in the sink. There was no dishwasher, I like that. No TV, I like that. And no wedding ring on her finger, I like that.

"Most men could care less about rings," my Guardian Angel said. "But, I forgot, you are Mr. Morals."

"And proud of it," I said.

My Guardian Angel stuck his finger down his throat.

"Who would want to kill your sister?" I asked Ann point blank when she sat down. There was no polite way to start.

Ann got up from the table. She came back with an ashtray and set it on the table. "I only have one ashtray," she said. "I don't smoke much and when I do, I take the ashtray with me. I think they are disgusting lying around the house all full of butts and ashes." She made a face like she had just stepped in cat poop.

I quit smoking years ago. Not so much because I didn't like to smoke, but because it cost so much.

Ann rummaged through a kitchen drawer and took out a pack of Lucky Strikes, lit it with a stick match, and inhaled deeply.

I was staying with a Wrigley's Spearmint gum chewing, stick match striking, Lucky Strike smoking, sister of a girl who had recently been murdered, and to top it off I was falling for her. My Guardian Angel was standing in the corner butting his head against the wall.

I know one thing for sure this part of the world has the market cornered for Lucky Strikes.

"My sister was every man's nightmare," Ann said, sitting once again at the table. "She would go out with them, flirt, hang all over them, and then most of the time when the guy was howling at the moon she came home. She went out with every guy around here, not that there are that many. She had them all scratching at each other like tomcats during a full moon."

"Smoking makes her talkative," my Guardian Angel said done with banging his head against the wall, "and Barbara might have been my type of girl."

"Which one of the cowboys I met at the bar did she go out with?" I asked.

Ann looked at me like I must be the stupidest detective in the world if I didn't hear what she had just said. "Every one of them," she replied, arching her right eyebrow at me to emphasize the fact I was an idiot. A woman arching her eyebrow at me has always been one of my weak points.

Cowboy soup, I thought before I asked, "did anyone of them buy her the diamond tennis bracelet she was wearing?"

Ann laughed but it was not a happy laugh. "These boys don't have enough money to take a girl out to a movie. If they did have money they would spend it on their horse. The ranger, Brad Fisher, bought her that bracelet. He was so infatuated with her he was ready to leave his wife and daughter."

"Did she sleep with him?" I asked.

"She slept with him. I caught them on the sofa one day when I came home from work early. She got a kick out of sleeping with married men."

"I wonder if Ann is like me and likes to watch?" my Guardian Angel said.

There has to be loopholes for some people to get into heaven.

So Barbara had been a tease, a flirt, and liked to sleep with married men. Maybe it was because married men weren't a threat or maybe she liked causing a lot of grief?

"Who bought her that gold chain she wore around her stomach?" I asked.

"That highway patrolman from Alamosa. Let me think. His name is. His name is Hayworth, Gary Hayworth."

"Lord, Roosevelt," my Guardian Angel said.

"Do you think she slept with him?" I asked.

Ann smiled wryly at me. "Men don't buy girls gold chains to wear around their belly unless they plan on seeing them with only the chain on."

There is one nice thing about women in their forties. They're no fools. "And he's married," I added.

"Bingo, you win the ten thousand," Ann said, taking a deep drag on the cigarette. "She dated that other cop, Hoffman once or twice but I don't know if she slept with him or not. He's also married."

"Who do you date around here?" I asked Ann, hoping it was nobody.

"I came out here to get away from men, Roosevelt, right now I want a man like the House of Representatives wants a pay cut."

"Divorce?" I said.

"Yes," Ann answered, but not sounding devastated. "Men's and Women's, a friend of mine used to say. We are both as dumb cowbirds when it comes to each other."

I dropped the subject. "Did Barbara move here for any specific reason?" I asked.

"I don't know if you know it or not but my father runs topless bars all over Texas. He also has high priced call girls. By high priced I mean the best - two to three grand a night - some more. That doesn't count the tip. The girls work for 15% and get all of the tips. Most of them make more money than doctors. The women who work for him are housewives, lady lawyers, ladies with class and nice wardrobes, most people would never guess what they did. Barbara always craved excitement and she talked a man who runs daddy's business in Austin into setting her up. Daddy found out about it and sent her out here to stay with me."

"I bet the man doesn't work for your dad anymore."

"They found him in the bay covered with crabs," Ann said, with no emotion in her voice. "It was ruled a suicide."

I wanted to say he killed himself because it was easier to commit suicide than wait to be murdered. But, if I had a daughter, and somebody set her up to be a hooker, he might wish all that happened to him was he was tossed in the ocean. But, life being how it is, I have always had a great empathy for prostitutes.

“I love prostitutes,” my Guardian Angel said. “I think it is a much more honorable profession than being a banker or a stock broker. At least with a prostitute you know you are going to get screwed.”

"How long have you been out here?” I asked Ann.

I like to throw in trivia questions when I'm looking for information, sometimes I learn a lot from bits and pieces of idle conversation.

"I came out in early April. It was still cold. Daddy bought me this cabin. I opened the bar and cafe in May when fishing season started. I'll run it till hunting season is over and I plan on staying here all winter. The thought of curling up by the fire and reading a book really excites me anymore."

I looked closely at Ann, not frivolously, but past the skintight pants, past the two buttons open on the blouse. She looked tired and lonely. Tired lay underneath her skin like a dark robe - loneliness was behind her eyes. It was confusing. How can she be tired of men when she dresses the way she does? Around her gypsy eyes I could see tiny worry lines.

"Don't fall in love," my Guardian Angel pleaded. “Fall in lust.”

"It might be too late," I said.

"You are too impulsive," he said.

"I have always believed in love at first sight," I said.

"Grow up, one who is lost in the 60's," he said.

"How long was Barbara here?” I asked Ann.

"She came here about two months ago."

"There's no need to ask any more questions now," I said.

She looked relieved. She butted the cigarette, stood, and dumped the ashtray in the garbage, put the Lucky Strikes back in the drawer, and started to do the dishes. "What are you going to do now?" she asked me, seemingly happier doing a woman thing.

"I think I'll go see Ranger Fisher."

"If I'm not here when you get back the key to the front door will be in the barbecue on the porch."

For somebody who was supposed to be afraid of getting killed that was about the lamest place to hide the key to her house. But I was not going to be an idiot and try and tell a woman what to do - especially one who smokes Lucky Strikes and lights them with a stick match.

"Don't forget the Spearmint gum," my Guardian Angel said.

I was about to go out the door. "How about I buy a couple of steaks and we barbecue tonight," I called to Ann.

She came around the corner of the kitchen, drying her hands on a dishtowel. "Pick up some beer while you're at it," she said.

I started up Matilda and smiled to myself. I still had beer in the car. I am going to get off cheap.

It didn't take me long to drive to the Ranger Station. A sign in the driveway informed me that Smokey the Bear said fire danger was moderate. Two green government trucks were parked in the parking lot and a ten-speed bike was leaned up against a tree. A flagpole in the front yard proudly flew Old Glory and underneath it, a flag of Colorado. About a hundred yards behind the Ranger Station was a log cabin with a heavily rusted Jeep Cherokee parked in the driveway. In the small front yard were a swing set and a bicycle with training wheels.

I went into the Ranger Station and a young woman, tanned, with rosy cheeks, sat behind a standard military type metal desk with a computer on it. There was a table with a variety of flyers stacked neatly on it. The woman stood. She had on a short sleeved ranger shirt with her nametag, green long pants, and cowboy boots. She wasn't wearing a pistol so I figured she was working during the summer as a volunteer while majoring in forestry at some Colorado college. She had red hair, cut only slightly longer than an army recruit. Although she wasn't fat, she was big boned and strong, about 5'4" tall. Her arm muscles were well developed and her shoulders looked like a man's. In Montana they call these kinds of wholesome looking outdoor women, 'Thunder Thighs'. In Wisconsin they call them, 'Two Bucket Women,' because they are strong enough to carry two buckets at a time. In San Francisco they call them, 'Men'.

"May I help you?" she asked pleasantly in a deep voice that sounded surprisingly like my Uncle Harry who had been a Marine Drill Sergeant.

"I'm looking for Brad Fisher." I read her nametag, Reeves.

"Brad is home eating lunch," she informed me and added, "His house is out back."

I went outside. I wanted to ask Fisher some questions but I didn't want his wife around. If his wife didn't know about his involvement with Barbara I didn't want to be the one to inform her, her husband had been sleeping with Barbara Maiden and spent about 1/3 of his yearly salary on a diamond bracelet that the money should have gone to the daughter's college fund. The bracelet seemed a little out of his monetary range - unlike most government jobs, forest rangers don't have a lot of opportunity to steal money from the public.

I waited for Brad to come back to the office after lunch. Ranger Reeves came out a few minutes later. I could tell she didn't like me. "He's home," she told me.

"I don't want to disturb him, I'll wait."

"He won't mind, a few days ago his wife and daughter went to Denver to see her folks."

Ranger Brad Fisher answered the door within 30 seconds of my knock. He was tall, clean shaven, and had short dark brown hair and blue eyes. He looked to be in his late twenties. His face and arms were tanned a shoe leather brown and his hands were used to work. He looked good in his uniform, but the pistol on his hip seemed out of place. Taking a guess I thought it was a Colt 357 - a man's gun, big enough to knock down a semi-truck at 100 yards. "Yes," he said, in a tone that he thought I was a salesman trying to sell the government some common sense.

I could see no reason to not get to the point. "I'm Bob Roosevelt. I'm a private detective. Ann Maiden hired me to help solve the murder of her sister. I'd like to ask you a few questions."

Brad's shoe leather tan seemed to pale and he glanced over my shoulder like he thought the F.B.I. was about to start a full-scale assault on his house. "I don't think I can help you," he said nervously, adding, "I've already talked to the Sheriff."

"Ann told me about you and Barbara," I said.

Brad looked at me like I was the grim reaper and motioned me to come in. The house was clean in a lived in sort of way. The only thing out of the ordinary was the blanket and pillow on the sofa. I figured Brad had been sleeping on the sofa longer than the few days his wife has been gone. Affairs with pretty young blonds have a way of getting in the way of a man's sex life with his wife.

"Unless the wife is into threesomes," my Guardian Angel said with a crooked grin.

I followed Brad into the kitchen. He was halfway through a sandwich and we sat at the kitchen table. A window faced into the deep woods behind the house. A gray squirrel sat on a limb of a tree looking at us like we are the weirdest things he has ever seen, which, to Mother Nature's creatures, we probably are.

"I didn't kill Barbara," Brad told me as he picked up his sandwich but his hands were shaking.

For some strange reason I felt sorry for him, or maybe not sorry for him, but sorry for the mess he had created in his life.

"Did your wife find out about you and Barbara?" I asked.

Brad nodded sheepishly. "I was stupid," he said.

"You only feel stupid because you got caught," my Guardian Angel scolded him.

"I kept making up excuses about why I had to be out at night. One night I met Barbara by the river, that camping area with the stand of aspens and footbridge, my wife caught Barbara and me."

"That diamond bracelet you bought her must have cost you a nice chunk of change," I said.

Brad looked out the window. "I was stupid," he said again.

"You should have taken her to Denver," my Guardian Angel said. "Every idiot knows you don't mess around in your own backyard. And if you want another tip, if you are going to have an affair have it with a married woman, they can't talk."

"Where did you get the money to buy the bracelet?" I asked Brad.

For an instant it seemed Brad was offended by the question. I looked at him and let him know I was trying to solve a murder, not become the most popular guy in southern Colorado.

"I had saved for two years and bought it for my wife."

God, I thought, he sure had it bad.

"My life was fine until Barbara showed up," Brad said and he seemed like he was about to cry. "I've been here two years, have a good wife, a beautiful 5 year old little girl and a great job. Then I met Barbara one day by the river. I was checking water levels and came around a bend on the river and there she was sun bathing in the nude. She didn't even try to cover herself when she saw me. She sat up, smiled, and then lay back down. The next time I saw her, she was working at the bar in Platoro. One thing led to another."

"Were you jealous of her dating other men?" I asked.

"Not enough to kill her, Mr. Roosevelt," Brad said.

For some reason I believed him, but I've had more than one of my beliefs shoved back into my face.

I stood. "Don't get up," I told him, and added, "Listen, I hope it all works out with your wife."

Brad couldn't look me in the eyes.

Ranger Reeves was standing outside the office as I walked back to my car. She walked over to me. "You're that private eye everybody's talking about," she said. "Brad couldn't have killed Barbara. He isn't that kind of man," she informed me.

As I got into Matilda I said to Ranger Reeves, "Somebody killed her," and noticed she was wearing three small gold loops in each ear.

The look Reeves gave me would have made Attila the Hun pale.

As I drove away Ranger Reeves was standing with her feet apart and her hands on her hips.

"Did you take note that she is wearing boots and has small feet?" my Guardian Angel asked.

"No, I didn't. Thanks."

I drove to Antonito to see the Sheriff and also to pick up two steaks at the store.

Sheriff Rogers was at the jail sitting in the office, looking bored, and still being rude by wearing his cowboy hat indoors. "Nobody in jail you can play basketball with," I joked, pushing his rudeness out of my mind.

"Not funny, Roosevelt," he said.

Some people have no humor in their lives.

"I suppose you stopped by to see the autopsy report?" he said, and handed me a large manila folder. "There's photographs in there also."

There were photographs of Barbara laid out on a stainless steel table. I hadn't noticed when we had pulled her out of the water but there was no doubt she was a natural blond and her golden body was evenly tanned all over. There were close ups of the bullet hole in her temple - so close you could see the three holes in her ear lobe for earrings. I thought it strange she didn't have earrings on.

"It was a 22," Rogers said. "Not enough left of the slug to get any rifling's. The bullet disintegrated in her head, and there are no powder burns around the hole so she wasn't shot at point blank range."

There was nothing in the report that caught my attention until the end. ‘Semen found in anal tract, probably not forceful as there are no signs of struggle on body and lubricating jelly was used. Also traces of semen found in vagina. Semen samples have been sent to the state laboratory to see if they match.'

"How long will it take to get the lab report?” I asked Rogers as I placed the folder on the counter.

"Sometimes a day, sometimes a week, it depends on how many golf games the lab boys have set up."

"Have you found out anything?" I asked Rogers, perplexed by the lab report.

"I know she dated every man around here."

"What about Brad Fisher?" I asked.

Rogers fumbled around in his shirt pocket and pulled out his Lucky Strikes. He took a stick match out of his pants pocket, struck it underneath his desk and lit his cigarette. "Brad didn't do it. He isn't the kind. He's a small town boy who met him a city girl that took him for a ride and he didn't know how to handle it."

"I'm staying at Ann's. When you get that report of the semen, call me," I said.

Sheriff Rogers face looked like he'd just been told his 56-year-old girlfriend was pregnant. I don't know if it was nerves or not but he did a strange thing. He took the burned match out of the ashtray, stuck it in his mouth like a toothpick, and started chewing on it.

"Oh boy, oh boy," my Guardian Angel whistled.

I had the door open when I remembered. "Did you find any prints on those shotgun shells?"

"Not a one," Rogers said, like it was the best news he'd heard in weeks.

I went to the store and picked out two T-bone steaks and to be on the safe side, bought a head of lettuce, two tomatoes, a cucumber and some radishes.

After I turned off the paved road from Antonito onto the dirt road leading to Platoro I pulled off the road. I took out my notebook and pencil and added some clues. When I was done, I had 51 clues. I read them carefully. I put my notebook in the glove box and started to drive to Ann's, only one thing really disturbed me, I had a strange feeling that the semen in Barbara's orifices was not going to match.

"Remember what I told you, Roosevelt, murder, pornography, adultery, and your chances of living not good," my Guardian Angel said like he had never been wrong in his life.

"Pea Brain, it's hard to forget when you tell me all the time," I said.

"I don't want you to forget before you get killed," he said. "I don't want you to think you can lay a guilt trip on me."

Turning into Ann's driveway I was no longer thinking about the case. I was thinking about Ann and wondering what it was about her that made me feel good inside, when, if I had any sense, I would be cautious of her.

"Very, very, very, cautious," my Guardian Angel said.

"Very is not a good modifier," I said. "There is always a word that can be used in its place to better exemplify what you are trying to say."

"Dimwit, be cautious," he said.

"Better," I said.

CHAPTER SIX
MOUNTAIN AMBUSH

Ann's Ford Explorer was parked in the carport. I knocked on the door not wanting to walk right in, after all, I'd only been a guest for a few hours. There was no answer so I tried the doorknob. The door wasn't locked. I walked gingerly into the house, fighting back fear that something might have gone wrong. What, I wouldn't know, but something. I heard the shower running, and Ann singing, and I relaxed. She was singing an old cowboy song, "If I had the wings of an angel, over these prison walls I would fly, I'd fly to the arms of my loved one, who'd be kissing some other guy." She had a great country western voice.

"If you like twangs and people who sing through their nose," my Guardian Angel said disdainfully but started running toward the bathroom.

"Pea Brain, no," I ordered.

He turned sadly, "I'm more into bawdy old ballads, sung by ladies with low cut blouses who are half drunk on ale and their husbands are out of town," he said.

I was putting the groceries in the refrigerator when I heard the shower go off. "I'm here," I called loudly.

I didn't want Ann to walk out of the bathroom in all her glory, with me standing there holding a bag of radishes in my hand. Holding radishes isn't much of a manly thing.

I went and got the beer out of Matilda. It had been out of the river so long it was hot. Back in the house, I put a twelve pack in the freezer to chill quickly.

When I turned, Ann was in the kitchen. She had on a red robe, was barefooted, and her wet hair was hanging straight down her back. Under the robe were miles and miles of scrubbed pink skin. She was so lovely it made me smile.

My Guardian Angel licked his lips but kept his mouth shut.

"You don't know how much I'm glad you're here," Ann said, making me feel all warm and fuzzy inside.

"I have the steaks and beer, and some salad makings," I said, trying to ignore the thought of Ann's freshly scrubbed body.

She turned and walked away. I hoped to get dressed.

I ambled around the living room. There were no photographs of family, no little nick knacks that women collect, no elephants, unicorns, cats, pigs, spoons from different cities or countries hanging on the wall in their own special rack. The house looked more like a motel room and didn’t have a lived in feeling.

I was standing in the middle of the living room when Ann came back. She had on an above the knee light green dress, with string straps. The material clung to her body like pollen to a bee. She was wearing blue cowboy boots. Her lipstick was a pale red and she had put on turquoise stud earrings that complimented her dress. "You're lovely," I said, breathlessly.

Ann tried not to show she was pleased by my comment, but I could tell she was. "I have to run to town for a few minutes, relax, I'll be back soon," she said.

I felt like a little boy who wants to give a girl a flower, but was to shy. I listened to the Explorer start and the grinding of gears as she put the stick transmission into reverse. After she'd backed out of the carport, she ground the gears into first and drove away.

"Whoever shot at you was driving a vehicle that the gears ground," my Guardian Angel said suspiciously.

"It wasn't Ann," I said. "I have no doubt."

"Don't let your budding feelings cloud your reasoning," my Guardian Angel replied.

I waited for a few minutes, making sure Ann hadn't forgotten something and would turn around. I headed to Barbara's room as fast as a junkie heads for a methadone clinic.

Barbara's room had a single bed with a solid brown bedspread. A dark blanket with an Indian design was folded at the foot. There was a small dresser with various lipsticks and other cosmetics on top, and jewelry box containing several gold bracelets and various earrings. In the closet was a variety of clothes, from fancy dresses - expensive - to a dozen or so Levi's of various colors and several dozen western shirts. On the floor of the closet were six pair of expensive cowboy boots. The kind lizards and pythons and large dumb birds give their lives for. The boots were black, brown, white, red, green, and blue. She had spent more money for boots than Matilda had cost. On the closet door was a full-length mirror. There were no photographs or prints on the walls, no curtains over the window just white blinds. I started going through the drawers to the dresser. The first one was full of panties, all silk, all sexy, all colors. Pea Brain's eyes were the size of small plates. The second was full of bras, all silk, all sexy, all colors. Pea Brain was rubbing his forehead. The third drawer was full of teddies, boob-exposed kind, crotch exposed kind, rear end exposed kind, and one black leather one with a leather collar.

"I really like her choice in clothes," my Guardian Angel said in a hoarse voice.

The fourth drawer had massage oils in every flavor and color imaginable.

I was about to go into Ann's room but changed my mind. A woman can always tell when her things have been disturbed.

I stood in the living room and looked out the window. It was peaceful. The meadow the cabins are in is green and lush. The mountains are like good dreams. I know there is a trail running along the river back towards Platoro, and I wondered how long it would take to ride a horse to the campsite where I had camped and found Barbara's body.

I went out to Matilda and got my note pad out of the glove box. I was starting to get confused, which is nothing new, but I figured it would be a good idea to go over my notes.

Sitting on the sofa with my note pad, I wished I owned a cabin in the mountains - a place with all the modern conveniences so I could really enjoy the quiet and the outdoors.

I have gathered a lot of information since leaving the campground and I read through my clue book and added more clues. Somebody tried to turn me into dead with a twelve-gauge shotgun loaded with buckshot. I found a stick of gum by the murder scene - Wrigley's Spearmint gum. Ann has enough Wrigley's Spearmint gum around the house for a Girl Scout meeting. I also found a pack of Lucky Strikes and a chewed on stick match. Ann smoked Lucky Strikes and lit them with a match. I wondered if she has a tattoo on her perk little rear, something about non-filtered cigarettes and tattoos go together. Also, Willie Hood, the cowboy who reminded me of a bear smokes Lucky Strikes. I know Ranger Fisher had had a thing going with Barbara and had bought her a bracelet that he told me he'd saved for to give to his wife. But then, Barbara also slept with both highway patrolmen in the area, Hoffman and Hayworth. Hoffman is married. Barbara had also gone out with the four cowboys I met in Platoro. Barbara had been a hooker in Austin, Texas and judging by her dresser contents didn't leave all of her profession back in Texas. I know Ann's and Barbara's father is the topless bar king of Texas and probably doesn't give to the United Catholic Fund or give a dang about orphans or third world countries that are starving to death. I know Ranger Fishers' wife had gone off to Denver with the daughter, probably after she'd caught Brad and Barbara doing the naked two step. I know Barbara had semen in every orifice of her body except her ears and she had been killed by a 22 short. Sheriff Rogers also lit one of his Lucky Strikes with a stick match and chewed on it - he might only use his Marine lighter for special occasions like when he's locking somebody up. I know Sheriff Rogers seemed disappointed when I told him I was staying and he'd driven over any tracts that might have been left in the dirt from the person who shot at me. I also think he is holding information back from me. I know the two detectives from Denver could care about some sexy tart that got herself killed in the boondocks of Colorado and would never be back. The lady ranger, Reeves, is protective of Ranger Fisher and wears small cowboy boots. Ann's Ford Explorer is a manual transmission and she can't drive without grinding gears. I put the notebook down and then picked it up again to write another note. Neither Sheriff Rogers nor the Highway Patrolmen had taken photographs of the crime scene.

I keep my notebook in the same condition my mind is in - scrambled.

I put my notebook in my suitcase with my pistol. Out of boredom, or the desire to see my face, I went into the bathroom and looked in the mirror.

"You are still ugly, Roosevelt," my Guardian Angel said with a grimace.

I opened the medicine cabinet and besides the normal assortment of headache pills, menstrual pills, dental floss, there were two tubes of KY lubricating jelly.

As I went back into the living room Ann was turning into the driveway. She came in with a smile on her face the size of Texas, like what she had in the brown paper sack was going to make me want to marry her. "I'm starving," she said, "You barbecue and I'll pour the wine."

She took two bottles of red wine out of the sack and sat them on the dining room table. "I thought we'd celebrate you taking on this case and coming to my rescue."

"I have a feeling she and her murdered sister might not have been close," my Guardian Angel said out of the blue.

I suddenly remembered the beer in the freezer and dashed to the kitchen. The beer wasn't frozen, but it was close. Ann stood behind me as I took the beer out of the freezer and put it in the lower part. "I guess I'll make a salad also," she said, seeing all the veggie's I had bought.

It sounded like she liked salad as much as she liked her ex-husband.

"She's a Texas girl, people in Texas don't eat no stinkin' salad," my Guardian Angel said.

"Salad eaters are from Berkley and Boulder and cities like that."

There is nothing to compare with cooking steaks outside on a barbecue, looking at the mountains, knowing there is a tossed salad on the kitchen table, even if ladies from Texas don't like them, sipping wine, and talking to a woman that I feel I am growing close to.

Ann and I had already drunk three glasses of wine. It took one to light the fire, one to wait for the fire to die down and the coals to form, and one to hold while we watched the steaks. "I like mine rare," she said, as the sun was going down.

"You have beautiful hair," I told her, as I flipped her steak. I am brave after three glasses of wine. "Your hair is as black as a starless night."

"You sound like a poet who can't even place his poems with a literary magazine that only pays in copies," my Guardian Angel said.

Ann turned from the rail and smiled at me, giving no hint that she had heard my beautiful hair line so many times it was boring.

Standing close to me she examined the steaks. Her perfume swam around my head like a narcotic.

"Go for it boy," my Guardian Angel coached. "Ask her if she wants another glass of wine, then skip dinner and hot foot it to the bedroom before she falls asleep."

"They're done," Ann said, smiling at me, "and I need another glass of wine."

"Pea Brain, you need patience," I told my Guardian Angel.

"You're as sexy as a smashed turtle on the highway," he said.

"I can't help it if I'm not French," I replied.

I took the steaks into the kitchen, feeling as proud as a cave man hunter who had returned from the wilderness dragging in a bison.

Ann refilled our wineglasses, lit a candle she had put on the table, and turned off the lights. Through the window the sky over the mountains was a pale crimson, its last blaze of color before its death and the birth of night.

Ann sat. The flickering candlelight danced around her face. Her dark eyes held me. She was a gypsy fortuneteller who would tell me what direction to take with my life. She held up her glass of wine to toast. "Life and love and money," she said.

We clinked our glasses together. "Love is enough," I said.

"Only in a fairy tale," my Guardian Angel said with a sad look, remembering his lost love riding off with the knight.

We ate a few bites in silence. "Did you find anything out today?" Ann asked while pouring herself more wine.

I was so intent on being a carnivore I'd lost my manners.

"I don't think Ranger Fisher did it," I said.

"He's an idiot," Ann said. "He met Barbara and thought his safe life, his family, everything that was good was now boring. He found out. Now he's sitting at his Ranger Station hoping his wife comes back and feeling sorry for himself. It serves the jerk right."

Ann's voice was so cold that if I hadn't had four glasses of wine I would have shivered.

"I hope it all works out for him," I said. "I don't think he's a bad guy."

"You men all stand up for each other," Ann said, arching her eyebrow at me, which was a rebuke, but was also sexy and made my Guardian Angel start dancing over the possibilities.

"We really don't have to talk about the murder tonight," I said, trying not to sound angry that Ann had told me I was like all the other men, even though I do try to stand up for all my stupid, low life, sex crazed, men brothers, in our endless battle to be more than a bumbling 16 year old kid to every woman we meet.

Ann ate a few more bites of her steak. She had ignored her salad. I'd eaten my salad first, which is the proper thing to do.

"Well, what do you want to do?" she asked me, sipping on her wine and giving me a sexy look.

Private detectives are supposed to be like doctors, you don't mess with your clients. Myself, I have made a vow I will not sleep with a woman unless I feel I love her and she loves me.

"Don't have an attack of right and wrong oh knight in shiny armor," my Guardian Angel groaned.

I smiled at Ann and felt my heart melting, but couldn't think of how to answer her question.

Pea Brain beseeched me. "Tell her you want to sleep with her. Tell her you idiot. Can't you see she's ready to jump into bed with you as fast as a bored housewife from Kansas would jump into bed with Robert Redford?"

"Let's sit in the living room and talk," I said to Ann.

My Guardian Angel gagged.

Ann gave me a funny look. "You must be a nice man," she said.

"No, he is an idiot," my Guardian Angel said shaking his head.

Ann shut the curtains in the living room, leaving a small slit between them. She poured us two more glasses of wine, lit several candles and sat down on the opposite side of the couch. My

Guardian Angel sat down beside her and put his hand on her knee. "Pea Brain, get away from her," I ordered.

He ignored me.

"Tell me what you believe in," Ann asked. A question that took me off guard.

I felt like I was 22 and sitting in a candle lit room with some old hippie friends, discussing questions that could never be answered. "I believe in peace and love, I suppose," I said.

"You don't sound sure," Ann said.

"I'm not anymore. At one time I was, but not now. Time is a cruel teacher. Peace is for people with peace in their hearts and love is fleeting."

"Do you have children?" she asked.

"I've never been married," I said, feeling a moment of sadness.

"You are a lucky man," Ann said.

"Some people think so," I said. "But I don't feel lucky."

Ann sipped her wine. She was beautiful sitting in the glow of the candles. Her face radiated something to me that made me feel warm. Her dark eyes penetrated my eyes and gazed into my thoughts.

"I would sleep with you," Ann said casually, like sleeping with me would be dessert.

"It would be nice, maybe lovely, but it isn't the right thing to do," I said.

"You are such a big disappointment," my Guardian Angel said, sliding his hand under Ann's dress.

"It will be the right thing to do one day," Ann said, with confidence in her voice.

"I hope so," I said truthfully.

Ann stood and on the way to her bedroom she stopped and kissed me on the forehead. Her lips felt like hot coals but they also soothed me.

"How touching, how quaint," my Guardian Angel said sarcastically.

"Pea Brain, you had better keep your hands off of Ann," I warned him.

"What will you do if I don't?" he asked tauntingly with his hands on his hips.

“Don’t push your luck,” I replied pointing my finger at him.

He turned his back to me.

I gazed into the candle flames. The silence of the house was like a refuge. The flickering candle flames were good spirits reaching out to try and save mankind. Finishing my wine I went to bed.

It was still dark when I woke up. The clock on the end table read 4:30. I got out of bed quietly. My head throbbed and I needed a drink of water so badly I knew what a man dying in the desert feels like who only has beer. "If I was you I'd stay thirsty," my Guardian Angel warned.

I ignored him. I put on my pants, went to the kitchen, turned on the light, and drank two glasses of water. I turned the light off and headed back to the bedroom, noticing the moon's soft light filtering through the slit in the living room curtain. Enraptured by the light I walked into the living room table and stumbled to the floor at the exact same moment the living room window exploded like it had been hit with a 105 recoilless artillery piece. Glass sprayed through the air. Another blast reverberated. I low-crawled as fast as I could to the hall, jumped up, ran the rest of the way to my room, dug out my pistol and started to run back to the living room. Ann, wearing a full length white nightgown, started to come out of her bedroom. Her eyes were as big as coconuts. I pushed her to the floor, "Stay put," I ordered. My Guardian Angel fell on top of her.

I moved to the edge of the hall where it entered the living room, peered around the corner, and fired two quick shots through the shattered window, and then dashed to the door, yanked it open, fell to my knees and pointed the pistol with both hands out into the darkness. In the distance I heard the sound of somebody running and I didn’t think it was the UPS man hurrying to his delivery truck. I darted off the porch, pistol ready, and scampered around the house. Lights from two of the other cabins blinked on like a slow strand of Christmas lights. Satisfied the shooter was gone I went back into the house and turned on the living room lights, being careful to not walk on glass. I had been lucky when I ran through the room. I hadn't cut my feet. Shotgun pellets dotted the living room wall. I helped Ann up but to my surprise she didn't look terribly shaken. Maybe she had been in the infantry. "You give a girl an exciting time," she said, taking a deep breath

"I want to buy your living room table," I told her. "I want to drill a hole in it and wear it around my neck for good luck."

Ann looked at me, for some reason her eyes looked like cat's eyes, and I felt like a wingless sparrow.

A siren blared. I wondered how the police got here so fast as I put my pistol back into my briefcase and hurried to get dressed.

As I pulled on my boots I had a sudden disturbing thought. Why had Ann left her living room curtains slightly open if she wanted me around to protect her?

"She was also taking a shower with the door unlocked when you came back from the store," my Guardian Angel said looking confused.

"Not good," I said.

"I think Ann wants to kill you," my Guardian Angel said like he had to pick his words carefully because he didn't know if he believed them himself.

Why?" I asked, also confused.

My Guardian Angel shook his head, rubbed his chin, scratched his hairy leg, and then shrugged his shoulders. He didn't have an answer.

CHAPTER SEVEN
HONORABLE COWBOYS

Sheriff Rogers, wearing his trusty black cowboy hat, rushed through the door with his gun drawn. My Guardian Angel held up his arms like he was under arrest. Ann and I were sitting at the kitchen table drinking instant coffee. Since I was still alive the Lucky Strike she was smoking even smelled good to me. I wondered how Rogers had gotten here so fast. I don't think the police in Antonito would normally be driving around at 4:30 in the morning. Rogers looked at me, looked at Ann, looked at the window and the glass all over the floor, and put his pistol away. "If this keeps up, Roosevelt," he said, walking toward us, "one of these times your secret admirer isn't going to miss."

"He must be the world's worst shot with a shotgun," my Guardian Angel said.

"This isn't the friendliest corner of America I've been in," I said to Rogers.

Rogers gave me a look that I read to mean, "Then why don't you get out of here."

"I keep telling him the same thing," my Guardian Angel said. "But Roosevelt has a death wish. Down deep I really don't think he likes me."

"How did you get here so fast?" I asked Rogers.

"I happened to be on the highway. I went to Chama, New Mexico to a friend's house, and was coming home when the call came through there had been a shooting. When I heard where it was I had a hunch you'd be involved."

I didn't want to tell Rogers that police weren't supposed to use their squad cars to go on personal trips, especially across state lines, and that most cops don't answer questions. "One of your neighbors called in," Rogers added.

I wanted to say, "No kidding, I figured it was a raccoon who reported the shooting," but common sense told me to shut up.

"Did you see a car or a truck on the highway on your way in?" Ann asked.

Besides being beautiful, she might have a trace of private detective in her, I was about to ask the same thing.

Rogers shook his head which was strange to me. It is about five miles to the highway from the cabins. But thinking about it, I hadn't heard a vehicle drive away. I'd only heard the sound of somebody running down the gravel road away from the cabins, which didn't rule out the fact the shooter might have parked a car on the road and driven toward Platoro and not Antonito.

Rogers walked around the living room, but said nothing. When he headed for the door I got up as he turned on the front porch light. I followed him outside and it didn't take us long to find two shotgun shells a few yards from the front window. "Don't touch them," he ordered me.

He must have forgotten I was the one who gave him the other shotgun shells.

He went to his car and came back with a paper sack, picked up each shell by sticking his pen in the end, and looked at them. It didn't surprise me they were 12 gauge buckshot. "Whoever it is, is a bad shot," Rogers smiled at me as he put the shells in the bag.

"I already said that," my Guardian Angel said with a frown. "I hate it when people steal my lines."

I didn't tell Rogers that I'd tripped over the coffee table and fallen on my face causing the blast to go over my head.

As we went back into the house I noticed people standing on the porch of the first cabin. This was probably the most excitement they had seen since a deer got hit by a pickup truck on the highway. The lights to the second cabin were not on. But the lights to the last cabin were.

Rogers looked at the glass on the floor of the living room and the holes where the shotgun pellets went into the wall. "We won't find anything important here," he said. "You can clean it up," he said to Ann.

I didn't bother to tell Rogers I had fired twice at the shooter. Nor did I tell him maybe he should take photographs of the crime scene.

"I'll send these shotgun shells in for prints, but I imagine they'll be like the last ones," Rogers said, adding, "But before I go back to town, I'll go talk to your neighbors."

As soon as Rogers left Ann got out the vacuum cleaner and started to vacuum up all the glass. I found my two spent cartridges and then pulled the half blown up curtains over the shattered window.

"Who are your neighbors?" I asked Ann after she turned the vacuum off.

"Two of the cabins are owned by older married couples from Denver who are retired. They don't come over."

I could understand that. City people would come out to the mountains to relax and be left alone. Plus, the women might be intimidated by two beautiful single women and not want their husbands coming over and being tempted. Not implying that older men can be tempted by two gorgeous younger women.

"The other one is owned by Jesse Killton, one of the men you met at the bar."

My heart skipped six beats. "Is Killton the red headed cowboy who drives a lumber truck in Chama?" I asked.

"I told you he had a cabin here," Ann said, looking at me like I should never ask her the same thing twice.

I knew what I had to do when the sun came up. I am going to see Jesse Killton.

I opened the door and saw Rogers' car in front of the first cabin.

Ann put the vacuum away and turned off the living room light. "Want some early morning fun?" she asked me and winked.

"You bet he does," my Guardian Angel almost yelled, reminding me of a male cheerleader for U.C.L.A.

I shook my head.

"I would like to slap you one time," my Guardian Angel said sadly.

"I like them hard to get," Ann told me, blew me a kiss, and went to her room.

I went back to bed. I thought about how casually Sheriff Rogers and Ann responded to me getting shot at. Most women, if their living room window was blown out by a shotgun would babble on for weeks and live on a steady diet of Valium and diet coke. I also thought about the slight gap that had been left when Ann closed the curtains and how convenient it made it for somebody to look in. But, it was only an accident that I had gone to the kitchen. I couldn't see somebody standing by the window all night waiting to take a pot shot at me.

"Weird," my Guardian Angel mused.

But even the strange questions did not dent my feelings for Ann. I then slept the sleep of a man who was supposed to be dead.

A sliver of light came through the blinds making the back of my eyelids turn red. I rolled over, not ready to get up and meet the day. Birds began to sing, which at the moment sounded like a lousy punk rock band out of Seattle that hadn't eaten for three weeks, and were wondering why they couldn't tune their guitars. What did get my attention was the command, "Scoot over, Roosevelt."

I opened my eyes and Ann was standing by the bed completely naked. She did a slow turn, showing off a tattoo of a small butterfly on her rear. She laughed, "Only kidding," and walked out of my room.

"Dear lord," my Guardian Angel said breathlessly. "That is my idea of how to wake up."

I took a shower, dressed, and went to the kitchen. There was a note on the kitchen table. "Decided to go to work, see you tonight, you had better eat some vitamins and drink a lot of orange juice so you have the power to say no."

"Your morals get in the way of good sex," my Guardian Angel said.

"Yes, but they keep me disease free," I said.

"A little bit of disease is good for the immune system," my Guardian Angel said.

He must have forgotten how many people died from disease in the 14th century.

I made a cup of instant coffee from hot tap water, slurped it down, and headed for the closest cabin.

I was almost to the porch of the first cabin when a man and a lady walked out. They were in their late 60's, and smiled at me like I was their eldest son who never seemed to be able to get his act together, but they still loved me. The man was plump and bald, and the lady had white, tightly curled hair that reminded me of a Midwest schoolteacher. "What happened last night?" the lady asked me.

I gathered country people aren't used to the sound of gunfire at night like city people are. But I figured Sheriff Rogers had told them what had happened and she wanted to check out his story.

"I really don't know," I half lied. "I wanted to thank you for calling the police."

"We didn't call them," the man said gruffly. "If fool headed people want to kill each other that's their business."

They guy must be from New York and wouldn't stop to help somebody who was hurt because it would make him late for lunch.

"I'm Ann's brother," I said.

"We know who you are," the lady scolded me. "You're that private detective that was on TV not Ann's brother."

She said, private detective, in a tone that I am about one inch higher than stale potato chips.

"At least you're not one of the many men that used to go in and out of that house at all hours of the day and night," Mr. Whoever-He-Was said, they had not introduced themselves.

"And that woman," Mrs. Whoever-She-Was said.

"Kind of heavy set with short red hair," I said.

The lady nodded her head yes and added, "That Barbara was a tart but I didn't want to see her get killed."

"There were two highway patrolmen that used to drop by all the time," Mr. Whoever-He-Was said.

"Did the Sheriff come by often?" I asked.

Mrs. Whoever-She-Was looked at her husband like this was the toughest question she had ever had to answer in her life. "No, but he does go and see Jesse a lot. That Jesse is such a nice young man."

"Sorry to have bothered you," I said, and waved good-bye as I walked toward the closest cabin to theirs, taking note of the new Chevy Suburban in their driveway.

"They seem like a nice couple," my Guardian Angel said.

"Looks can be deceiving," I said.

"Don't play your wise prophet game with me," he replied.

There was nobody home at the other cabin. I had a strange feeling nobody has been there for a while, which was also strange as Ann had told me a couple lived there. The cabin furthest away had a corral by it with two horses looking like they are two protruding ribs away from either becoming a steak in France, or glue for a second grade class in Philadelphia. There was a metal shed by the corral with a padlock on the door. There was a beat up Ford pickup under the carport with the bed full of junk a cowboy would have - wire, fence posts, a half rotten hay bale, various bolts and nuts, beer cans, empty cigarette packs, two flat tires, and bits and pieces of broken rope. The pickup had not been parked in front of the bar in Platoro the first time I met Ann and the four cowboys.

Jesse Killton answered the door within ten seconds of my knock. I had a feeling he'd seen me walk up. I also thought it weird he didn't have a dog. Most single cowboys have some kind of dog so they can have something to kick and cuss at when nothing else is around.

I remembered Jesse as soon as I saw him. He'd sat the furthest from me at the bar in Platoro. "Come on in," Jesse said, a big smile on his face. He was tall, red headed, clean-shaven and had blue eyes that seemed to jump out at me. I don't think he is much over 25 or 26 years old. I went into the living room. There was no doubt it is a single cowboy's house. There was a beat up table in the middle of the living room with four chairs around it. The chairs were resting places for dirty Levi's, shirts, newspapers, and several saddle blankets - the expensive woven kind that look like small rugs. The table had boxes of shotgun shells on it, dirty dishes, fishing reels, and other odds and ends. There was a sofa that looked like it had been reclaimed from the dump. On the wall was a gun rack with two rifles with scopes, and a 12 gauge Remington semi-automatic shotgun. Scattered in no pattern on the walls were pictures of naked women that were torn out of high-class magazines like Gent, Biker's Dream, and other literary magazines.

My Guardian Angel examined the pictures closely, muttering something about cutting edge art and the excellent use of light and tone.

"Clear some room and sit down," Jesse said. "After last night your legs might be a little wobbly."

"You call the police?" I asked as I sat, noticing that the shotgun shells were buckshot.

"I called the dispatcher in Alamosa, they put out the call. Antonito doesn't have a dispatcher at night. I wouldn't have called if I hadn't heard two different kinds of gunshots. The shotgun woke me up and the pistol shots sent me scurrying to the phone."

"How come you didn't come over?" I asked, trying not to make it sound like he was a coward.

Jesse laughed. "I don't stick my nose in anybody's business, for all I knew you were having a shootout with some guy who came over to put the moves on Ann. Or Ann was filling you full of holes for trying to do more than be a nice roommate."

I bet all the deer and bears in the mountains know I am staying at Ann's.

"Well, thanks for calling," I said, not bothering to tell him what had happened. I figured Sheriff Rogers had told him everything.

"Want some coffee?" Jesse asked, as jovial as Santa Claus after Christmas.

Being a cowboy Jesse probably drinks at least six pots of coffee a day whether he needs it or not and the coffee would be black and as thick as cheap oil. I nodded my head. I didn't want him to think I was some wimp and drink water instead of coffee. Jesse brought two cups of lukewarm coffee. My cup had an old grizzled cowboy's face on it and the words. "I spent all my money on beer and women. The rest I just wasted."

"That's funny," I said after reading it.

"The truth," Jesse said.

"Roosevelt is too cheap to spend his money on women," my Guardian Angel said and went back to looking at the pictures on the walls.

The coffee was blacker than old oil and smelled like it had been brewing for at least ten days. I took a sip wondering if it would peel my tongue. It didn't but the caffeine jolt almost made my toes curl.

"I suppose you came over here to ask me some questions?" Jesse asked and then gulped two swallows of oil.

"You know all about me I take it?"

"Sheriff told me about you being a private detective and an old hippie. He even told me you got shot in Iowa."

I wondered how the Sheriff had found out about Iowa. I also marveled at how differently cowboys think about long hairs now. Years ago, when most cowboys wore their hair in the same style Hitler's S.S. did, they took turns beating the hell out of long hairs. Now that almost every cowboy in the world has hair touching the back of his collar it's all different.

"Cowboys have learned chicks like to rub their fingers through hair on the back of a man's neck," my Guardian Angel said. "That is the ones who will let them," he added, giving me a, 'you are lower than a cow pie' look.

"I bet you get your share of babes," Jesse grinned at me.

"Not Mr. Victorian," my Guardian Angel said.

I didn't say anything to either one of them.

"Staying with Ann has to be hard on you," Jesse said. "Although she's nothing like her sister was."

I was about to ask how was she different but Jesse went on. "Barbara would go out with anybody, which didn't mean you were going to get her in the hay, but you at least figured you had a chance. Ann will smile and tease, but I haven't heard of her going out with anybody. Whenever Barbara had parties Ann would always leave."

"I heard Barbara went out with all you guys," I said, trying not to sound like I was digging too deeply for information, but I was happy about the information concerning Ann.

"Willie took her out first but Barbara only went out with him once or twice. I took her out three times but she never even let me kiss her. Then Frank and Ray took her out together. They went out all the time. The three of them would go dancing, go out to eat, go fishing. They were really disgusted when they found out she was going out with those two cops from Alamosa."

I remembered Willie, Frank and Ray, the other cowboys at the bar. "Did she go out with the two cops at the same time?"

"I think she did, but I really don't know. I saw her a few times with both of them and several times with only one of them."

"I take it Barbara was hard to put a halter on," I said.

"I didn't want to halter her," Jesse said, and gave me a sly grin.

I went over to Jesse’s gun rack and took the shotgun down. Cowboys always like to show off their guns. I pulled back on the receiver and locked it open, there was powder residue. I looked down the barrel. The gun smelled like it had been recently fired. "Shot at some stray dogs the other day," Jesse said, "haven't cleaned her yet."

"Nice gun. These other two are deer rifles."

"30/06 Winchester and a 308 Sako."

"You know who might have wanted to kill Barbara?" I asked Jesse, looking right into his eyes.

"Any jealous type," he said, not affected by my eyes. "Maybe even the same person who has tried to kill you twice.”

He laughed like me getting shot at twice was the funniest thing he had heard of since his mother married his father.

"I have to get going," I told him. I would ask him what went on at the parties another time.

Jesse opened the door. I noticed his boots. His feet were no larger than most women. He stood on the porch as I started to walk away. "By the way," I said, "did you ever give Barbara any presents, jewelry, earrings, anything?"

"I learned a long time ago, if a woman likes you, you don't have to buy her things to get some of that loving.”

Maybe Jesse was smarter than I gave him credit for.

"I have a question," my Guardian Angel said as I headed back to Ann's cabin.

"Yes," I said.

"If Ann never went to any of the parties, why would she want to jump in bed with you right away? And don't tell me you are irresistible to women."

"Maybe it's love at first sight," I said.

"Roosevelt, you're not 14."

I was back at the cabin and looking at the shattered window when Jesse drove by. "I don't know about that guy," my Guardian Angel told me.

"I don't either. Friendly people have always made me nervous," I answered.

"I do know one thing," my Guardian Angel said. "That Ann is something else. I can see why you are falling for her. But I still think she wants to kill you."

"I like her," I said.

"You more than like her," he said.

"Maybe," I said.

I decided to take some time and go over my clues. I read and read, and read, and read, and read some more. I felt like chocolate pudding that had always wished it was strawberry. I was reading again when through the hole that was supposed to be a window I saw a truck pull up with sheets of glass in the bed. The men didn't bother to knock on the door but went right to work fixing the window. When they had to come inside they walked right in without knocking. Seeing me on the sofa they didn't even flinch but one said, "Buddy, you must be one happy camper, you could be lying to St. Peter right now."

News in the mountains travels fast. The chipmunks must have an underground gossip network.

"You should be doing the comedy club circuit," I told the man.

"My wife keeps telling me that," he said seriously.

When they were done the funny said to me. "Tell Ann we'll send the bill."

I was never a studious student, one reason why I joined the Army and went to Vietnam, but I decided to read my clues one more time. I now have 64 clues but I am as stumped as a male dog trying to find a tree in the arctic. But, I do know one thing - somewhere in my 64 clues is the key that will open up the case as fast as a person following the Jenny Craig plan for two months will open up a box of chocolates.

I was about to leave and go visit Willie Hood when the phone rang. It's always a perplexing thing when a phone rings in a house where you are only visiting. I felt guilty about answering. I drove my guilt away and answered the phone on the fifth ring. "Roosevelt," Sheriff Rogers' voice boomed. I could see his moustache flapping on his lip and I wondered if he had his hat on. "Those semen tests came in sooner than I thought. I figured you'd like to know they came from two different men."

I didn't know what to say so I said, "thanks," and hung up.

Blond, good looking, gold chain and diamond bracelet wearing Barbara, had been into threesomes.

"I would have liked to see her in action," my Guardian Angel said and looked at the ceiling like he had the worst luck in the world.

Matilda started up on the first turn of the key. She is the most reliable lady I have ever been with in my life and I know she loves me.

As I drove toward the highway I tried to rid my mind of all thoughts. At times when I'm not thinking about a certain subject I can be hit with deep insights that have been overlooked. It usually doesn't work, but anything is worth a shot. I was empty-headedly driving down the road when I drove by the Ranger Station. About a 1/4-mile later I slammed on the brakes, did a U-turn, and drove slowly by the Ranger Station. I hadn't seen them before, but, beside the Ranger Station, and mostly hidden by trees, was a large stack of cinder blocks. There had to be enough to make the footings for a small house. I drove on and then did another U-turn and headed back toward the Ranger Station. I drove by the Ranger Station again and did another U-turn. It is tough being indecisive. I turned into the Ranger Station.

"Are you turning into a woman?" my Guardian Angel asked.

Ranger Reeves didn't greet me like a representative of our forest service should. "I was hoping I wouldn't see you again," she said. "But, I'm glad whoever tried to shoot you missed."

"You're not the only one," I said.

She got up from behind her desk. I looked at her hands as she walked toward me, no rings, and no bracelets. I smiled at her and noticed she hadn't changed her earrings, three tiny gold loops. She wasn't wearing any make-up. "I was wondering where you lived?" I asked.

"You know he didn't do it," she said. I figured she meant Ranger Fisher.

I didn't answer her question and after a few awkward moments she answered my question. "Before you get to where Ann lives there are two cabins. I live in the second one. I rented it for the summer," she said. "The people who own it got tired of the country and moved to Phoenix."

"Why are all those cinder blocks next to the building?" I asked, like cinder blocks were something I really care about.

"I don't know they've been here since I came in the spring. If you really want information, you should talk to Ranger Fisher. I only work during the summer. I go back to school in the fall. I only have one more year then I'll be full time."

I felt proud. During our first meeting I had pegged her correctly as being a student.

"You are still dumb as a post," my Guardian Angel said.

"Has Fisher's wife returned?" I asked.

"She came back yesterday," she said tentatively.

There was no need to go see Fisher right now. I would see him at another time and I also wanted to talk to the Mrs.

"Don't do anything Smokey the Bear wouldn't do," I told Reeves as I left.

I drove toward Antonito.

The old Mexican man at the grocery store told me where Willie Hood's trailer was. "He ez not up in the mountains. Fishing ez still bad," he told me.

I took it Willie wasn't guiding this week.

Willie's trailer was off a dirt road and behind several houses. The houses looked like they hadn't been lived in since Poncho Villa decided sleeping with young Mexican women was more fun than being a revolutionary who could never win.

There was a beat up Chevy truck parked by an old silver trailer that looked like it had seen too many dust storms. The trailer had tires on the roof. A rusty horse trailer was by a corral with three horses in it that looked so tired they could barely walk. There was a stack of hay, tossed haphazardly by the corral. There was a black cur dog chained to the porch that was big enough to eat a cow and mean enough the only thing he really enjoyed was getting kicked and biting people's faces off. He started barking as soon as I turned onto the rutted dirt driveway. I don't know what he is guarding, if this was all my stuff I would want somebody to steal it.

I got out of Matilda a safe distance from the dog. I knew the safe distance since he was at the end of his chain, straining for all his might, and snapping his jaws so hard spit was flying around his face. My Guardian Angel was behind him pulling on his tail. Willie came out of the trailer. "Shut up," he yelled at the dog.

The dog cowered and started whining. Willie scowled at me and walked past the dog. I wasn't going to be invited inside his trailer to sit around all afternoon and drink beer and discuss how outfitters were getting shafted by the government. Willie, once again, reminded me of a bear. He was wide enough and powerful enough to run through a barn wall. His eyes surrounded by his shaggy black hair and full dark beard looked like black embers. I figured Willie was a lot like his dog, only nobody had kicked him lately. The first thing he said was, "Jesse called me and said you'd probably bring your nosy rear over here."

"Nice guy," my Guardian Angel said, adding, "But I didn't know you had a nose on your rear."

I had the urge to ruin old Willie Hood's day. There's nothing more I like to do than kick the stuffing out of big guys with attitudes, but I smiled weakly. "You might be able to help me solve the murder," I said.

"Go ahead and kick his rear," my Guardian Angel said. "He needs it. Forget that old peace and love stuff."

"A broad throws her body around like she did somebody's going to kill her," Willie grunted.

"I thought broad is something that is wide," my Guardian Angel said, modern English confuses him at times.

"I heard you took Barbara out a few times," I said to Willie.

"I took her to eat, took her dancing, she wouldn't even kiss me."

Poor cowboy, I thought. With a way with words that Willie has, I am surprised women don't see him and immediately rip their clothes off and gasp, "Take me you dirty mouthed, low class, idiot."

"You ever go to any of her parties?" I asked.

Willie grinned, or I thought it was a grin, because I couldn't see his mouth because of his beard. "I went to a few, they were something. She'd dance after she got lit, it was something."

"Was there any group sex going on at the parties?"

"I'm not into any group stuff, it isn't right," he said.

"How about Ann? Did she ever stay for the parties?"

"Ann never stayed. She left or went to her room. The only time of day she ever gave me and any of the boys was when we were at the bar."

I couldn't see sitting around chewing the fat with Willie nor did I think he would be a wealth of information. "I'm sorry to have bothered you, but I thought you might know something that would help me," I said and started to get into Matilda.

"I got something, but I don't know if it means anything, you being a private detective and all might think it means something. There's an older couple living in the second cabin from Ann. One night I was going over to Barbara's house, uninvited, I wanted to ask Barbara out. Well, my truck broke down about a mile away and I had to walk in. When I got there, there was a small crack open in the living room window and I happened to look in. The guy was sitting on the sofa and Barbara was down on her knees between the guys legs and she wasn't playing the French Harp."

I didn't know what to say, but there was an undertone in Willie's voice that was sad as he told me the story.

"It was better than renting one of those X-rated movies," Willie said, still unable to hide all of the sadness. "But, unlucky for the old boy, his wife found out and she left him. He moved away a few weeks ago."

As I drove away I had a hollow feeling in my stomach.

"No, it's a hollow feeling in your head," my Guardian Angel said.

I drove to the jail. Sheriff Rogers, dedicated cop that he is, was in the office, investigation isn't one of his strong points. I did want to tell him wearing his cowboy hat inside was just not right. "I'd like to see those photographs of Barbara again that were in the autopsy report," I said.

"I take it the only naked women you ever see are dead ones," Rogers said, but not trying to be funny.

He rummaged through his drawer and handed me the folder. I looked closely at all the photographs for several minutes and then handed him back the folder.

"You know something I don't?" the Sheriff asked.

"I know the sky is blue," I felt like saying. Instead, I smiled at him and walked out. There is something about his moustache and his cowboy hat bad manners that is beginning to bother me.

"You shouldn't be a smarty pants to the police," my Guardian Angel said.

"I know," I agreed.

"Then why were you?"

"I think it's revenge for all the times the police hit me in the head when I was a hippie," I answered.

"You should have known that protesting leads to getting knocked around," he said.

"Not in a democracy," I said.

"All governments lie," he said. "Even though your government is the best, they still lie."

"It's a strange world," I said.

"Without a doubt," he replied. "When good is bad and bad is good, it is beyond strange."

"Would you ever feel strongly enough about something to protest peacefully, knowing you were going to get beat up by the police and dragged to jail?" I asked my Guardian Angel.

He thought for a moment. "I really don't know. Being that I'm dead it's really hard to say."

"It takes a brave person to make change," I said.

"Then the world needs a lot of brave people," he said.

I drove slowly back toward Ann's trying to think.

As I turned into Ann's driveway, I knew there was far more to this case than a sex crazed blond getting her brains scrambled after two guys used her as a pincushion.

CHAPTER EIGHT
BREAKING AND ENTERING

It was late in the afternoon and I figured Ann wouldn't be back from the bar until after dark. I got my notebook and scribbled away for a while. I didn't bother to read over my clues and when I was finished I flopped on the sofa. I needed a nap like a guy on death row needs a new lawyer.

I slept the sleep of an old wino who had begged money all day for food and made so much he bought himself two good bottles of wine - no dreams, no memories, no regrets. When I woke up, I showered and trimmed my beard.

I went outside. Whoever had shot at me ran toward the river, so I headed in that direction. I stopped on the bridge and looked up the valley in the direction of Platoro. I know where I had camped is 10 miles from Platoro. I know the camp is 11 miles from Ann's. I have no doubt Barbara didn't walk 11 miles so she could sunbathe in the nude and see how many positions she could get into with two guys.

"There's a lot more to this case than murder," my Guardian Angel said.

"Pea Brain, I said that a while back. Why bring it up again?" I asked slightly annoyed.

"I felt you needed a little conversation," he said. "You've been talking to yourself a lot lately."

"You stick with being my Guardian Angel and let me be the detective," I said, adding, "and, if I want to talk to myself that's my business, not yours."

He gave me an, 'up yours,' look.

I went back to the house and decided to go to the Ranger Station. As I was about to leave, a guy drove up in an old paint splattered pick-up and got out. "Ann wants me to fix the wall," he told me.

"Go on in," I said.

I had forgotten to lock the door anyway.

By the time I got to the Ranger Station it was closed and there was no vehicle in front of Ranger Fisher's house. I looked at the pile of cinder blocks discovering there were two missing from a perfectly square stack. I had a good hunch where the other two went to.

"Well, duh," my Guardian Angel said.

I was heading back toward Matilda when a woman called, "Hey you, mister, what do you want?"

Now was as good a time as any to talk to Mrs. Fisher.

Mrs. Fisher was big-boned, wide-hipped, had shoulder length brown hair, plain features, and was wearing little makeup. She was about 5'7" and had on a loose-fitting, light blue dress, which did about as much for her figure as putting a sack over a potato, and she was wearing tennis shoes. She had three earrings in each ear - two small colored studs and one loop - and was wearing a gold wedding band. Around her neck was a dainty chain with a gold cross. She looked like the type of woman who is a good cook, does the dishes, weeds the garden, is an exceptional mother, and goes to church at least fifteen times a week.

"Sorry to bother you," I said. "I need some cinder blocks and I saw that stack from the road."

"You must be that private detective," she said, eyeing me like she didn't trust me. "You're trying to find out who killed that whore." Her voice had an edge to it that could have cut through solid steel.

"Yes," I replied, taken aback by the harshness in her voice.

"My husband was an idiot, a fool, and a weak man."

"Sounds like the normal modern man to me," my Guardian Angel said.

I agreed with Mrs. Fisher. "Yes, your husband was an idiot."

She smiled triumphantly and crossed her arms in front of her. For a reason beyond me she reminded me of Mussolini.

"I do have a duty, though," she said. "I'm his wife, we have a daughter, and I've forgiven him."

"That's admirable of you," I said.

"I can see Mrs. Fisher a hundred years ago, dressed in black, storming into all the bars in town and breaking open the kegs of beer and whiskey with axes," my Guardian Angel said.

"That whore Barbara got everything she deserved," Mrs. Fisher went on. "She will never be able to break up another home. Whoever killed her has saved a lot of good decent people pain."

"It was still murder," I said, thinking that her statement was not at all Christian - but, a lot of people have been killed in the name of God.

Mrs. Fisher glared at me like I am a cousin to the devil, spun on her heels and stomped toward her house. I take it she doesn't like to be disagreed with.

I drove back towards Ann's. I felt about 197 years old. If one of my old hippie buddies would happen along I'd gladly truck off to the mountains to roll in the dirt for a few weeks. Afterwards, I would come back to the real world, find out I'd taken my mind so far from reality I'd start making dream catchers for the gas station market.

"Dream catchers have been selling well lately," my Guardian Angel said, "and at least you would not get shot at."

"Few people realize their dreams in our modern world," I said. "We spend all of our time working - hoping we can buy our dreams."

I was about to pass Ranger Reeves driveway, when on impulse, I turned in. I really didn't have anything I wanted to ask her. I really didn't want to see her. But, budding feelings or not, I didn't feel like going back to Ann's either.

Ranger Reeves was sitting on the porch drinking a beer. She watched me walk toward her with an expression on her face like she was trying to decide if she wanted to see me or not. She had changed out of her uniform and had on baggy Levi's, a black T-shirt, and was wearing a well-used pair of cowboy boots. I noticed, once again, she has small feet. "You look like you lost your last friend," she said, adding, "But I doubt you ever had one."

"Working for the government hasn't helped your sense of humor," I said to Ranger Reeves.

"Have a seat, I'll get you a beer," she smiled, obviously amused by her own funny.

Her smile took me off guard.

"Whether I act like it all the time or not I am your friend," my Guardian Angel said.

"I know you are," I replied.

"My only problem is you can't count on me all the time," he said looking down at the ground.

"What are friends for?" I asked with a grin.

Reeves brought a beer for me and another one for her. "I know you didn't stop by to try and seduce me," she said, as we sat in two old wooden rocking chairs. "I could tell the first time you met me you knew I am a lesbian," Reeves said matter-of-factly.

"No closet hang-ups for Reeves," my Guardian Angel said.

"It used to bother me but it doesn't anymore," Ranger Reeves said. "People always think lesbians are different. People are all the same, we fight with our girlfriends as much as straight people fight with each other."

Reeves thought she was going to shock me. "What people do with their own lives is their business," I said.

"How come people want to make judgments?" she asked.

"They are afraid," I said.

"You might not be such a bad guy," Reeves said.

"Why don't you show me your cabin? I'd like to see it. Someday I want to build one," I said.

Reeves was happy to show me the cabin. Even though it wasn't hers I could tell she was proud of it.

The cabin inside was old and rustic. The logs were stained a dark brown and the mortar between them was painted white - making the small rooms seem bigger than they were. The floors were dark wood and crooked. Reeve's home was immaculately neat, everything in place, everything folded, it looked like dust would be afraid to settle anywhere. The kitchen had an old wood cook stove next to a gas range. I noticed an electric clock radio. The furniture in the living room was handmade from pine and everything faced a large rock fireplace, stained black from years of soot. There was a small TV in the corner that sat on a table with a video player below it. There were two bedrooms. Her room was like the rest of the house, neat and tidy. There was a large revolving stand on the dresser with numerous earrings. In the bathroom was an old bathtub with legs and a clear wraparound shower curtain. A small wood stove was in the corner for use during the winter. There were books in every room.

"I bet you would like to own this," I told her as we walked back outside. "It's beautiful."

"I'd give my eyeteeth for her."

I set my empty beer down. "You want another one?" she asked me with an undertone to her voice she would like the company.

"Only one more," I replied.

She smiled like she'd won the Fairy Princess award in San Francisco.

She brought two beers and we sat looking out over the meadow. It would be dark soon and the light was fading, blending in the colors, soothing the earth. "Did you and Barbara have a thing going?" I asked.

Reeves didn't bat an eyelash. "I would have liked to, she was gorgeous, but she liked them more than one at a time and I'm not into any group stuff."

"Me either," I said.

"You're not into any single stuff either," my Guardian Angel said.

"Do you think Mrs. Fisher could have killed Barbara?" I asked Reeves.

"That woman has God on her side Roosevelt. In her mind God will do all her killing for her."

"Why are you so protective of Ranger Fisher?"

Reeves sipped on her beer and I watched two red-winged blackbirds land on top of a stand of cattails by the river. "He's been nice to me, never any words about my sexual preferences. He is a nice man. There aren't many of them as you well know?"

We sat on the porch and talked about many things: How the government was selling off all the timberland. How the endangered animals might as well take out funeral insurance. How the river water is so polluted fish are placing orders for scuba gear. How greedy people are cutting down the rainforest so in time they could make more money by selling us cylinders of oxygen so we can breathe. How dolphins have to be the smartest creature alive.

Reeves is concerned about what mankind is doing to the world. Being an old hippie, my worry is that nothing will ever change until it is too late.

"You care Roosevelt. You have hope," my Guardian Angel said.

"Cynical hope," I said.

"Still hope."

As I drove away Reeves waved at me and I waved back. Years ago and after Vietnam, when there was no gray in life, only black and white, I knew a lady like Reeves. She fell out of the hippie movement and moved to San Francisco and got involved with the Gay Rights Movement. I ran into her years later and she was as miserable as most of the straight couples I knew. "My girlfriend has been seeing another lady for five years," she told me. "I just found out about it."

"At least you won't get Aids," I told her.

My statement seemed to cheer her up. The last I heard, she was teaching poetry at a private girl's school in Northern, California and was writing a book titled: TWO MEN, TWO WOMEN, ONE WOMAN AND ONE MAN, PHOOEY. From the title I figure it has a chance of being a bestseller.

To my surprise Ann's car was in the driveway. Mr. and Mrs. Whoever-They-Was were standing on their porch barbecuing and waved at me. Jesse's truck wasn't by his house, although his horses were chomping away on hay, so either he had come back to feed them or somebody had fed them for him.

I didn't bother to knock on the door. When I walked in I could hear Ann in the kitchen. The wall had been patched and freshly painted.

Ann had on a pair of short pants that should have been illegal and a white blouse that was more cleavage than fabric. She smiled at me like a French girl smiling at a young American G.I. who had helped free Paris. Pea Brain couldn't keep his tongue in his mouth.

"Have a beer," she said. "I'm making us a Denver omelet."

I drank a beer while Ann scurried around the kitchen. I felt my heart stirring again.

The omelet was delicious. Ann looked delicious. "How was work?" I asked.

"The two Colbert boys came by and that's it. They had a few beers before they headed into the mountains to set up a fishing camp for a trip they've booked for next week. Some guy and his wife from Chicago who want to get a taste of the wilderness. How about you, you find anything out?"

"I know enough to know I don't know anything," I said.

"Three knows in one sentence. Why didn't you merely say - I don't know anything?" my Guardian Angel said.

Ann, not being an English teacher, like my Guardian Angel thinks he is, did not have a reaction to my answer.

"Aren't you afraid, Ann?" I asked. "You wanted me to stay here because you thought the killer might also want to kill you."

"Why would the person who killed Barbara want to kill Ann?" my Guardian Angel asked himself more than me.

I didn't like the question or the possible answers.

"That was silly," Ann answered. "I'm over that, besides, whoever shot at you obviously didn't want to kill me."

Ann sounded as calm as an old infantry sergeant after a firefight, who was surrounded by a bunch of 19 year old privates, who now knew war isn't fun and you can't shout at the enemy, "Na, na, you missed."

"I saw Jesse and he told me you went to see him," Ann said.

"I talked to him and Willie."

I didn't tell her I was going to Alamosa and look up the two highway patrolmen.

"How come you told me an older couple lives in the third cabin when nobody is living there?" I asked as evenly as possible.

"I forgot they moved out," Ann replied simply.

I didn't bother to tell her I knew why they moved.

Ann cleared the table. I really didn't want to trust her, but, "You want to help me tonight?" I asked Ann.

Ann's eyes lit up like a college kid about to go on a panty raid. "Is it dangerous?"

"If you consider killer dogs and cowboys the size of small trucks dangerous, yes it is."

"You bet," Ann agreed.

"First off, you have to put on some long pants."

"I thought you would like me dressed like this," she pouted.

"I do, but while I'm trying to break into a trailer, I don't want to be distracted."

Ann kissed me on the forehead.

While Ann was changing clothes I looked in her freezer and found a frozen roast. I put it in the microwave on defrost.

I went into the living room and noticed there were new curtains. Anything without shotgun pellet holes in them is an improvement. I tried to close the curtains. When I pulled on the cord the curtains wouldn't close all the way and left about a six-inch gap. I tried to pull them together by yanking on the curtains, but it was no use.

Ann came out. "They don't close. They never have. I need a new rod."

When I bark up a wrong tree I do it well. I can scratch off a couple of my clues.

Ann was wearing regular Levi's, black boots, and a long sleeved shirt. "You look wonderful," I told her.

"Only for you," she said, with a twinkle in her eye.

"You lie well," I grinned at her.

I went back to the kitchen and took the meat out of the microwave. I cut the roast into many small pieces, got out a frying pan, turned on the stove, and put the roast in the pan.

"We already ate," Ann said.

"Dog bait," I told her.

Ann sat at the kitchen table. "Have you heard from your father?" I asked her.

"Not a word. But I called the Sheriff today and my father had Barbara's body taken to a funeral home in Denver."

"You and Barbara were never close, were you?" I asked.

"We were sisters," Ann replied coldly.

By her tone, there was no need to pursue the topic further, but one day I would have to.

"Where are you taking me on this dangerous mission?"

"I want to break into Willie's trailer. I'm guessing because he is single he won't be home in the early evening."

"That's dangerous," Ann said. "He is a mean guy. Willie is known from Taos to Durango for having never lost a fight."

"If he catches us you fight him and I'll run," I joked.

Ann didn't see the humor in my comment and probably thought I am some kind of girly boy. I didn't see any need to tell her I spent years doing karate until I got tired of wearing pajamas all the time. I'm not the best, but I'm not the worst either. But I do know how to cover myself, I bought a 9 m.m. I've never seen a karate chop yet that will stop a 9 m.m. unless it is in the movies, although tonight I'm not going to take the pistol.

After it was dark I took my time driving into town. Ann was quiet.

"You be one, dumb idiot," my Guardian Angel said.

"I know," I said.

"You be one, dumb, simple-minded idiot," he said.

"I know," I said.

"You be one, dumb, simple-minded idiot, who has dog food for brains," he said.

"It's the company God has saddled me with," I said.

"Not nice," he said.

Willie's truck was gone and all the lights were out. I hadn't seen his truck in town. His dog was home though, as we drove by his bark bounced off Matilda like an Israeli concussion grenade.

I parked behind an old abandoned house, not far from Willie's, took a flashlight and a screwdriver out of the glove box, and Ann carried the sack of meat. "We'll go up to the trailer. When we get there, I want you to talk quietly to the dog and then toss him one piece of meat. I think he'll settle right down," I told Ann.

Most mean dogs, unless they are trained to attack, are only mean because their owners are mean to them. Dogs have weird loyalty when they protect those who abuse them, but then, many women are the same way with abusive husbands.

"Men get abused too," my Guardian Angel said. "But being men they are ashamed to admit it."

As we got close to the trailer the dog started to bark. The only house on the block that looked lived in was three houses away. The people who live there were probably so used to hearing the dog bark they don't think anything of it. It's like burglar alarms on cars in the big city - nobody pays any attention to them - half the time the thief can sell them for more than the car.

"Why do you want to break into Willie's trailer?" Ann whispered to me.

"He might have killed your sister," I replied, truthfully.

The dog was at the end of his chain, snapping and barking. "Do your stuff," I told Ann.

Ann took several steps forward, barely out of reach of the dog. "Nice doggie, nice doggie," she said in a low soothing voice that could have seduced the Pope.

The dog stopped barking, but moved around uneasily. "You're a good boy," Ann cooed. "Such a nice boy. I have something for you."

Ann tossed a piece of meat to the dog. The dog sniffed it and gobbled it up. "Good stuff," Ann said. "Do you want more?"

The dog's tail started wagging so hard I thought he might fly. Ann tossed him another piece of meat. He ate it without chewing. Ann held a piece of meat in her hand and walked up to the dog. He sniffed it, and then gently took it out of her hand. She started to pet him. "See, you're not so mean," she said.

"That's impressive," my Guardian Angel said.

I walked past Ann and the dog to the front door. The door wasn't locked. "Stay here with the dog and slowly feed him the meat, if somebody drives up the road, whistle twice and we'll beat feet," I told Ann as I went into the trailer.

"Are you going to hit your feet with a stick?" my Guardian Angel asked, looking confused, but he did not come into the trailer with me and sat down by Ann.

I turned on the flashlight. To my surprise the trailer was neat. On a coffee table by a small sofa were several stacks of outdoor magazines and a clean ashtray with an open pack of Lucky Strikes next to it. There was a TV with a plastic potted flower on top of it. The kitchen table had a bowl of oranges on it and two place mats with outdoor scenes on them. The dishes were done and stacked in a dish drainer. There was one bedroom in the back of the trailer. The bed was made. In the corner was a 12 gauge semi-automatic

Mossberg. I picked it up, ejected a shell, it was buckshot. I slid the shell back into the gun. In the closet, Willie's clothes were all hung neatly and his boots were in a line. There was a lamp on top of the dresser. I opened one drawer, all socks, another drawer, underwear, another drawer, T-shirts. I opened the last drawer and there was a small wooden box in it. I took out the box, opened it, there were six lady's earrings - four small diamond studs, and two medium sized gold loops. I put the box back in the drawer and started for the door. Halfway to the door Ann rushed into the trailer. "A truck is coming," she gasped.

"Big bad Willie," my Guardian Angel said. "I was watching Ann so intently I didn't do my job."

I quickly shut the door. "Get behind me," I ordered Ann. Pea Brain got behind her.

I stood where the door would open into us. Ann was closer to me than my shadow. Truck lights shone through the window as a truck pulled into the driveway. "Maybe it's not him," Ann whispered.

The dog didn't bark. It was him. "What are you doing, dumb dog?" we heard Willie grunt to the dog.

I tensed as the door started to open. The light came on. But before Willie could turn to shut the door, I clobbered him in the back of the neck, he groaned, sagged, but didn't fall. I kicked him behind the knee and moving sideways, kneed him in the chin, slammed both hands down on the back of his head, and kneed him once more in the chin as he crashed to the floor. I grabbed Ann's hand and we darted out of the trailer. The dog was sitting back from the door looking at his master, cold stone out on the floor, like it was the happiest day in his life.

Matilda, lovely lady that she is, started right up and we sped away.

"Holy smokes," Ann said, once we were out of Antonito and headed back towards Platoro, "that was close."

"You were supposed to warn me, not run into the trailer," I told her.

"Boy you sure put Willie down. I've never seen such a thing. I figured you'd be a puss," Ann said.

"He is, but he's always lucky," my Guardian Angel said. "Plus he cheated. He bushwhacked Willie."

"There are a lot of things you don't know about me," I told Ann, somewhat angry at both her and my Guardian Angel.

"Roosevelt," she said. “I don’t want to know anything about you. All I want is for you to take me home and take my clothes off."

"Oh boy, Roosevelt," my Guardian Angel wheezed.

I thought about how soft her skin would be, how warm she would be, how beautiful she is. "I can't," I said.

Ann started to chuckle. I looked over at her and she had taken off her blouse and bra. By the time we got to her house she had squirmed around and taken off her boots and pants. "Still no, soldier boy," she teased.

Pea Brain was barking at the moon.

"No," I said, sounding like a frog with laryngitis.

Ann laughed as she got out of the car. My Guardian Angel went and stood on the porch but I know he was not contemplating God or the endlessness of space. I sat in the car for a long time. There are times when this moral thing is hard to take.

CHAPTER NINE
COPS

When I got up in the morning Ann was gone. She had not left me a note. "Women do not like it when men reject them," my Guardian Angel said. "If you would have slept with her she would have left you a short story."

"Pea Brain, why don't you go find some traffic to play in," I said. "I'm really not in the mood for your dribble this morning."

"Cars would only go through me," he said with a, 'I got you look' on his face.

I made some hot tap water coffee, cleaned up, and got my notebook, added a few clues and skimmed over them.

I know Barbara was a natural blonde and Ann has natural black hair. Barbara had pierced ears, but had no earrings on when she was found dead. Ann doesn't like Ranger Fisher and has no sympathy for him. I'd once again been shot at by somebody with a 12-gauge shotgun firing buckshot - which was a clue I would rather not have. Sheriff Rogers arrived at Ann's house rather quickly after I'd been shot at. Barbara used to have parties at the house and Ranger Reeves had been to the house at least once. Jesse Killton has a 12-gauge shotgun, a box of buckshot, and has small feet. The Sheriff had to have run a check on me in order to find out I'd been in Iowa. Ann doesn't date, but she has taken a shine to me. Barbara had two different types of semen in her. Two cinder blocks are missing from the stack of blocks at the Ranger Station. Reeves is a lesbian and she and I enjoy talking. Mrs. Fisher has God on her side and wears three earrings. Ranger Reeves' house is neat as a pin and she has small feet. Ann's father still hasn't called her although he had Barbara's body moved to a funeral home in Denver. Willie Hood has earrings in his drawer, owns a 12-gauge shotgun loaded with buckshot, and is hard to knock out, even with a sucker punch. I suspect everybody I've met as being the killer except me. And last but not least Ann hasn't paid me. I now have 73 clues.

"If you keep working for no money you are going to have to get a real job," my Guardian Angel said.

“I am not materialistic, money means nothing to me,” I said proudly.

"I don't care," he replied. "I work for free also, but there is a big difference between you and me. I don't have to eat, buy gas, clothes, insurance, beer, need I go on."

"I think I am truly falling in love with Ann," I said, changing the subject, knowing that everyone is materialistic in one way or the other.

My Guardian Angel was silent for a few moments. "I have told you before, I think you should be careful with Ann. I think she wants to kill you," he finally said.

"Why?"

"It's a gut feeling."

"I haven't had feelings like these for a woman in years," I said.

"Love in this modern world is scary," he said.

Deciding to drop the subject I scrambled some eggs to go along with the condition of my brain, ate quickly, and drove to town.

Sheriff Rogers was doing what he does best, sitting in his office with his bad manners hat on, twirling on his moustache and smoking a Lucky Strike. "Nothing on the shotgun shells yet," he told me.

"I was wondering if you ran fingerprints on Barbara." I asked.

"The morgue did. She was Barbara Maiden, no doubt about it. I even ran a background check on her.”

I was impressed.

"She was arrested twice for prostitution in Texas - once in Austin and once in Houston. She was picked up once for possession of a small amount of pot. All the cases were dropped. She was also in some deal concerning porn films, but Texas doesn't seem to know much about it. It's a federal deal and the Feds haven't answered my request for information."

"Have you had many dealings with those two highway patrolmen from Alamosa?" I asked him - thinking at the same time my Guardian Angel had warned me about a pornography ring.

"I take it you mean Hoffman and Hayworth. I see them on the highway a lot. I do know they both had the hots for Barbara. I ran into Hoffman once at a coffee shop in Alamosa. I had to take a prisoner up there and he told me he thought Barbara would sleep with anybody wearing a uniform."

"Do you think they're crooked cops?" I asked him.

"No," Rogers replied. "They both might chase women but neither one of them is crooked."

"Do you think they were into threesomes?"

"Somebody was," Rogers said, giving me a crooked smile.

"Who do you think killed Barbara?" I asked Rogers, for nothing better to say. If I don't know who killed her how could he?

"I can only figure it was some guy who felt he was getting jilted or he was jealous. She might have told somebody she was going to marry him and then he found out she was changing the oil on two guys at a time. Roosevelt, nothing goes on in a little community like this without everybody knowing. There are no secrets around here. I know she played around with everybody but I don't see her murder being a random act of violence done by some drifter."

"It was no drifter," I said, but I doubt Rogers knows Ranger Reeves is a lesbian - people don't know everything in little towns and, as of this moment, no one knows who killed Barbara.

"I figure one thing for sure, whoever is taking pot shots at you is probably the killer," the Sheriff said.

I didn't tell Rogers I might disagree with him on that, nor did I tell him why.

"Have you been sleeping with Ann?" Rogers asked me, with more than a casual interest - proving my point - people don't know everything that goes on in little towns.

"Not Mr. Moral who might be falling in love," my Guardian Angel said rolling his eyes back in his head.

"She's as tough to approach as a lady married to a doctor," I answered.

"I don't know if I believe that," Rogers said, lighting up another Lucky Strike only this time using his lighter and not a stick match.

"Have you ever been married?" I asked.

"No. Been close a few times but never married. Too old now to even think about it. When I retire in a few years, I might find some lady. I plan on moving out of here and going to Hawaii. No more long winters, no more jails, no more late night calls. I plan on sitting on the beach and watching the ocean."

"It might be hard to sell a house around here. This isn't exactly a booming community."

"I don't own a house," Rogers said. "I have a room in the back of the jail."

"Like most people he's married to his job," my Guardian Angel said.

"Willie Hood's trailer got broken into the other night," the Sheriff said, giving me the, 'I can tell if your lying, you low life criminal punk. So you had better tell the truth or I'll beat the dog snot out of you where I know there are no video cameras,' look.

I shrugged my shoulders like I didn't know what he was talking about. Silence is golden when you're guilty.

"Whoever it was knocked him out. Funny thing though, they didn't steal anything."

"Kids must have done it," I said, nonchalantly.

"No, whoever did it must have known what they were doing. They got by that mean dog of his."

I wanted to tell him thanks for the compliment, but this conversation had gone on long enough. "If you hear anything, let me know Sheriff."

The Sheriff didn't bother to get up to shake hands goodbye and tell me it had been nice to see me. I think he was wondering if I was lying to him about Ann. But I have never been one to brag about my love life. At least I have one redeeming trait.

"You don't have any friends to talk to is why you don't brag," my Guardian Angel said. "And your love life is nil."

"You told me the other day you were my friend," I said.

“It was a weak moment,” he mumbled.

I drove toward Alamosa on Hwy 285. About ten miles north of Antonito I passed a gate to the Forked Lightning Ranch - the only reason I knew it was the gate was by the name COLBERT on the mailbox. Ann told me the Colbert boys would be up in the mountains for a few days setting up a fishing camp so I didn't turn in.

I figured I would drive to the Highway Patrol Headquarters and find out what shifts Hoffman and Hayworth worked. I didn't want to call and tell them I was coming because I felt they might not want to see me. If I was into blackmail, I could make some good money off of them, people don't really like to hear about their married protectors messing around with other women.

"I don't think you should push Hoffman or Hayworth too far," my Guardian Angel said.

He was right, but if I took everyone's advice I'd be selling cars in Dallas.

The Highway Patrol office was right next to the highway, which made sense, and had a dozen or so squad cars parked in front of it. Like most government buildings, it was brick and had a flagpole flying the state flag and Old Glory. There was a large Colorado Highway Patrol insignia on the side of the building made out of colored tile. The floor inside was polished brown linoleum that would make any army barracks jealous. Along the walls were glassed-in cases, with various awards for excellence from the state. They are really awards for giving tickets to tourists and drunken cowboys and for the most reflective sunglasses. There was a visitor’s desk with a highway patrolman behind it, wishing he could be in the thick of things. He wanted to be hiding beside the highway behind a tree, waiting for three college girls wearing halter-tops and short shorts, to speed by.

Most road cops stuck with desk duty find it hard to talk civilly to the public because they've forgotten what to say except, "Do you know how fast you were going?” They also hate to work inside because they can't wear their sunglasses and have to take their pistol out of its holster, which makes them feel naked.

The highway patrolman behind the counter looked like he spit shined his body. "Don't you know how fast you were going?" he said to me. Then stammered, "I mean, sorry, may I help you sir."

"Only if you have probable cause," I said.

He thought that was as funny as a woman trying to join the police force.

"I'm trying to locate Officer Hayworth and Hoffman," I said.

"You're that dick, Roosevelt," he blurted out.

My Guardian Angel started to pick up his robe and shake his wanger at him but I gave him a no look even though I didn't like the insinuation. The police officer hadn't known me long enough to call me derogatory names.

"I'm him," I said, not insinuating I was a dick.

"Well, you're in luck, they're both in the back drinking coffee and waiting to go on duty, go on back and take a left at the second door. That's the break room."

When I went into the break room, Hayworth and Hoffman looked at me like I was the Wicked Witch from the North who had come to steal their squad cars - none the less, they both forced a smile and Hayworth said, "Caught anymore bodies while fishing?"

"No, I've been fishing for a murderer," I said, and sat at the table with them.

They glanced at each other like it was secret time and didn't offer me a cup of coffee. I decided to come right to the point. "I understand that you two guys both had a deal going with Barbara Maiden."

"Listen Roosevelt," Hayworth said. "We're both married men...." I cut him off. "I'm not going to tell anybody, I'm only wondering if you know anything about Barbara that might help me."

They both relaxed. "I met Barbara while I was fishing," Hoffman started. "I'd parked close to the bridge by the cabins where she lived and I was fishing upstream. I came around a bend and there was this gorgeous woman, young, blonde, naked as the day is long. When she heard me, she just rolled over, leaned up on her elbows and smiled and asked me if I'd caught anything. When I started to walk by her she asked me to sit down and talk to her for a while."

"I wouldn't have said no," I commented, adding, "did you two guys pay her?"

Hayworth gave me a dirty look, which I took to mean, no.

"You guys ever do a threesome with her?"

It's a known fact cops have to live by the buddy system so I didn't think the question was out of line.

"You jerk," Hayworth snarled, and started to stand up.

"Sit down," Hoffman ordered him.

"We're not sick," Hayworth said, sitting, but looking at me like I didn't want to visit his part of the highway at night.

I was glad he cooled down - beating up a policeman in self-defense is a hard case to win, especially when another policeman is the only witness.

"Either one of you guys buy her presents?" I asked, looking straight at Hayworth.

Hayworth shook his head. I could tell he was still angry, but according to Ann, he'd given Barbara the gold chain she wore around her stomach. Why would he lie? Or did Ann lie? Hoffman hesitated for a mere second before he also shook his head.

"I understand Barbara used to have some wild parties at her house. Did you guys ever go to any of them?"

"We never went to any parties," Hoffman said.

"Word gets out, neither one of us could afford it," Hayworth said. "We have to be careful."

"It's a stressful job," I commented. "People have to have ways to burn off the stress besides going home to the same old ham and egg sandwich."

Both of them reminded me of little boys who had been caught smoking in the backyard. Only these little boys carried great big pistols that fired more than caps and long black sticks filled with lead that weren't made to hit baseballs.

"Did any other officers get in on the fun?" I asked.

Hoffman shook his head.

There really wasn't anything else to ask them. I doubted either one of them was ever in love with Barbara and ready to leave their wife and change careers. "If you ever think of anything that might help me, call. I'm staying at Ann's. I know you have the phone number."

As I walked out all I could hear were my footsteps and their breathing. If they hadn't done a threesome with Barbara I have never really existed.

"Maybe everything is only a dream and nothing really exists," my Guardian Angel said.

"Good thing you were never a hippie," I told him. "That question could have sent you on a one way ticket to Mars."

I drove to downtown Alamosa looking for a jewelry store and to try and think.

On Maine St. I saw a sign - LIFE'S TREASURED MOMENTS - JEWELRY FOR THE DISCERNING. The lady in the store, who I guessed to be the owner, was middle-aged, attractive in a plump way, had on a green velvet dress and blouse, a Concho belt the size of Maryland, and so many turquoise rings I don't know how she lifted her hands. Most of the jewelry in the store was turquoise, a lot of silver, and a few gold rings and watchbands. She smiled so warmly at me I smiled back. She also didn't follow me around the store trying to help me. I dislike clerks who want to help me. I like to go into a store, browse around, and be left alone until I'm ready to buy.

"There is only one problem," my Guardian Angel said. "As cheap as you are, you never buy."

There was a large display case filled with earrings, there were beaded ones, turquoise ones, feather ones, and on and on. I bent over and looked at the case. The lady walked over. "We have more in the back," she said.

"Actually," I said. "I'm here because there was a small robbery in town and I'm the insurance adjuster. Officer Hoffman, a Highway Patrol Officer from here told me he had bought some rather expensive earrings from you, but he lost the receipt."

In small communities, most storeowners know the names of all the policemen. "I know Officer Hoffman. I also know his wife. But I haven't heard about a break in," the lady said, sounding slightly annoyed either about the break in or the fact none of her friends had told her. "But yes, he did buy some earrings, although I wouldn't call them expensive. They were rather cheap."

She said cheap like you would say, "There's cat hair on my food."

I followed her to the register. By the register was a small computer. She pushed some buttons, looked at the screen, pushed some more buttons, looked at the screen, pushed some more buttons, looked at the screen and smiled. "Yes, here we are, six weeks ago he bought 1 pair of turquoise studs, 1 pair of small unicorns, also studs, and 1 pair of beaded earrings. He spent $32.00 total."

"He was cheap," my Guardian Angel said wrinkling his nose.

"That isn't much of a claim," I said, "but can I have a copy of that receipt?"

"I'll make you a copy, but if you drove down from Denver you wasted your time."

"Part of the job, you know how people are?"

Having to deal with the public all the time she gave me a knowing smile.

"I'll only trouble you one more time. Officer Hoffman wants to insure his wife's jewelry since Officer Hayworth's misfortune. He bought a gold waist chain but I don't know if he bought it here."

"He did buy it here," she grinned. "It was beautiful - nine hundred dollars beautiful."

She handed me the receipt.

I thanked her for her time as I put the receipt in my pocket.

Across the street was a fast food hamburger joint and I decided to fill my body with saturated fats. Full of French fries and beef patties I drove out of town, making sure I was doing the speed limit the brotherhood of police can be nasty if you get on their bad side although Matilda is hard pressed to go much over 65, and that is downhill.

It felt good to get out of the belt of billboards and headed back into the secluded Antonito Valley even if a murderer did live here. I drove along enjoying the scenery and solitude when I passed the road to the Forked Lightning Ranch. I put on the brakes, backed up, and decided to check it out - there was a chance the Colbert boys hadn't made it to the mountains.

I bounced over the rutted dirt road that would be all but impassable if it rained. The grassland has been overgrazed and the grass was sparse. The fencing was rusty and badly in need of repair. It wasn't a ranch that was making a lot of money, but then, most don't. After going over three cattle guards, I went down one long dip in the road and when I got to the top, I could see the house about a 1/4 of a mile away. It was an old white frame house badly in need of paint. There was a front porch with a slanting roof with deer racks nailed to the support posts and a stack of split firewood by the door. A bent TV antenna was on the roof. There was a large propane tank beside the house, but there were also two stovepipes for wood stoves. Not far from the house were a series of empty cattle pens. There was a small barn with several corrals with half a dozen horses milling around discussing their bad luck. Not far from the corral was a large stack of hay bales. Parked by the hay bales were three horse trailers of various sizes. They looked like they were used by the army for artillery practice. To the side of the house was a 55 gallon drum with an old saddle tied to it that was tied between two half dead trees with ropes. The ropes could be pulled to imitate a bucking horse. A man sits on the barrel and people pull on the ropes and laugh when he falls on his head and gets a concussion. Not far from the drum was a hay bale with a set of cattle horns attached to it to practice roping. There were two pickups parked in front of the house that looked like they were in a contest to see which one could be more beat up and rusty. Three medium-sized cur dogs lazed around the trucks.

I drove over a cattle guard near the house. As I pulled up to the house the dogs ran around the car barking and growling. An old man, at least 70, cowboy to the bone, as thin as a pencil, wearing faded Levi's held up by a belt with a silver buckle the size of his head, a many times patched blue work shirt, and boots that looked like they'd been on his feet for 53 years, ambled, bow-legged, out of the house. "Get out of the car," he hollered. "Them dogs nothin' but bark."

I gingerly got out of the car. The dogs yipped and danced around like I'd known them ever since I was a little boy. "If I'd wanted guard dogs, I'd been a gangster," the old man said, and held out his hand. "I'm Mr. Leroy Colbert, welcome to the Forked Lightning Ranch, land rich but dollar poor."

His voice was cracked and gravely like the land around us.

"I'm," I started to say but he cut me off. "I know who you are. You're that fake cop that fished up that pretty blonde filly who had my two boys wishing they had money."

He chuckled slightly, winked at me, and held out his hand to shake.

"At times it's not good for everybody to know you," my Guardian Angel said.

Mr. Leroy Colbert's eyes were a blazed green with the twinkle of a merrymaker. He had two days' worth of whiskers the color of dirty snow on his wrinkled and weathered face. His mouth looked like it always had a wry smile plastered on it. One hello and I knew he was the salt of the earth and working 16 hours a day in snow, rain, sleet, hail, or the hot sun was all part of it. He had a grip like iron and his hands were as rough as a cedar post. He was the kind of man that during the war I would have wanted at my back. When the shells started popping I would know he would be there and not doing the boot scootin' boogie back toward camp. "Glad to meet you sir," I said. "And yes, I'm that fake cop."

"Beats being a cowboy," he said. "Come on in, it's time for a drink. I'll answer your questions. I know you didn't come out here for the view."

If Mr. Colbert said it was time for a drink, it was time for a drink.

The inside of the house was as rundown as the outside. He led me through a small living room painted some color between red and pink. There was a pot-bellied wood stove and several chairs and a sofa covered with army blankets. On an old pedal Singer sewing machine was a TV that looked so old it had to be a black and white. The floor was cracked linoleum with a few throw rugs tossed on it. The kitchen had a beat up wooden table in the middle of it. A saddle was set up in the corner that needed mending and there were leather working tools on the table. A potted Geranium on the windowsill looked like it hadn't been watered since Iowa won a Rose Bowl.

"Sit down, take a load off," Mr. Colbert ordered.

"He would have to take his head off," my Guardian Angel said.

Mr. Colbert brought a bottle of Old Scarecrow Whiskey and two water glasses to the table. I wasn't about to ask Mr. Colbert if I could have a glass of water for a chaser. I figured he'd tell me water was for brushing your teeth and for Girl Scouts to drink.

He sat, poured the water glasses half full, and picked up his glass. "Screw the government," he toasted, and we clinked glasses.

"I didn't know the government was female," my Guardian Angel said.

Mr. Colbert took two gulps, wiped his lips with the back of his hand, shook his head, and smiled. "That's some good stuff."

Taking one small sip I thought my tongue was going to fall off, my esophagus turn inside out, and my eyes flip backwards in my head.

Mr. Colbert laughed. "It gets better after a few swallows," he said, adding, "When your tongue is numb and your lips burn."

He took another swallow. I took a swallow. He took another swallow. I took a swallow. His glass was empty while mine was only down about two inches. He refilled his glass and poured a dab in mine.

"It's a weird thing," he said. "You some big shot fake cop who comes all the way out here to the middle of no man's land to do some fishing and you hook a dead body. What are the odds of that? Bet it made you stand-up and take notice."

"No, it made him decide to stay here and get killed," my Guardian Angel said as he bent over and sniffed my glass of whiskey then shook his head like a dog that had just bitten a stink bug.

I took another sip of the whiskey. Mr. Colbert wasn't right, it didn't taste any better. "Finding Barbara's body put the damper on my vacation," I said.

"Son, I ain't never had a vacation. When my wife was alive, once a month we'd go to Durango, eat dinner, go to a dance hall and dance and drink till the place closed down. That woman could dance. Dance in more ways than one I tell you."

He drank some more whiskey - either enjoying the memory or trying to wash it away.

I took another swallow of the whiskey and started to ask Mr. Colbert where his sons were but didn't have a chance. "You think one of my boys killed that girl?" he asked me point blank, and started rolling a cigarette from a package of Top rolling tobacco.

Some people I can lie to, some people I can't, some people take life how it is, others want to paint a picture of life and call it real. Mr. Colbert didn't want lies and he didn't want any painting on his wall, but he could have used help rolling his cigarette. His finished cigarette looked like a joint my grandmother would roll.

"I figure those boys were out of their league with Barbara," I said. "But, Mr. Colbert, I'm trying to find out who killed her and for your sake, I hope they didn't."

Mr. Colbert lit his cigarette with a stick match that he ran over the top of the table. After the cigarette was lit, he blew the match out and put the match in his pocket to use for a toothpick later. "If they did, I'll kill them myself, even if it means there'd be nobody to inherit this ranch. My family takes care of its own, good and bad. Always have, always will," Mr. Colbert said in such a calm, dry tone, I knew he wasn't kidding.

"I heard they're up in the mountains guiding a fishing trip. I stopped by in case it got cancelled."

"They'll be up there a few more days. Trip was supposed to be for a week but the couple changed it to three days."

I sipped on the whiskey. I had a feeling Mr. Colbert would do enough talking I wouldn't have to ask any questions.

"Those boys never fought a day in their lives. They've shared everything. They're good boys, hardworking, not too smart, not too dumb. They love this cowboy life. Not many cowboys left in the West. We got rich people moving in and buying five and ten acre parcels of land and thinking living out in the sticks is fun and easy. But living out here is hard and tough, takes a certain breed. But, when that Barbara hooked them, they changed. That city lady shook her little finger and those two country boys started yapping at the moon. They stopped talking to each other for a while. They even argued. One day I had to stop them from fighting. I told them she didn't love either one of them and just to go on and take turns seeing her naked until they got it out of their systems. They listened to me I think. But I know she hurt them both. I can't truthfully say they didn't kill her."

Mr. Colbert drank some more whiskey.

I drained my glass and stood, feeling sorry for the old man. "If you don't mind I'll come back out in a few days and talk to your boys."

"They'll be here," Mr. Colbert said. "I'll make sure they're here."

He walked with me toward the door. It was then I noticed the shotgun in the corner. "What kind of shotgun is that?" I asked.

"It's an old J.C. Penney's 12 gauge, shoots as good as the day I bought her 55 years ago. Paid five bucks. I've killed enough coyotes with that gun to make coats for every woman in New York City."

"Use buckshot?" I asked.

"It's the only thing that will roll a coyotc."

"Roll you too, Roosevelt," my Guardian Angel said. "And not in flower."

As I got into Matilda I noticed hanging from a gun rack in the window of one of the trucks were two rifles, but, I couldn't tell what type they were.

I drove away half pie-eyed and half-sad. We've almost killed off the real cowboys. They're not something that can be put on the endangered species list and saved. But, even sadder, I trusted Mr. Colbert about as much as I trust a banker.

CHAPTER TEN
DUMB AS A POST

When I got back to Ann's I walked over to Mr. and Mrs. Whoever-They-Was' house.

Mrs. Whoever-She-Was answered the door. "Yes," she said, looking at me like I was interrupting her favorite TV soap, which is a no, no, in the modern world.

"I was wondering if you ever saw an older man visit Barbara. He is about 70 years old, thin, has a scraggly beard and drives an old beat up truck," I asked, referring to Mr. Colbert.

She thought for a moment. "No, never saw an old man visit Barbara except for that dumb old coot that lived next door to us."

"How about the Sheriff?"

"A few times, but he never stayed long."

"Did you see one or two cars when the Highway Patrol Officers came?" I asked.

"Sometimes one and sometimes two," Mrs. Whoever-She-Was said.

"Most of the time it was cowboys and younger guys who were at Barbara's," I said. "Yes, Mr. Roosevelt, most of the time it was cowboys and also that lady ranger, but she always came over by herself and she never came over when Ann was around. If you would not drink during the day, you smell like cheap whiskey, you might be able to solve Barbara's murder," she scolded me.

I apologized for bothering her, but didn't try and explain to her it wasn't my fault I smelled like whiskey.

"Sure, Roosevelt, Mr. Colbert twisted your arm to drink," my Guardian Angel said rolling his eyes back in his head like he had never had too much to drink while he was alive.

The first thing I did, once I was in the house, was unpack my watch, set it and put it on. The watch makes me a certified member of society. I will have to start punching a time clock and only take 15-minute breaks or be docked. I will have 30 minutes to eat my lunch, go to the bathroom and smoke 3 cigarettes. I will now have to worry about my future, pay my taxes and social security, and invest in mutual funds.

It was 4 o'clock. I paced around the room. It was 4:01. I paced around the room. It was 4:02.

"See what an advantage having a watch is? Now you know how fast you are dying and how fleeting life is," my Guardian Angel said with a look on his face that at least to him his statement was profound.

I made a cup of coffee, remembered I smelled like a brewery, brushed my teeth, slurped the coffee, and went out and started Matilda. I had time to go to the Ranger Station and look at some maps. It beat sitting around looking at my watch for the rest of the afternoon.

Ranger Fisher was in the office. He looked tired and depressed. There were dark circles under his eyes. "His wife being back doesn't seem to have helped him out," my Guardian Angel commented but I could tell he really didn't care.

"Do you have a topography map of the wilderness area around Platoro?" I asked Ranger Fisher.

"We have one the forest service puts out but we don't have a real good one, you'd have to get one of those from the National Survey."

He picked up a map from the stacks of printed folders on the counter and handed it to me. I put it in my back pocket. "Had any luck yet on Barbara's murder?" he asked me, sounding a little nervous.

"Nothing I would consider earth-shattering. The more I find out, the less I know."

"It was a terrible thing," he said, but not looking at me when he talked.

"Where's Ranger Reeves?" I asked.

"This is the third of her three-day leave. She told me all she was going to do was sit around the house."

I was about to ask him about the cinder blocks when Mrs. Fisher walked into the office. She glared at me and didn't say a word. I nodded at Ranger Fisher and smiled at him sadly as I left. Being married to God has to be tough, especially a jilted God - ask the Jewish people.

Seeing her, my Guardian Angel made the sign of the cross and knelt down on one knee and faked a prayer.

I drove to Ranger Reeves' cabin. Her bicycle was on the porch. I knocked and the door opened almost immediately. I smiled at her and noticed a suitcase just inside the front door. "Sit on the porch, I'll get us a beer," Reeves said like she was glad to see me.

She came out with two beers, handed me one as we sat down. "The lesbian and the stud, this could be some story," she commented dryly but with a slight twinkle in her eyes.

"She thinks you're a stud," my Guardian Angel laughed.

"Enjoying your three days off?" I asked Reeves.

My question seemed to bother her, but she answered after a moment, "I've done nothing but sit around, take naps, and drink beer."

Sounded like a good vacation to me. One I should have taken instead of going trout fishing. "You ever see Mrs. Fisher smile," I asked.

"She laughs when she puts on her hair shirt and flogs herself," Reeves said.

"Maybe she's a repressed homosexual," I said.

Reeves pondered the insinuation. "No," she finally said. "Not even another woman could live with her."

"Whoever killed Barbara I think they stole her earrings," I said.

Reeves jaw line tightened for an instant. "Why do you say that?" she asked, not looking at me but toward the river.

"She had on jewelry and her ears were pierced, but she wasn't wearing any earrings. A woman with pierced ears will normally wear earrings."

"Roosevelt, do you always wear underwear?" Reeves asked.

She had me on the wearing underwear question, but my rear isn't pierced so her statement didn't make any sense to me.

"You know what I think, Roosevelt. I think not you, not the F.B.I., not anybody, are going to find out who killed Barbara," Reeves said.

"I agree," my Guardian Angel said. "Especially when it comes to Roosevelt."

"Why do you think that?" I asked Reeves, looking at her closely.

"There are no witnesses"

"How about that smarty-pants?" my Guardian Angel sneered.

"Yes there is," I replied. "Whoever did it," I said to Reeves and my Guardian Angel.

"I wish you were a woman," Reeves said.

"I have to be honest," I told her. "If I was a woman, I don't know if I could stand men."

We both laughed.

I drank another beer with Reeves. She was upset that the Japanese had bought most of the hardwood forests in Asia and were cutting them down. She was also upset people could still kill whales. She thought people who thought tiger bones made them sexual supermen should have their love sticks cut off. She was tired of politicians always saying what they were doing is for the good of the people - which everybody in the world should know is a lie - what they are doing is good for the politician.

We drank another beer. I don't know why, but I am comfortable around Reeves.

"You had better not be too comfortable," my Guardian Angel said.

"Why?"

"I don't know exactly."

"Advice with no foundation is not advice," I said, adding, "Which you have been good at lately."

"If you don't listen to my no foundation advice you might end up dead," he said with about as much emotion as if he was flossing his teeth.

The sun was about to go down, time had gone by without me looking at my watch, and Reeves and I had further discussed - the sardine crises, the owl crises, why one day Christians and Arabs would fight, we both agreed China would rule the world, and Canada was probably the best country in the world to live in, but in a close run with Sweden, Norway, and Finland.

Driving away from her house I felt good. When I got to Ann's it was dark and the lights were on. Ann was sitting at the kitchen table, her arms folded across her chest, her legs crossed, and her foot was bobbing up and down a mile a minute like she was ice fishing for perch. "You didn't leave me a note," she said angrily.

My Guardian Angel tip-toed into the kitchen. I take it that sometime in his six hundred years of being alive and dead he had caught a women's wrath.

"There's no need to worry about me," I said to Ann. "If I get killed, you won't have to pay me, and besides you never told me to leave you a note."

"Don't do it again," she threatened.

This was the type of situation, that if we were a married couple, we would have sat in our own chairs and watched TV all night while ignoring each other. But, since there is no TV and we are not married we have to communicate.

"My father called today," Ann said, changing her tone. "He has arranged for Barbara's body to be shipped back to Texas." She didn't sound sad and I wondered if she would wear black or white at the funeral.

"It took him long enough to call," I said.

"He's been indicted for racketeering. Word reached him before the indictments came down and he hid out so his lawyers could arrange his bail before he turned himself in."

Another player bites the dust. When the Feds move in and arrest mafia dons, hit men, cartel members, and other outstanding members of our society, they're either going to snitch out all their associates or do a flat 40 years. 40 years in a 4 foot by 12 foot steel hole with only a commode for company will make the most hardened criminal start singing like a love sick parrot - especially when he knows it will only take about six months of him behind bars before all his friends will take over his operations and start sleeping with his wife and mistress. Big Abe Maiden now felt like Little Sally Maiden.

"You don't sound too put out," I said to Ann.

"My father divorced my mother shortly after I was born. He married Barbara's mother not more than two months later. He never sent my mom enough money to live on," she said bitterly.

"Interesting, Ann and Barbara were stepsisters," my Guardian Angel said.

"I knew that," I said.

"How?"

"When I first came to the house Ann made a statement about Barbara's mother, she didn't say, our mother."

"Good, Roosevelt," my Guardian Angel said, but gave me a sour face like giving me a compliment upset his stomach.

Now was as good a time as any to dig into Ann and Barbara's relationship. "You didn't know Barbara as you were growing up did you?" I asked Ann.

"She lived in a big house with maids, wore great clothes. I lived with my mother in a small house. My mother worked two jobs to support us. Barbara and I would see each other off and on when I would go see my father for a few days. But, no, we never knew each other. I hated her, she was spoiled and haughty, and treated me like scum."

"Then why were you crying when I first met you and you had heard about her death?"

"I really don't know. Maybe I was crying for the tragic way she lived and died. From the day she arrived here it was a big pain. Before, I had the house to myself. I was enjoying being alone. Then she shows up and starts bringing men over. She would only work at the bar occasionally, it was below her dignity to work, all she wanted to do was sunbathe and run around."

"Your sister went both ways, didn't she?" I asked.

Ann looked at me and her shoulders sagged. "I think she and Reeves had a thing going," she said.

"Barbara got around," my Guardian Angel said. "And Reeves is a liar."

"Maybe, maybe not," I told him.

"Did Barbara ever want you to join in all the fun?" I asked Ann.

"I'm not that kind. And for your information, she also asked me to take photographs. But I didn't."

"I would have," my Guardian Angel said and grinned so big I thought his cheeks might crack.

"When she had parties I left," Ann continued. "I would go park in a camping area and look at the stars, or go sleep in the bar. I've been around Roosevelt, don't get me wrong, but group things aren't for me."

I know she has been around, who hasn't in this modern world?

"Sister Mary McDonald from St. Louis," my Guardian Angel said. "Her soul is so spotless she already has a go straight to heaven card."

"Barbara did tell you everything that was going on though, didn't she?" I asked Ann.

"I told her I didn't want to know, but she told me almost everything, every detail."

"Who was she doing trips with?"

"That, she never told me."

"After your mother died, did your father help you?"

"I was 19. Mommy was killed in a car wreck. Big Abe Maiden didn't even come to the funeral. I went to travel agent school, got married, lived a boring life and then got divorced. One good thing was I never had kids. Broke and at with nowhere else to go I contacted my father and he bought me a car and told me to come out here and run his bar. He said he would send me enough money to live on and to enjoy my life."

"Then Barbara shows up."

Ann nodded.

"You don't have $7,500 to pay me do you?"

Ann was quiet for a moment. "Abe sends me $500 a month. I spend it all. I make about $100 a week at the bar from cowboys and fishermen. Does that answer your question? And now, with him in trouble, he might not be able to send me anything. I was going to ask him for the money to pay you when he called. I figured he would pay to try and figure out who killed his daughter, but what with his problems, I didn't."

I know Big Abe Maiden has enough money to send half the women in Colorado $500 a month. And, being a real gangster, his concern over his family was all a disguise to let people think he had a heart.

"If Ann hates her sister why does she want you to find her killer?" my Guardian Angel asked me looking puzzled.

"That is a good question," I replied feeling puzzled myself.

Ann came over to me. "Hug me Roosevelt," she said, putting her arms around my neck.

I hugged her. I wanted to tell her she made me feel warm and how bad it made me feel that her life had not been happy. But I didn't.

After the hug, Ann sat back down. "Did you know Barbara might have had something to do with porn films?" I asked.

There was a momentary look of alarm on Ann's face, which she quickly covered over like age lines with make-up. "No," she said. "Was she?"

"Just a rumor," I replied.

Ann and I made a gourmet dinner of chicken soup and crackers. After she'd eaten three crackers, she said. "I thought of something Barbara told me I'd forgotten. She made a comment one night she was going to make the moves on Ranger Fisher's wife. She thought it would be fun and ironic. She told me there was no way Mrs. Fisher liked men."

This case is like trying to find a Q in a can of alphabet soup.

When we were finished eating I went to the porch. I noticed Jesse's lights were out and his truck was gone. Ann joined me. "Ready for a little danger?" I asked her on the spur of the moment.

"Being with you is dangerous," Ann said but with a mischievous grin.

"Let's go break into Jesse's house, only this time, whistle if you see a car coming."

Ann giggled like a little girl sitting in a dark closet with a little boy and for the first time they were going to play you show me yours and I'll show you mine.

I got my penlight and my trusty packet of private detective breaking and entering tools from my suitcase. I ordered them out of a catalog from a company in Florida that specializes in things criminals need: debugging tools, phone scramblers, lock picking kits, code books, alarms that tell you when your phone is bugged. The funny thing is though, criminals aren't their main customers - large corporations are.

Ann and I walked behind all the cabins until we came to Jesse's. "You stay on the porch," I whispered to her.

"Check," she said.

"I'll stay with Ann," my Guardian Angel said putting his arm around her shoulder and kissing her neck, ignoring my earlier warning of never touching her again.

It took me six seconds to open the lock. This wasn't a big city with 27 dead bolts to each door and a buzzer. I flipped on my flashlight and headed for the bedroom. Jesse's bed wasn't made and clothes were tossed everywhere. There wasn't anything in his closet, except, if I would have been a thief and they fit, I would steal his pair of lizard cowboy boots. There wasn't anything of interest in the top drawer of his dresser. There was nothing in the second. But in the third there was a Colt Woodsman pistol, a 22 that could fire shorts or longs. I didn't pick it up, but it lay in the drawer looking as deadly as a shedding rattlesnake. Moving aside a stack of T-shirts there was a set of Polaroid photographs, but they were not of the mountains. They were photographs of a naked Barbara like she was posing for Gent, or High Society - no Playboy material here. Jesse might not have slept with Barbara, like he said, but he had gotten more than an eyeful. The photographs had been taken in his living room. There was no mistaking the table. I put the photographs back and walked out of the house, locked the door, and Ann and I circled back to her house. When we got to the porch Ann said, "That wasn't too exciting."

She didn't bother to ask me if I found anything that might help. Thinking back, she hadn't asked me if I found anything at Willie's either.

We went inside and I sat on the sofa. Ann got us each a beer.

"It really doesn't make any sense to me that somebody would want to kill Barbara. The way she was, I don't see who could have fallen in love with her. The only reason she might have been killed was if she found out something about somebody around here and they thought she might tell," I said.

"Or she was blackmailing them," Ann said.

"Why didn't you think of that?" my Guardian Angel asked.

"Pea Brain, I don't tell you everything I think," I said giving him an, eat a cow pie look.

"Do you have any idea how she got to the camping area where she was killed?" I asked Ann.

"I let her off on my way to work. A lot of times I would let her off and she would walk back to the house. She was a physical fitness nut."

"All the belly slapping she did you wouldn't think she needed anymore exercise," my Guardian Angel said.

The phone rang and Ann got up to answer it. I finished my beer and got up to get another one. When I came back into the living room Ann looked distressed. "What is it?" I asked.

"That was one of Big Abe's lawyers. Big Abe was found in his backyard several hours ago. He had two bullet holes in the back of his head and his tongue had been cut off. I'm going to bed Roosevelt." She wasn't crying.

Ann shut the bedroom door quietly. From what she had told me, she had never been close to her father, but still, he had been her father and I figured she should have shown some form of emotion, even if it was satisfaction at his death. But as to Big Abe's murder. He had been a gangster and the death of a gangster never chokes me up.

I sipped on my beer. Obviously Big Abe Maiden hadn't been the biggest fish in the fish bowl. I wondered if Ann would get anything in the will. After a few moments I went to Matilda and got my notebook and remembering the wilderness map I'd picked up from the Ranger Station stuck it in my pocket.

I unfolded the map on the coffee table and traced the trails leading from Platoro. I was right. One trail went from Platoro to Red Lake and circled back to the footbridge at the camping area where I had camped. Another trail went from the back of Ann's cabin community, climbed over some steep hills, and then followed the little river that ran into the Chama River below where I found Barbara.

I started writing in my notebook. I wrote, erased, wrote, erased, and wrote more. I went back and read my clues and erased a few, added others. I read again. I now have 84 clues and numerous other notes that might be clues.

In the last 24 hours I'd learned Barbara had been picked up for prostitution and pot, but let go. She had been involved with porn films. I know Sheriff Rogers has never been married. I know Officer Hoffman had lied to me when he said he hadn't bought Barbara a present - he had given her the gold chain. Officer Hayworth had also lied, he had bought three pairs of earrings - at least I figured it was a lie - there is a possibility he had given them to his wife. I know Mr. Leroy Colbert owns a 12-gauge shotgun and keeps stick matches for toothpicks. I know Mrs. Fisher doesn't like me. Mrs. Whoever-She-Was told me no old man had been to the house that she had seen, but the Highway Patrol guys had come together and alone. She had also told me Reeves had always come alone. Ann told me Reeves and Barbara had a thing going, but Reeves said they didn't. I know Barbara and Ann were stepsisters, and not close, and Ann feels like Cinderella. Ann told me Barbara was going to put the move on Mrs. Fisher. I'd found a 22 pistol at Jesse's house and a stack of photographs that any Frenchman would love to buy and reproduce for his booming tourist trade. I know Ann had driven Barbara to the area where she was killed. Big Abe wasn't going to have to do any jail time. And I know there are two trails leading to the area where I'd camped. I also know I am one confused, not going to get paid, private investigator who might never go trout fishing again.

"Not going to get paid is a good reason for you and me to get out of here," my Guardian Angel said.

"I can't, money or no money, I am going to solve the murder," I said.

"Do you still feel strongly for Ann?" he asked.

"At times, but there are some doubts."

"Good," he said.

"Maybe, maybe not," I said not sadly but not happily either.

"Did you ever think about becoming a career beach bum?" my Guardian Angel asked.

How love and beach bum are related I have no idea. I didn't answer him.

I drank my beer and read my notebook. I read it backwards to the front - sometimes it helps. I read and read and read. I was about to read it again when Ann walked out of her bedroom. She had on a robe and came and sat down by me. She rested her shoulder on my head. "I want you to hold me," she said.

She reminded me of a kitten that had been left beside the highway. "I'll be happy to," I said.

I held Ann and stroked her hair. Ann seemed to relax in my arms. "I didn't love him but he was my father," she sniffed.

"It will work out, Ann, everything always does," I said.

"No it doesn't," my Guardian Angel said trying to undo Ann's robe.

CHAPTER ELEVEN
MRS. FISHER - MRS. FISHER

When I woke up Ann was gone. Sleeping through noise isn't a good practice for private investigators, especially since I had been shot at twice in one week. My Guardian Angel should have woken me up. "Pea Brain, you'd better start doing your job," I warned him. "You've already let Willie sneak up on me."

"I thought you needed your rest," he said, shrugging his shoulders like 'what's the big deal?' "And besides, I'm bored."

"When I die, or get killed, no thanks to you, I hope you get reassigned to the most boring person in the world. A person that is so boring they think oatmeal is exciting."

My Guardian Angel got all huffy. "I pulled you through Vietnam didn't I? I helped you quit drugs. I made you famous for 15 minutes. I've saved you from bodily harm so many times I've lost count. I warned you not to go fishing and twice this week I told you when you were in harm's way. I can't do everything, Roosevelt. I don't think you realize how taxing a person you are."

"You are going to think taxing if you don't shape up," I told him.

He went off to sulk, but I had gotten his attention. Putting up with all of his lamebrain, one-liners I occasionally have to lambaste him to let him know he's not getting the upper hand on me.

I got out of bed and took a shower. Ann had left me a note on the kitchen table. How sweet I thought as I picked it up. It said: "In your detective work today go by the store and pick up some food."

The little lady was all heart, but she had forgotten to mention beer. But, even though I knew her father hadn't been a perfect role model, I still thought it was strange how little she was reacting to his murder.

"Barbara's either," my Guardian Angel said apparently over his bummer.

I made a cup of hot tap water coffee, slurped it down, and went back to the bedroom to make the bed. Going by Ann's room I stopped and looked at Ann's chest of drawers. I felt guilty, but went into her room anyway. I looked at my image in the mirror over the dresser. I didn't look guilty. There were a lot of cosmetics on top of the dresser and a dark wood jewelry box with two carved dragons on it. In thc top drawer were panties, panty hose, and one set of panties with no crotch, which have always seemed a waste to me - why not just take them off? I moved the items around carefully and found nothing else. I tried to put everything back exactly as it had been.

In the second drawer were neat stacks of T-shirts and cotton socks. I moved each pile and found nothing, once again being careful to put everything back the way it had been.

The third drawer was empty, which is odd, most women have enough clothes there are never enough drawers, corners, or boxes for everything to fit in. The bottom drawer was depressing. There were three large brown bath towels and matching washcloths. Underneath the towels was a six-inch Smith and Wesson 22 pistol that had printed clearly on the barrel, 22 shorts, longs, or long rifles.

The pistol was loaded. I lay the pistol back in the drawer. "This is not good at all," my Guardian Angel said slightly shocked himself.

"Depressing," I said.

Looking under the bed there were two shoeboxes. The first box had a pair of blue pumps in it. The second box a pair of tennis shoes.

"It's a real case buster for shoes to be in shoeboxes," my Guardian Angel said.

I opened the drawer to Ann's nightstand. There wasn't anything. I went back to the dresser and opened the jewelry box.

There were many sets of earrings: turquoise, silver, gold loops, beaded, silver feathers, and several diamond studs. There was also a wedding band.

"Earrings seem to be in great demand in this part of Colorado," my Guardian Angel said.

Back in the living room I gazed out the window. It was peaceful, it was quiet - my budding love, now wilting, owns a 22 pistol.

Mrs. Whoever-She-Was was hanging out laundry. I saw Jesse's truck and wondered when he drove a logging truck to make any money? Feeling as low as a flat tire on a Cadillac in Death Valley I decided to go talk to Jesse.

Mrs. Whoever-She-Was waved warmly at me. I waved back. "Wait, wait," she called and hurried over to me.

"I was sitting around last night and I thought of several things. I don't know if it will help you or not, but I figured I should tell you. I was going to come over but you saved me the trip," Mrs. Whoever-She-Was told me excitedly.

I was thinking about Ann's pistol and wasn't really paying any attention. "You keep asking me who has been to the house and I told you who all the people I've seen since Barbara moved in. It was silly of me, but I only thought about Barbara because she was murdered then in dawned on me before Barbara moved in Ranger Reeves used to come over to see Ann about every other night. It was always dark when she came. At first, after Barbara arrived, Ranger Reeves would come over like normal, but after a while she only came over when Ann was gone."

"How do you know she was gone?" I asked, now completely paying attention.

"Easy, silly, her car was gone. Mr. Roosevelt, no matter what time of night, if a car is leaving here or coming in, it wakes me up. I'm a light sleeper and a lot of the times I sleep in my recliner in the living room."

I didn't know what to say. "Roosevelt, you are as stupid as they come," didn't seem harsh enough.

"And then this morning, when I saw Ann leaving, I remembered something else. Before Barbara came, Mrs. Fisher used to come over some evenings and see Ann. I haven't seen her in over a month."

"Interesting," my Guardian Angel mused scratching his head like he was one of the Three Stooges.

"Did Ranger Reeves and Mrs. Fisher ever come over at the same time?" I asked.

Mrs. Whoever-She-Was wrinkled her brow like she was a finalist in a spelling bee and had to spell zucchini. "Well, yes, as a matter of fact, they came over together three times that I can remember."

Mrs. Whoever-She-Was had spelled zucchini right.

"I suppose it was always at night."

"Yes it was, Mr. Roosevelt. But women have to have quality time with other women you know."

"Some people's idea of quality time is different," my Guardian Angel said.

"If I think of anything else I'll be sure and tell you," Mrs. Whoever-She-Was told me and walked off as happy and carefree as a CEO's secretary in a palimony suit.

"Roosevelt," my Guardian Angel said to me as I headed toward Jesse's, "You sure we're not in San Francisco?"

Jesse was standing by the corrals filling a water tank for the horses. They were munching on hay, one of their favorite past times. Their second favorite is crapping and watching people shovel it up.

"If man is so smart and has dominion over the earth and the animals, how come not one animal on the face of the earth picks up your poop?" my Guardian Angel asked.

"God likes to screw with our minds," I replied.

"Roosevelt, you look like somebody told you your divorce was denied by the judge," Jesse grinned at me.

I wanted to tell him I know now why he grinned all the time. He was a photographer for a raunchy magazine and never paid the girls. Instead I said, "I think it's the mountain air, too clean."

He didn't laugh. I take it he has never been to a big city and doesn't know what real air looks like.

"Come on in," he said. "I've got some fresh coffee."

Jesse poured us some real coffee, by real I mean real. It was black enough and bitter enough to tan leather. "All right," he said sitting down, "who did it?"

"The only thing I know is, it wasn't me," I said.

"I've heard different. Sheriff told me the only person in the area where Barbara was killed was you. He told me the body hadn't been in the water long enough not to make you a prime suspect."

"I guess that's true," I had to agree.

"But, I know you didn't do it. You would have never gone to see the police."

It seemed to me the Sheriff had told that to the two detectives from Denver. What was the Sheriff up to?

"Does the Sheriff own his own car?" I asked Jesse.

"No, he doesn't need one driving a car the taxpayers pay for," Jesse answered.

"I take it you haven't been driving a log truck lately," I said, trying to sip the coffee and not let it touch my teeth. I don't want to stain them - a pearly white smile is important in our country.

"It's been really slow. The government found out the company was cutting in some areas they were not supposed to. They've been shut down until a suitable fine can be figured out. It's not hurting me right now though, I'm drawing unemployment and in a few weeks the hunts will start. I make do."

"Why did you kill Barbara, Jesse?" I wanted to see if he would stammer or be shocked.

He did neither. He laughed. "Roosevelt, nice try, but it wasn't this cowboy. The only thing I wanted to do was crawl all over her naked body. I'll tell you a secret though. Barbara would let me take photographs of her naked in every position you could imagine, but she wouldn't let me touch her. It was tough, let me tell you. I even offered her 50 bucks once. She laughed and told me I was like a brother to her, somebody she could feel comfortable with."

"How did you handle it, being like her brother?"

"Roosevelt, I didn't love her, do you think I'm some kind of fool. That kind of woman will only get you in trouble."

"What went on at those parties Barbara would have?"

"Most of the time there would be me, the Colbert brothers, Willie, and sometimes that ranger lady. Barbara would get drunk and start dancing and before you knew it she would be naked. That was about it. It was like a topless bar, a whole lot of looking, no touching, but you didn't have to pay her for a table dance."

"Willie told me Barbara wouldn't have anything to do with him." I said.

"That's true, only Willie took it real hard, especially when he found out Ray Colbert was sleeping with her. I think Willie loved her, he even gave her earrings."

"What kind were they?"

"I don't know, he never told me. The only reason I knew he gave her some earrings was he told me one night when he was drunk. Ray and Frank and Barbara came into a bar in Chama where Willie and I were at and she was wearing his earrings. He didn't say anything then but when they left he angrily told me and everyone else in the bar about it. He was mad enough to fight the whole city."

"Willie had earrings in his trailer," my Guardian Angel said. "I wonder if he took them out of Barbara's ears."

"Barbara was doing threesomes, did you know that?" I asked Jesse.

"The Sheriff told me. But one time I was over at the house and Barbara, Ann, and I were sitting around talking. Reeves came over and when Barbara let her in Ann got up and left, like she was mad about something. It wasn't ten minutes later that Barbara asked me, point blank, "Jesse, you've always wanted to sleep with me. Well, here's your chance. Only you have to let Reeves watch. Reeves looked like she was high on something and she was almost drooling. I couldn't do it. I wouldn't do it. I'm no freak. I left the house and after I shut the door I could hear them laughing. After that, I never went back to the house."

"I'm into some weird stuff," my Guardian Angel said shaking his head, "but these people are even beyond my tastes."

"How long ago was that?" I asked Jesse.

"Three weeks, maybe."

"One more thing then I'll leave you alone. Did you ever see Mrs. Fisher at Barbara's?"

"Used to, she used to come and see Ann, but when Barbara showed up, she only came a few times and then quit coming over."

"Did Ranger Fisher and his wife ever come over together?"

"Not that I know of."

I couldn't tell Jesse I had broken into his house and knew he had a 22. The photographs didn't mean anything now that Jesse and told me he had taken them. For some reason I figured Jesse was telling the truth about not sleeping with Barbara in front of Reeves. Most cowboys, underneath their tough exterior, are softies at heart and have this thing about what should be private - they also put women on a pedestal, especially their mothers. When I left the house Jesse was smiling. I was not smiling.

Headed back to the house I felt deeply troubled about Ann. Also, Ranger Reeves was proving to be an elusive little fairy, and Mrs. Fisher, who has God sitting on her shoulder, had been hanging out with the wrong crowd.

I felt like I was at an amusement park, but there was one thing wrong - I was the ride.

"The women you fall for are always suspect," my Guardian Angel said.

I decided to go see Sheriff Rogers. Matilda, true to form, started right up. Driving I felt assured with one fact - there was no way Matilda is a lesbian - she has always been good to me and has never blinked her lights when a pink Porsche sped by.

Sheriff Rogers was in front of the jail watching two inmates dressed in orange pants and T-shirts washing his squad car. He didn't have a rifle or shotgun cradled in his arm to guard them. He also, for some strange reason did not have his cowboy hat on. He smiled at me - slave labor must do a thing for his heart.

"This here is Matty Rodriguez and Jimmy Slaughter. They figured they needed a few days in jail to catch up on some physical skills," Rogers told me.

The two inmates grinned at me and kept washing the squad car. They both looked like they got put in jail on purpose so they could have a decent meal.

"How come you told Jesse you thought I was a suspect in the murder?" I asked Rogers, slightly peeved.

"I wanted to see what his reaction would be."

"How many people have you told the facts of this case to?"

"I'm doing an investigation myself, Roosevelt. You seem to forget this is my County and I'm a cop."

"You're right," I said. "I apologize."

Sheriff Rogers lit a Lucky Strike with a stick match. "Take a smoke break," he told the two inmates.

Rogers gave them each a cigarette and a stick match. The men sat down by the car smoking to their heart's content.

"You know in Texas a prisoner can't smoke in jail anymore," I said.

"The only things Texas is good for are smugglers, illegal aliens and peanuts," Rogers said.

"Watermelons and onions, too," my Guardian Angel said. "Not to forget oil and cattle, Tex-Mex food, barbecue, the Alamo."

"Would you be quiet," I cut in.

"Are you holding any information back from me?" I asked the Sheriff.

Rogers shook his head and laughed. "The main thing I'm doing is waiting for somebody to kill you, leave some evidence, so I can pin Barbara's murder on him, too."

"Sheriff," I wanted to appease him by calling him by his title, before I asked the next question. "Sheriff," I said, "did you ever sleep with Barbara?"

There was no mirth in Rogers' eyes. He looked at me like he was a chain gang boss in Georgia in the 1930's and I was a black man who had been framed for raping a white girl, who in reality had been raped by the leader of the Klan, because she wouldn't go out with the bigoted jerk.

"Roosevelt," he said, coldly. "I've been and always have been a servant of the people. I take my job seriously. I would have liked to have slept with Barbara, but I never did. You idiot, I'm old enough to have been her father."

"Sorry," I said.

"I've never seen anything wrong with younger women, even if they do talk too much," my Guardian Angel said.

"You are a strange man, Roosevelt," Sheriff Rogers said.

"He knows it," my Guardian Angel said.

"Did you happen to get any prints off of the shotgun shells?" I asked.

"They were as clean as my car is going to be," he replied, while he field dressed his cigarette.

There was no need to say goodbye before I drove away. I knew one thing as I headed for the Forked Lightning Ranch. I believe Rogers. He is a straight arrow cop and for him to take out a younger woman was against his grain.

"I don't know if he is that straight and narrow," my Guardian Angel said, "The day you found Barbara he was turning onto the Antonito road."

"I already have that written down as a clue," I said.

"I was only trying to help."

“Pea Brain, you could help a lot if every so often you would just shut up,” I said.

He stuck his tongue out at me which was a lot nicer than flipping me the bird.

Mr. Leroy Colbert was out by the corrals looking at the horses. He waved at me. The dogs barked and growled at Matilda, but when I got out all they wanted was to be petted.

Mr. Colbert had a hand rolled cigarette hanging out of his mouth and hadn't bothered to shave since I'd last seen him. He also hadn't bothered to change clothes. "Roosevelt, you look like your dog ran away," he hacked.

We watched the horses for a while. They were good-looking quarter horses, strong and well fed. Neither one of us said anything for a few moments. "Come on in the house," he finally said. "It's getting where I hate horses."

I prayed he didn't want to drink any whiskey. "I got a fresh pot of coffee on," he said.

Cowboy coffee is their crystal meth. My heart was still pounding from Jesse's home brew. We sat in the kitchen and I tried to read my future in the dark-as-life coffee. It said: Roosevelt, you will be a failure. Roosevelt, the I.R.S. will catch you one day for cheating. Roosevelt, you should open up a health food store, and get you an older girlfriend who has money. Roosevelt, if you were smart, you would pack your bags, not pass go, not collect $200 and get your old hippie body out of Colorado. I looked up, all I could see was the truth.

"When one accepts the truth in life, life is much easier," my Guardian Angel said.

"Pea Brain, if I want philosophy I'll buy a book," I told him.

"The boys will be here soon. They called me from Platoro about an hour ago," Mr. Colbert told me slurping his coffee.

"Life is tough," I blurted out for no reason at all.

"You can say that again," Mr. Colbert said.

"Life is tough."

"How about we say it together," Mr. Colbert said.

"Life is tough," we said together.

"It ain't never been any good boy," Mr. Colbert said. "Now, in the future, in the 12th century, the 14th century, before Christ, when there were cavemen, and even before cavemen when we were only monkeys trying to figure out how many bananas we could hold in our hands without dropping one. It's always been tough."

"Is there any hope?" I asked.

"Nope," Mr. Colbert said. "The sooner you figure out it's all a losing situation the better off you will be."

"He's a smart old geezer," my Guardian Angel said.

I wanted to go somewhere and sleep for three weeks. But after merely breathing Mr. Colbert's coffee and drinking half a cup of Jesse's I wouldn't be able to sleep for three days. If I could dry the coffee they made and put it in small wedges of tin foil I could sell it at truck stops to truckers for a small fortune.

"I don't know what your problem is son," Mr. Colbert said sounding like my father. "You're sleeping with Ann and you're not paying rent. What else do you need?"

I started to say, I'm not sleeping with Ann, but I didn't. Looking at Mr. Colbert's grizzled and experienced face he wouldn't believe me if I told him the truth.

"I know what it is," Mr. Colbert said, rolling himself another smoke. "You're not going to solve this case and you feel like a failure."

"Roosevelt is comfortable with feeling like a failure," my Guardian Angel said.

"I haven't solved every case I've ever worked on," I told Mr. Colbert.

Mr. Colbert finished rolling his smoke and lit it with a stick match, once again putting the burned out match in his pocket. "My father used to tell me there were some people in this life that need killing," Mr. Colbert said. "You ever think Barbara was one of those people?"

From what I have gathered, Barbara was self-centered, over-sexed and a home wrecker, but she didn't force men to poke her with their primary brain. "No sir," I answered, "I don't think she needed killing. Maybe she needed a real friend."

Mr. Colbert puffed on his cigarette. "We all need friends," he said in a faraway voice, as if his mind was traveling back when he and his wife were young and in love. "Sad thing is there aren't many real friends in a man's life. Most people want something. Companies want to break your back and pay you lousy wages. Governments want to take your money and lie to you. A good friend is hard to come by."

Thinking back on my life I realized it was devoid of the mystic figure called ‘good friend' - everything seemed to be merely a passing.

My Guardian Angel smiled at me. I smiled at him. Often times the ones closest to us are easily forgotten.

I drank a shot of coffee to whirl my mind back to the here and now, and not the realm of da da land, filled with questions and no answers.

The dogs started barking and I heard the banging and groaning of a truck pulling a large horse trailer. "Boys are here sooner than I thought," Mr. Colbert said, inching himself out of his chair. His old joints were as stiff as a new pair of boots.

I followed Mr. Colbert outside. Frank and Ray had gotten out of the pickup truck and were playing with the dogs. When they saw me neither one of them smiled. "Boys, this here is Mr. Roosevelt," Mr. Colbert introduced me.

The taller of the two brothers stepped forward and we shook hands. "Frank," he said.

Ray didn't shake hands. "We met you in the bar, you bought us a drink. Willie told us you were a private detective working on Barbara's murder," he said.

Both of them had on well-worn leather chaps, boots with spurs, blue Levi shirts many times patched, and stained white felt cowboy hats. I could tell they were as happy to see me as a guy on parole enjoys seeing his parole officer.

"After you get the horses put up come on in the house, Mr. Roosevelt wants to ask you boys some questions," Mr. Colbert told his sons.

Neither Frank nor Ray made any form of protest to their father. "We can go back in and wait," Mr. Colbert told me.

I wondered why we had bothered to go outside in the first place.

Sitting back at the kitchen table Mr. Colbert seemed different guarded. He poured us more coffee and rolled himself another cigarette. We sat in silence like strangers in a big city who had to share a table for lunch.

When Frank and Ray came into the kitchen, I felt like a man in a business suit who had by accident stopped in a biker bar for an after work drink. Ray sat down at the table while Frank got two coffee cups and filled them and put one in front of his brother before sitting down. My usual blast of short questions lay stuck in my brain.

Frank broke the silence. "I went out with her first," he said quietly and slowly, as if each word was picked from a list of words before he spoke. "I thought I was in love. I tell you, when I touched her, it was like another person came alive. She was wild."

He drifted off into visions of Barbara and him.

"Barbara came on to me," Ray said, not looking at me but down into the depths of his fortune telling coffee. "I knew it was wrong, she being my brother’s girl and all, but I don't know what happened to me. It was like I lost my mind or something." Ray's words trailed off.

"She told us both she liked us the same," Frank started again, "but she didn't love either one of us. Ray and I would take turns taking her out and then we started to take her out together."

"Did you guys ever do a threesome with Barbara?" I asked.

Frank looked at his father. Ray looked at his father. They looked like two teenagers who had been caught sneaking the car out of the driveway. "One night at her house, we all got drunk and did a threesome," Ray said. "It was her idea. After that, we did it a few more times."

Mr. Colbert looked at each of his sons - his eyes were hard - almost hateful.

"We didn't kill her," Frank said.

Ray peered into the depths of his coffee.

I stood. "No, I don't think you men did," I said, and walked out of the house. I was tired of talking to cowboys.

As I drove toward town I felt sorry for Mr. Colbert.

I stopped at the grocery store and bought some pork chops, two cans of apple sauce, a can of peas, and a 12 pack of beer. The old Mexican man who ran the store once again didn't say a word to me.

Sheriff Rogers was standing by Matilda when I came out. He was wearing his hat. "Why didn't you tell me Big Abe had been killed in Texas?" he asked, like he felt like taking out his pistol and hitting me upside my head a few times.

"I'm not family," I said. "That's up to Ann."

"Do you think that Barbara's murder might be tied in with him? Maybe he owed some money to some guys and they killed his daughter to let him know they weren't playing around?"

"Colombians and Jamaicans do that," I said. "Even our famous Mafia with their fake code of honor kill women it anymore. But for some reason, I don't think so."

"Maybe you and I should work on this case together," Rogers told me.

"Sheriff, nothing personal, but I work alone."

"You find something out that you think is important you had better tell me," Rogers warned.

I smiled at him, got in Matilda, and drove away.

I stopped at the Ranger Station. Neither Ranger Reeves nor Ranger Fisher was in the office and one of the trucks was gone. I went to Fisher's house. Mrs. Fisher opened the door before I knocked. She gave me a look that would wilt an oak tree and started to say something. I didn't give her a chance. "You like Ann the best or Barbara?" I asked her.

She started to slam the door, but I reached out and stopped it. "Maybe you should talk to me or I could have a talk with your guilt-ridden husband," I said.

If her eyes had been machine guns, I would look worse than a raccoon on the highway that had been run over by 27 cars. She could tell I was not bluffing and stopped pushing against the door. "I'll come out," she told me like I was the Black Forest and she was acid rain.

I knew my worst nightmare was true.

Mrs. Fisher stood on the porch with her arms folded across her stomach and her face set in a granite grimace. "So you found out," she said curtly.

"Purely by accident," I confessed.

I really didn't know until her statement.

The granite of her face turned to sandstone, then to limestone, and finally drifted into sand. I hoped I was not in for the crying victim routine, with tears and a lot of sniffing. "You must believe me," Mrs. Fisher said, like she was an orphan and I was Daddy Warbucks, "I've never done that kind of thing before."

"I wonder if a married woman having sex with another woman is considered adultery?" my Guardian Angel asked.

"How did Ann seduce you?" I asked her.

Mrs. Fisher took a deep breath. "We met one day in town at the grocery store. She seemed nice and she asked me to drop by one day. A week or so later I was sitting at home, bored, so I thought I would go over. We drank coffee, talked, the little things women talk about, and before I knew it I went over again. One day we drank wine, got a little tipsy, and Ann brought up the subject about how men never understand women. My husband and I've never really been close, who knows, maybe I was feeling sorry for myself, I don't know, but the next thing I knew we were in bed."

"Mrs. Fisher, Mrs. Fisher," I said.

"Mrs. Fisher, Mrs. Fisher, Mrs. Fisher," my Guardian Angel gasped.

"I know, it's hard to believe," she said.

"Nothing is hard to believe for an old hippie who happens to be a Vietnam vet," I said. "Try putting those two worlds in your brain."

She grinned a 'guilty little girl' grin at me.

"Before you knew it, you and Ann, and Reeves, were all playing pin the tail on the donkey," I said.

"I only watched them," Mrs. Fisher said. "I never did anything with Reeves. I do know that Reeves and Ann had a thing going before me, but Reeves never minded Ann and me."

"How about when Barbara showed up?"

"It got to be too much for me. I couldn't take it anymore. I stopped, confessed my sins, and I am now living in the grace of our Lord, Jesus Christ."

"Do you think Barbara went after your husband because you wouldn't join in all the fun?" I asked.

"If it would not have been Barbara, it would have been somebody else. It's different now, much different."

"Mrs. Fisher, I won't tell your husband, believe me."

Mrs. Fisher looked like she wanted to hug me so I stepped back. "Thanks for your time," I told her and headed towards Matilda.

Who knows, maybe now she will be a good wife, maybe Ranger Fisher is now a good husband, maybe they will stay together for 67 years, have three more kids, 14 grandchildren, and when they are 97 die together in a plane crash.

"Not if one of them gets life for first degree murder," my Guardian Angel said.

"I don't think either one of them killed Barbara," I said, driving toward Ann's.

Ann was sitting on the sofa. She wasn't happy. "You went through my things you low life," she stormed her eyes shooting fire bolts at me.

Her anger did not even faze me, all I felt was disillusioned. My budding love for her had been killed by an early frost.

"It's too bad, even if I've never trusted her and still think she wants to kill you," my Guardian Angel said sadly.

"It is too bad," was all I could say.

"Oh well, life goes on," my Guardian Angel said patting me on the shoulder.

"I will always believe in rainbows," I said but not with a great amount of resolve

CHAPTER TWELVE
BY THE SKIN OF MY CHINNIE CHIN CHIN

I didn't know what to say to Ann. I'm sorry for going through your room you lying sexy thing, who I can't fall in love with now after what I've found out about you, didn't seem like the right thing to say.

So I stood, looking at her like a big dumb idiot, hoping some lame excuse would pop into my mind. Of course one didn't, excuses to a woman would be like telling a drill sergeant I had to go home because my girlfriend was dating my best friend and joining the Army was one big mistake.

Ann looked at me with eyes that were pins and I was a pincushion. After a few moments and I hadn't spoken she stomped out of the house. The slamming door her goodbye.

"At least now if she kills you, you know you don't love her," my Guardian Angel said.

There's logic in that statement but I don't know what it is. Ann's Explorer ground into gear and she spun off.

I got a beer, went to my bedroom and got my note pad and pencil. I came back to the living room, but didn't sit on the sofa, anger vibes might eat me up so I sat in the chair. I read all my notes. They read like a cheap sex book that sells five million copies, while a well thought out book that is a shining testimony to the fulfillment of man sells ten. I read the notes one more time and then added what else I'd found out. I'd found out Ann has a 22 Smith and Wesson. Ann has one empty drawer in her dresser. Ann's jewelry box is filled with earrings. Mrs. Whoever-She-Was informed me Ranger Reeves used to come and see Ann. Also, Mrs.

Fisher used to visit Ann. I'd found out Sheriff Rogers doesn't own a car. Jesse informed me Willie had given Barbara earrings and had been angry the night he saw Frank and Ray with Barbara when she was wearing the earrings. Jesse told me Barbara had offered to have sex with him if Ranger Reeves could watch - not a thing that would make Smokey the Bear happy. Sheriff Rogers informed me, in no uncertain terms, he wouldn't sleep with anybody that was young enough to be his daughter. Mr. Colbert always puts his used stick matches in his pocket and informed me some people need killing. Ray and Frank had played threesome with Barbara and neither one of them could look me in the eyes. Mrs. Fisher had confessed she'd had an affair with Ann but wasn’t into trips. I now have 100 clues but my cheap sex book has no plot and no main character.

"Modern books don't need a plot or character development," my Guardian Angel said. "Cheap sex and violence sells. You have a lot of that."

I finished my beer and went and got another one. The sun was beginning to set and I sat on the edge of the porch. Man doesn't see too many sunsets anymore - the new name for sunset is happy hour.

The beer tasted good. The sunset was pretty. There was something I was missing that would crack this case open like a watermelon falling off of a truck.

"You have to find the truck first," my Guardian Angel said.

"Pea Brain, the watermelon would also help," I said.

There is something deeper to this case than women who like women, men who like women, women who like women and men, men who only get to take photographs, or jealousy. Barbara had been killed for more than sleeping with every moving creature in the area. Big Ed had been killed because it was the normal for a gangster to get murdered.

The sun disappeared behind the mountains. There was no moon and the stars blinked at me like one of those mica-filled ceilings in a cheap motel room somewhere in Nebraska - the type where cigarette burns on the bed spread and carpet are considered part of the ambiance. I went into the house and got another beer. I was on the beer path to Zen. If I reach it I will buy a pickup, put confederate flag decals on the bumper, hang a 30/06 in the window, let my beard grow scraggly, have a tattoo on one arm that states "Born to Die" and on the other arm "Mom", start chewing tobacco, kick dogs, beat my wife or girlfriend, and hate all minorities - a minority being anybody who isn't like me.

Deciding to go for a walk I headed toward the bridge. I noticed Mr. and Mrs. Whoever-They-Was lights were on. Leaning against the rail of the bridge I wondered what fish do at night since they have to keep their eyes open all the time. Think what a burden it must be to not be able to shut your eyes and ignore the world. Below me were all kinds of little fishes wishing they could get a good night's sleep and praying that one day God would give them eyelids.

I let the sound of the water and the faint sound of crickets fill my mind. There had to be a break in this case, something small, something barely beyond the reach of my fingers, and if I could grasp it I could get out of Dodge. It is something beyond, beyond, beyond, beyond what? After a few minutes I gave up and ambled back toward the house.

"I think you should stay here longer and contemplate why fish don't have eyelids," my Guardian Angel said. "Why, I don't know? But I think you should."

I ignored him.

Mr. and Mrs. Whoever-They-Was house lights were out, but for some reason I didn't think they were in bed reading The Joy of Sex.

I was about five yards from the house when a large, dark object, rushed at me from behind Matilda. My Guardian Angel's warning came to me as I froze in my tracks. The large, dark object, looked like a bear, a growling, fangs-bared grizzly, too late I realized it wasn't a bear, it was Willie. Willie slammed into me like a train hitting a cow. It was a perfect shoulders-square-to-the-target tackle. My half-empty beer can went flying. The air came out of me like a cheap carnival balloon after being hit by a truck and my ribs felt like they were touching my backbone. Willie and I rolled over and over like we were one large bowling ball. "You sneakin' jerk," I heard Willie grunt through my fog-filled mind.

We were no longer rolling. Willie was sitting on me trying to hit me in the side of the head with left and rights. I had my arms up around my head, absorbing most of the shock with my arms. Willie was too heavy for me to bounce him off. He pulled his right arm back to try and drive his fist down into my nose. I had one split second. I took my right arm away from my face, and luckily, found my target. My hand circled his family jewels and I squeezed as hard as I could. Willie screamed. I squeezed harder. I pushed him off me with my left hand, my right hand still holding onto his now slightly oblong family jewels. The sounds coming out of Willie's mouth could have been mistaken for the monkey room at the zoo. I started to stand up and while doing so I released my grip. Willie put his hands between his legs like a boxer who had been hit with a low blow. He was trying to cuss me out and moan at the same time. It came out - "Fuaghhhh, youashhh, O Godaghhhh."

It took several moments for me to get my breath. I didn't think my ribs were broken but I could feel a trickle of blood running down my face. "You should listen to me," my Guardian Angel said, not feeling sorry for me at all.

"You cheat," Willie moaned, rolling over and pushing himself up on all fours. I fought the urge to kick him in the face.

"Cheat, you bushwhacked me," I gasped.

Willie slowly stood. I stepped back, giving myself enough room to kick him as hard as I could if he wanted to continue. "You broke into my trailer," Willie groaned.

I started to deny the truth. "Don't say you didn't, I heard your Volkswagen driving away. No car in the world sounds like a Volkswagen."

"I'm trying to solve a murder, Willie," I said, which sounded like a lame excuse for breaking and entering and squeezing somebody's family jewels.

"All you had to do was come and talk to me."

"I did come over once, you were rude," I said.

"You could have come over again. I was having a bad beard day," he said.

Willie didn't seem to be in the mood to rush at me and I did what most cowboys do after they have been in a fight. "You want a beer?" I asked him. "We can talk."

He nodded.

I let Willie walk slowly into the house in front of me.

Willie sat at the kitchen table while I got two beers. I put one in front of him. "You got blood on your cheek," he told me, which I thought was thoughtful.

I sat, wiping my face with the back of my hand. "You could have broken my ribs," I told Willie.

Willie smiled a crooked smile, or what I took to be a smile through his bushy beard. "I wouldn't have hurt you too bad," he said. "I know you're trying to find out who killed Barbara."

Willie picked up his beer and drank it all. I got him another one. "I didn't kill her, Roosevelt," Willie said, "I loved her. I couldn't kill her."

He sounded like a little boy whose pet mouse had been eaten by the family cat.

I didn't say anything. Willie seemed to be in a talking mood and there was no need for me to ruin it by asking him any questions.

"When I took her out the first time, I thought I'd died and gone to heaven. Barbara was the prettiest woman I'd ever seen and she went out with me." Willie shrugged his large shoulders. "Look at me, I make ugly look good. It was her idea the second time we went out to go to the river and get naked. As she undressed I thought she was a goddess, all tanned and golden. I thought if I touched her she would disappear. The next thing I know I'd bought her earrings and was babbling how much I loved her. When I told her I loved her, she laughed at me Roosevelt - laughed at me like I was a silly little boy."

"Willie the grizzly bear is really a teddy bear," my Guardian Angel said giving Willie a look like he should be a man and get over it or move to San Francisco and buy a dress.

"When she told me she wouldn't go out with me anymore because I crimped her style she handed me back the earrings I'd bought her like I'd gotten them out of a Cracker Jacks box. I drove all the way to Albuquerque to get them Roosevelt. It took me all day and cost me half a month's pay."

I felt sorry for Willie. "Where is your truck?" I asked him.

"At Jesse's."

"I'm sorry about Barbara and you," I said.

"I can't blame you for thinking I did it, I suppose."

"Did you know Barbara went both ways?" I asked.

"About a week after Barbara told me she wouldn't go out with me again I drove over to try and talk to her. I parked down at Jesse's and walked back. There was a dim light on in the living room. The curtain wasn't closed all the way. Instead of knocking on the door I peaked in the window. Reeves and Barbara were naked and they weren't playing doctor. I felt sick at my stomach, and then I really felt sick because Ann was standing on the coffee table with nothing on but leather boots that came up to her knees. She was filming Barbara and Reeves with a video camera. I went back to Jesse's."

"I'm starting to get confused," my Guardian Angel said giving me a quizzical look.

"Did you tell Jesse?" I asked, trying to not show how shocked I was at his last statement.

"I never told anybody till you. Some things people don't talk about."

"That day I met you boys up at the Platoro bar, you didn't seem to upset with Ann."

"You been up in the woods for a week with no beer, you'd buy a beer from the devil," Willie said.

In Vietnam they told us not to buy the local beer because the Cong would put cut glass in it. It never stopped anybody I knew from buying it.

"Who killed Barbara?" I asked.

Willie looked me straight in the eyes. "I don't know anybody around here that would kill anybody unless it was in a bar fight and then it would be by accident."

Willie lit a Lucky Strike with a disposable lighter.

"Do you think Frank or Ray might have killed her?" I asked.

"She used them like she used me, but they wouldn't kill her. About the only person they might kill is their father. He's been a meaner than a cur dog to them for their whole lives. He made it hell for their mother and hell for them while they were growing up. The only reason they've stayed around these parts is because they keep hoping the old man will die and leave them the ranch."

"Lord help us," my Guardian Angel said.

"Do you think Sheriff Rogers ever took Barbara out?" I asked, my mind feeling worse than oatmeal - it felt like grits.

"Not that I know of," Willie said.

We sat in silence for a few more moments and then Willie stood and started walking painfully to the door. His family jewels would be sore for a few days. "Thanks for the beers," he said and opened the door.

"Happy to be of assistance," I told him and waved.

It wasn't more than two minutes later his truck went by the house.

I went to the bathroom and washed the dry blood off my face. It was only a small cut. I took off my shirt and looked at my ribs. They were bruised but not badly. Sitting on the sofa I wondered why I hadn't found a video camera in the house going through Ann's things.

It wasn't ten minutes later when Ann drove up. I felt like the husband who had stayed home and watched TV after his wife had screamed at him for ten minutes and then stormed out of the house. She would come back, ignore him being a zombie in front of the TV, go straight to the bedroom and go to bed.

Ann, to my surprise, was smiling. If we were married I would figure she had maxed the credit card. I still didn't say anything to her. I looked at her like the Court Jester would look at the King when the King wasn't laughing.

"I want to apologize," she said to me, "You were only doing your job going through my things."

I felt like an invisible Willie had slammed into my gut. When a woman apologizes there is something terribly wrong.

"I suppose you found the pistol?" Ann said.

"I found it," I said.

"Do you have any questions?" Ann asked me, in a tone like she was the old western town's favorite red light girl and would never hurt a flea.

"No," I replied, simply.

"Good," Ann said, "Let's drink a beer."

I was feeling the effects from all the beer I'd drunk with Willie. But what the hay? If I can't be a good detective I might as well be a good drunk.

Ann and I stood on the porch. "I've always had a big sex drive," Ann told me. "It started when I was 15 and has only gotten stronger as I've grown older."

"Are you Swedish?" I asked.

"Be serious," Ann said.

"Are you Greek?" I asked.

"I must be part of both the way I feel most of the time."

"When is Big Abe's funeral?" I asked - her sexual preferences aren't something I want to dwell on.

"I don't know and I don't give a damn," Ann said bitterly. "I'm not going to go. For all I care they can take his body and toss it into the ocean."

So much for honor thy father and mother. I felt like telling Ann I knew she'd been playing night games with Mrs. Fisher and Reeves, and I know she'd been into taking photographs, but I didn't. One thing a detective has to do is know when to keep his mouth shut and never let anybody know what he is thinking.

"You probably know, but won't tell me, but I seduced Mrs. Fisher," Ann told me, as nonchalantly as if she was serving me tea and crumpets - so much for me keeping information to myself. "I've always liked women, there is something clean about their bodies, something that is not invading. But, I like men also, in fact, I like men better most of the time. With women, I'm dominant, with men I'm submissive," Ann said giving me a crooked little smile.

I was speechless.

"What is it about life that gets things so twisted?" she asked me almost sadly.

"If I knew the answer to that I would be signing copies of my international bestseller and booked on a lecture circuit for the next 10 years," I replied.

"I don't want to get old, Roosevelt," Ann said. "I don't want to live on and on in some continual rerun of a grade B movie."

"How about skin flicks?" I commented, trying to sound humorous but in all truth, being serious.

For a mere instant, I felt electricity in the air, but Ann composed herself. "Are you ever serious?" she asked me.

"As serious as crawling through the mud on my belly with machine gun bullets flying over my head," I said. "As serious as trying to find out who shot Barbara in the head and tossed her naked body in the Chama River. I'm always serious Ann. I just look and act like a fool."

"I'll be back in a second," she told me.

It was more than a second, maybe a minute, maybe two minutes. I heard Jesse's truck start. Watched his headlights come on and then heard the grinding of gears as he put his truck into gear. The headlights missed me as he drove by.

When Ann came back she had two more beers and had put on perfume. The night air seemed to be enhanced. She stood so close to me our sides were touching. "A beer for your thoughts?" she asked, handing me a beer.

I sipped on the beer. "I was wondering if 40 years from now anybody will know who I was." I said. "I was wondering why man wants to kill himself and every other creature on the face of the earth. And how a person hired by either a defense attorney or a prosecutor can be considered a non-biased witness?"

"Deep stuff," Ann mused.

"About as deep as manure in a feed lot," my Guardian Angel said pinching his nose.

"Let's go for a walk," Ann said.

We started walking toward the bridge, at least this time I knew Willie wouldn't be waiting for me when we returned. Ann and I didn't talk. It was strange, or weird, or both, but I am okay with Ann even though I can no longer love her. I'd been shot at sitting in her living room. I know her sexual variations, at least some of them, and yet I am comfortable with her. I felt like I knew Ann, or what Ann had wanted to be in life. It is strange, but I've been to a few topless bars in my life and every time I see a young girl dancing on stage, and listen to the hoots and whistles of the men in the crowd I always feel sorry for the girls. I felt sorry for Ann.

When we got to the bridge we didn't stop but walked on. "When I was young I used to go for long walks," Ann said. I would dream that one day I would meet my prince and he would take me away to a far off land where we would live in a nice house. He would love me for what I was and not for what he wanted me to be. I would cook and we would have children, happy children, children who would love their parents and grow up and go to college, and get good jobs, and in turn have good kids. Dreams go to hell, Roosevelt."

"Maybe they get sidetracked," I said. "Maybe life is only what we feel inside and everything else that goes on around us is really the dream."

Ann gazed into the night. I wanted to believe her mind was out with the stars, reaching for a world that was beyond women who didn't like men, or standing around naked with black leather boots on, but I couldn't believe it. Ann's mind was somewhere I would or could never go.

We walked back to the house and Ann went to her room without saying goodnight.

I got another beer and went back to the porch. I thought about all the crimes going on right at this moment - the rapes, robberies, muggings, wars, battles, domestic fights. Maybe it would be best for the world if all of humanity was locked up. Voluntarily, all humans would go to a big barren island and build a fence around it and let the world go on in its own natural cycle. In about 1000 years mankind would die out and give tigers, and monkeys, and fish their chance to screw up the world.

I went to my room and lay down on the bed without pulling down the covers or taking off my clothes. I felt mentally tired, as if my brain had run away during the day and gone to Pago Pago. I fell into a dreamless, empty sleep, so deep fantasy didn't dare enter, and murder was never a part of the real world.

CHAPTER THIRTEEN
EARLY MORNING RAIDER

Waking up I felt helpless. I was still missing something about Barbara's murder that I should know. The clue was there but somehow I had missed it.

"Your mind and your common sense are all that is missing," my Guardian Angel said.

"Pea Brain, speak for yourself," I snapped back.

I got out of bed, dressed, and headed for the kitchen. Ann's door was closed. I turned on the light. It was 3:30 a.m. and I'd only been in bed for a few hours. Something was bothering me - something was beating in my empty head trying to get out. I sat on the sofa feeling like I'd spent two days in an airport trying to catch a plane that would never land. "If you would..." my Guardian Angel started to say, but I gave him a dirty look and he shut-up.

He turned around and wiggled his butt at me. I went outside. The air was chilly, a hint of fall, and felt good like a cold washcloth on a drunk's face. The endless expanse of stars only made me feel more helpless.

"If you would find out what was in that empty drawer of Ann's it might help you," my Guardian Angel told me. He must not know what shut-up means.

"How do I find out what was in an empty drawer?" I asked.

"Ask Ann," my Guardian Angel replied.

"That's why I'm the detective and you're the protector," I said. "You don't ask a suspect a question they can dodge."

"Then I think you should break into Ranger Reeves house."

"Why?"

"I don't know, just a hunch, and at least you would be doing something besides getting up at all hours of the night feeling helpless and being rude."

"You're not as stupid as I thought," I replied.

"It's easy to be smart hanging out with you," he said.

I went back to bed.

When I woke up in the morning, Ann was gone and the little bi-sexual hadn't even left me a love note. My Guardian Angel was tap dancing - he'd watched Ann take a shower. I slugged down two cups of hot tap water coffee before going outside. Matilda, never the girl of my life to say no, started right up. I drove past the Ranger Station slowly and saw Ranger Reeves bicycle. Several miles down the road I turned around and drove back toward her house. There would be no nighttime breaking and entering - it was going to be a full blown, daytime, frontal attack. "I don't think this daytime bit is a good idea," my Guardian Angel warned.

"I don't care what you think," I answered.

"It's a pity," he replied in a way that I didn't know if I should be angry or afraid.

I parked in front of Ranger Reeves' house. If anybody saw the car, I'd been in the area long enough nobody would think anything was suspicious. I sat on the porch for a few minutes and then tried the door. It wasn't locked - small communities are still trusting.

I looked in all the kitchen drawers first, then the cupboard. I even opened the oven door to the gas stove and the wood stove. There wasn't anything to go through in the living room, but it was strange there were no videos stacked by the TV and the video player. The hall closest had sheets, an extra set of pillows, and towels. There wasn't anything out of the ordinary in the bathroom. Ranger Reeves' bed was made and her drawers were as neat and tidy as her house. Her drawers had white cotton socks, men's briefs, and T-shirts. Her closet didn't even have one dress - even for a trip home to try and fool mom and dad. The guest room closet was empty.

"This is an extremely boring breaking and entering," my Guardian Angel said holding back a yawn.

I felt like Mighty Casey who had struck out. "So much for your advice," I told my Guardian Angel.

"You didn't look under her bed," he told me.

"Nobody hides things they don't want people to find under their bed," I said.

"Don't get wishy washy with me, you looked underneath Ann's bed," he said.

There was a long cardboard box under the bed. I pulled it out and opened it. There were 24 videos and a camcorder.

"The case of the empty drawer draws to a conclusion," my Guardian Angel beamed, and strutted around like he was the only rooster in a chicken coop with fifty hens.

None of the videos had names written on them, although they were numbered 1 through 24. I had no doubt the videos were not copies of old classic movies. Taking the box to the living room I turned on the V.C.R. and started video number 1. There was no lead in, no list of characters, no production company logo, no music, right off the bat there was Barbara, dressed only in a gold stomach chain, and naked Highway Patrolman Hoffman and Hayworth, but they weren't writing speeding tickets. The visuals were accentuated with enough groans and moans to wake up Cleveland, Ohio. The next five minutes were variations of threesomes, none of which would make a member of a sex club blush, and the tape ended.

"This isn't your normal high mountain small community," my Guardian Angel said with his face was only an inch from the TV screen.

"More like a bridge club in L.A.," I said.

Tape number 2 was Ranger Reeves and Barbara, and they weren't cutting firewood for the winter.

Tape number 3 was Barbara, Ranger Reeves, and Mrs. Fisher, and they were not giving quilting lessons.

"Mrs. Fisher lied to you about threesomes," my Guardian Angel said.

Tape number 4 was Barbara and Frank and Ray Colbert doing a repeat performance of - "I wish I was a Colorado Highway Patrolman."

Tape number 5 was interesting. Barbara, Ann, Mrs. Fisher, Frank and Ray were doing more than a square dance. I wondered who was doing the filming as I figured Ann had been filming the other videos.

Tape number 6 was Barbara and good old Jesse doing boring old straight sex. Jesse had told me a great big fib.

"I think people like to lie to you because you are such a sucker," my Guardian Angel said.

Tape number 7 was Brad Fisher, Barbara, and Ann, giving each other mouth-to-mouth in places that don't need oxygen. Once again I wondered who was doing the filming.

Tape number 8 was Barbara and Ann doing things to each other that half-sisters shouldn't do, or even second cousins for that matter.

Tapes 9 through 22 were repetitions of the same groups doing the same things. At least there had been no chains, paddles, rubber suits, or donkeys involved.

Tape 23 had Frank and Ray Colbert, Hayworth and Hoffman, Barbara, Ranger Reeves, Mrs. Fisher, and Ann.

Tape 24 was blank.

All the videos had been shot at Ann's house.

I put everything back in the box, checked to see if there was a tape in the video camera, there wasn't, and took it all back and placed it underneath the bed. I sat at the kitchen table. The mystery of the empty drawer at Ann's has been solved. But, nothing I'd seen in anyway gave me a hint as to the killer, or killers, although I did know there were three people I hadn't seen in the videos, any of which could have been filming the merrymaking.

I started to leave the house, but went and got the box from underneath the bed instead. I put the box into Matilda's trunk and drove away feeling as though I'd been at a dirty movie theater all day in Baltimore, from where, as I left, I could see the White House.

I drove to Ann's, packed my bag, and wrote her a note. "Dear Ann: Will be back in a few days."

"You would be smarter to say, Dear Ann, will see you in twenty years," my Guardian Angel said. "And let's get out of here. If you remember when I was trying to warn you about fishing, I told you murder, adultery, a pornography ring, and....."

I cut him off...."and a small chance of me surviving," I said.

"I don't think you appreciate how good I am at times," he said.

"I do, but don't let it go to your head," I replied.

Sheriff Rogers, once again being rude and wearing his hate inside, smiled at me when I went into his office. It took me off guard, old Marines don't smile often. "I'm going to Denver for a few days," I said. "I have few questions I want to ask those two detectives that came down here."

Rogers smile faded as fast as cheap house paint. "Why?" he asked with a hint of worry in his voice.

"I've stumbled onto something that might be important."

"What?" he demanded.

I didn't tell him, what is too big of a question. "Did the Feds ever get back to you about Barbara being in porn movies?" I asked.

"No," Rogers replied gruffly, angry I did not answer him, then added, "don't let the door kick you in the rear."

As I headed north I know that before I returned from Denver the proverbial bird doo would hit the fan, at least at Ranger Reeves' house.

It was late at night when I reached the outskirts of Denver and checked into a Motel Six. Being accustomed to cheap hotels I slept better than I had in weeks and thoroughly enjoyed the shower in the morning with lousy water pressure.

There is something about going downtown in any city to see detectives that makes me ponder all my past sins against society. After talking to a receptionist that would make a drill sergeant cringe it only took five minutes for Detective DeLong and Detective Chavez to have me sitting in front of one of their desks while they circled around me like buzzards. True detectives like private eyes about as much as rabbits like hawks. "You still catching bodies?" Chavez asked me, but not smiling.

"How much do you guys know about Barbara Maiden having been in the skin flick business?" I asked, sounding like a Boy Scout trying to get his skin flick badge.

"You have really been investigating," DeLong said, looking surprised.

"Surprises me, too," my Guardian Angel said giving me a thumbs-up.

Chavez went to his desk and brought back a large file. He opened it and rustled through papers. He closed the file and put it on the desk. "We know Ann Maiden and Barbara made amateur skin flicks and sold them through triple X magazines. There is a company in California that does all their distribution. Ten to fifteen minute flicks cost around ten bucks. From what we've gathered, they were selling about ten thousand flicks a year."

I was amazed. "Why would they live in Colorado?" I asked.

"They got into some trouble in Texas, something about getting a few girls involved who were under 18, and decided to head for the mountains. The case is still pending. Ann hired one of the best criminal attorneys in Texas so it could take years before she goes to trial."

"Do you think the fact her father was gunned down in Texas had anything to do with Barbara's murder?" I asked.

Chavez smiled this time. "You really have been doing your homework homeboy," he said.

"The old college try," I said.

"What exactly is a college try? Is it different from a high school try? Or a kindergarten try? Is it a smart try? Or a dumb dropout try?" my Guardian Angel asked like he really wanted to know.

"Pea Brain, get off it," I told him.

"From what we've found out," DeLong said. "Ann and Barbara had their own thing going, with nothing at all to do with their father. We do know they both worked topless bars he owned several years ago, and they turned some high priced tricks. We know the family wasn't close. We heard from the Texas authorities there were reports Big Abe used to molest his daughters."

"Nothing that could be proven," Chavez added.

"A lot of women who star in skin flicks were abused," I said.

"You have any leads on who did the trigger work on Barbara?" Chavez asked me.

"I haven't been able to find out anything concrete," I told the truth.

When I left DeLong and Chavez looked like they were ready for a coffee break.

"I wouldn't go back to Platoro," my Guardian Angel warned me as I pointed Matilda south.

"I know," I replied.

"When you're dead, my duty will be much easier," he said.

"I love you too."

"I wonder if I could get assigned to one of Hefner's old girlfriends?" he asked dreamily.

"I would imagine her Guardian Angel would have to be rich," I said.

"I suppose," he said with a frown.

The drive back to the mountains seemed like a drive through limbo.

When I went into the house Ann smiled at me like I was her long lost brother who owed her money. "I'm glad you came back," she said.

"With you gone she couldn't kill you," my Guardian Angel said shaking his head at my stupidity.

"Did you find out anything in Denver that will help solve the murder?" she asked me before I'd a chance to sit down.

It was obvious the Sheriff had told her about me going to Denver.

"Why would he tell her?" my Guardian Angel asked.

"Why would she let me know that he had told her?" I asked.

"It's not polite to answer a question with a question," he said crossly.

I could see no need to beat around the bush with Ann. "I found out about you and your sister's skin flick business and how you have a small problem down in Texas."

My words didn't even faze Ann. "I also found out you two used to dance at topless bars in Texas and you turned high priced tricks."

Once again Ann didn't seem fazed. "There is also a report that your father molested you and your sister."

Ann's look of indifference turned to a deep anger. "I told you before my father was a low life. The best thing that ever happened to him was getting murdered"

I felt sorry for Ann in a weird sort of way. Almost in the same way I feel sorry for a person about to be executed by the state for a heinous crime, they had to have lead a miserable life.

"Did you enjoy all the movies?" Ann asked me in a tone that was somewhere between anger and I don't really care, but at the same time letting me know I am a lowdown thief.

"I can't figure out how you could get all of these people to participate, the money you pay them couldn't be that good."

"They don't get paid," she said. "They live out their fantasies. They break out of their boring small town life with something they think is forbidden, so it's exciting. The people around here were as easy to seduce as a 16-year-old boy."

"Were you and your sister fighting over money?" I asked.

Ann shook her head. "There is no money to fight over. The attorneys have most of it. I haven't been working at the bar because I have money. The bar is going up for sale now that Big Abe is dead. I'm going to get out of here."

"Vegas would be good for your kind of business," my Guardian Angel said.

"Do you think Barbara might have been blackmailing someone?" I asked.

"If she was, I don't know anything about it."

I think Ann was telling me the truth. It was time for the big question. "What do you do with that 22 pistol in your drawer?" I asked her.

"Do you think if I had killed my own sister I would have kept the pistol?" Ann asked, making me feel as dumb as a punk rocker trying to tell his mother he didn't do drugs.

"I've have to tell you the truth Ann, I really have no idea who killed Barbara. There are many suspects, but no of them have a real motive. It's not money, not sex, not black mail, not a distraught husband, not, not, not. I think I'll leave and forget all about it."

"Give it a few more days, would you?" Ann asked me, almost pleading.

"No," my Guardian Angel screamed. "She hated her sister. She doesn't want the killer found. She might be the killer. Get grounded, Roosevelt."

I thought about it. "A few more days," my idiot mind forced my mouth to say.

Ann smiled at me. "I'm going to town and get some groceries, maybe this evening you and I can start over from the beginning."

As I watched her drive away through the window, I know there isn't anything in life that ever starts over from the beginning.

"You have done it this time, Roosevelt," my Guardian Angel said looking genuinely bummed out.

I went out to Matilda and got the box of videos and put them on the kitchen table. I got my notebook and a beer, sat down at the table and proceeded to add a few more clues. Willie had attacked me for breaking into his house. After the attack he told me he loved Barbara but he had been spurned and given back the earrings he'd bought her. He'd seen Ann taking videos of Barbara and Ranger Reeves. Willie had told me old man Clayton had been mean to his boys. I found out Jesse's truck ground its gears. Willie lit his Lucky Strike cigarette with a disposable lighter. Ann told me she'd seduced Mrs. Fisher. I'd found the box of videos under Ranger Reeves' bed and found out Ann and Barbara ran an amateur skin flick business based out of California. There was reason to believe Ann and Barbara had been molested by Big Abe. Ann's reason for having the pistol was a good one. Ann might not have any money but there was the question of Big Abe's will - I am going to have to find out who is going to get the majority of his money - but I have a hunch it is going to be Ann. I now have 112 clues. I feel like I am the world's worst speller playing scrabble for money. I got another beer. Maybe the best thing to do would be to get stone-faced drunk, roll around on the ground, puke a few times, and hope that the state of oblivion would make the answer I need jump out at me like a car salesmen trying to sell me a car for zero down, with 18% interest that I wouldn't be able to pay off until California fell into the ocean.

I read my notebook from beginning to end: cinder blocks, chain, padlock, clothes folded by the stream, Ann dropped Barbara off by the stream, bullet hole in head, no burn mark, enough semen in Barbara to start a fertility bank, cops, earrings, straight sex, lesbians, Lucky Strike cigarettes, stick matches, cowboys, gum wrapper, Sheriff, shotgun blasts intended for me, blah, blah,

blah.............it was like reading one of those short stories for a college literature class that the author had been so wasted on cough syrup even he didn't know what he was saying, but, professors had figured it all out - when the author said, "the sky is dark," he really meant he wanted to sleep with his sister while riding a train to Moscow. I got another beer.

It was dark outside and I was sitting on the sofa drinking my sixth beer when Ann returned. It had taken her three hours to get groceries, but when she walked into the house with a bag of groceries under her arm I felt domestic, the little lady brings back the bacon. "I brought more beer," she said. Ann does have a few redeeming qualities.

While I drank another beer, Ann started barbecuing steaks. I could eat mine raw. "You watch the steaks," she told me, "While I take a quick shower."

Pea Brain didn’t follow her down the hall, even he had seen enough of Ann naked.

I was flipping the steaks for the second time when a buzzer went off in my head. I was numb and in shock. "I have it all figured out," I told my Guardian Angel, "even Big Abe's murder."

"Tell me," he said, but sounding doubtful.

"Barbara was killed by.....” I said, but then Ann came out on the porch. She had on a yellow summer dress, she was barefooted and her hair was pulled back. A virgin she isn't, but a skin flick goddess she is.

Ann stepped close to me.

"Don't try, Ann," I said.

Ann stepped away from me, "Part of my nature," she smiled.

We ate in silence. I felt like her rich older brother who was going to have to put up the money to hire an attorney after she's committed a crime that was so bad mom and dad wouldn't speak to her anymore.

When we were done Ann cleared away the dishes. "Want another beer?" she asked.

"No, he doesn't," my Guardian Angel said giving me a stern look like my mother used to when she knew I was up to no good.

I wanted to say no, but I said yes. I was lost somewhere between Texas and Mars over my revelations when Ann set the beer bottle down in front of me. Taking a big swallow it tasted funny but everything tastes funny after seven beers.

"You should have solved this one," Ann said. "Everything has been laid out on the table for you."

She raised her right eyebrow, teasing me, making me feel stupid, weak - a mere man in her superior womanly presence.

"While flipping the steaks it all came to me," I said and took another swallow of the beer.

"Be careful, Roosevelt, be extremely careful," my Guardian Angel said to me, sounding like he was at the far end of a five mile long tunnel and his mouth was full of cotton balls.

"You should have slept with me," Ann said, once again raising her eyebrow. "I wish I could have gotten you on film, it might have been one of my bestsellers. I would have called it Stud Detective."

Ann laughed like the joke was on me.

I took another swallow of the beer.

"No, no, no," my Guardian Angel hollered trying to knock the beer out of my hand which is impossible.

Ann slid the straps to her dress down over her shoulders and let it fall below her breasts. She went in and out of focus, instead of two breasts she had four. I took another swallow of the beer. I felt hot, then cold, then hot again. Ann stood up and the dress slid down below her hips. I wondered if a four-breasted girl with three belly buttons would get big tips in a topless bar. I didn't hear Ann make a phone call. I didn't feel Ann push me out of the chair. I didn't feel my arms being bent behind my back and lashed together with a piece of rope. I didn't hear Ann say to the man dragging me toward the door, "Don't kill him right now, we have to be more careful this time."

I also didn't hear my Guardian Angel say, "I'll be, I hit 100% on my predictions this time," nor did I see him give himself a high five.

CHAPTER FOURTEEN
DOG POOP CREEK

When I woke up it felt like my head had been the bass drum for a college marching band. The inside of my mouth was as dry as the belly of a rattlesnake. After a few minutes the cobwebs cleared out of my head and I surveyed my situation.

I was lying on a bed and my left wrist was handcuffed to the metal headboard. Whoever had put me here at least had a small amount of decency. There was a pillow under my head and a light blanket over me. I squirmed around and sat on the edge of the bed. Pea Brain was lying on the floor pretending he was sleeping. I was in a small room with the bed I am on, an end table with an unlit kerosene lamp on it, and a closet. The floor is untreated pine - dirty from years of use - the walls are unpainted cut timbers chinked with crumbling concrete. There was one window with an army blanket hanging over it. The door was closed. The only light coming into the room filtered around the edges of the army blanket, making the room a dark army green, but also letting me know it was still light outside. I had a bad feeling that the cavalry wasn't going to ride in and rescue me. "I told you not to come back," my Guardian Angel chastised standing up and stretching.

"Don't say anything unless you can pick the lock on a set of handcuffs," I warned him.

"You're not in the position to tell anybody what to do," he retorted.

"If you weren't such a smarty-pants I might listen to you more often."

"Fat chance, hardheaded one," my Guardian Angel said.

"Is anybody out there," I hollered at the door.

There was no sound, only the steady beat of my throbbing head, and the feeling in my stomach that this time this old hippie was headed for the big commune in the sky.

I really don't want to die with my boots on. I don't want to die period. Living forever is fine with me, even if I get arthritis and prostate cancer and have to run my food through a blender because I cashed in all my teeth to the tooth fairy.

"Room service," I hollered.

There was still no reply.

"I'll never stay in this place again if you don't get in here," I threatened.

"The room is kind of cheap anyway," my Guardian Angel said.

I heard boot steps moving toward the door. The doorknob turned and the door slowly swung open. "Jesse, you run a lousy hotel," I said, not surprised one bit to see him.

Jesse had a 12-gauge shotgun in his right hand. He looked as confident and as cocky as a prison guard on tower duty.

"The world is in real bad shape when you can't trust a cowboy," my Guardian Angel said and punched Jesse, which of course Jesse didn't feel, inanimate beings don't have much of a right cross.

"That's the shotgun you used to shoot at me," I told Jesse.

"I won't miss this time," he grinned.

"When this is all over you're going to wish you had never met Ann," I said.

"When this is all over I'm going to have more money than I ever dreamed I'd have in my life. I'll leave this burg of a place and start a new life."

"Ann is only using you. I don't know what she has told you, but I wouldn't trust her."

"Save your breath Roosevelt, I'm in too deep to worry about it now. The way I feel about it, you should already be dead, but Ann wants you alive."

"How did you know it was Jesse that shot at you?" my Guardian Angel asked.

"It will all come out in time," I said.

"I hate strung out endings," he frowned.

"I'm hungry," I told Jesse.

"Strange time to be hungry," my Guardian Angel said, but he doesn't have to eat.

Jesse, with the shotgun pointed at my chest, unlocked the cuff attached to the bed and left them dangling from my wrist. "Walk toward the door and don't be a fool," he said.

A fool I am, but it wasn't time to be a dead fool. I went into a large room. Jesse handcuffed my left hand to a chair, got a rope that was hanging on the wall and wrapped it around my body, but not underneath my right arm so I could at least eat or pick my nose.

There was a wood stove against the wall with a pile of wood beside it, and a picnic table in the middle of the room with two benches and two chairs. I was in one of the chairs. There was a water cooler on the table along with two Coleman lanterns. There was no sink. Along one wall were shelves with canned goods, a few pots and pans, a coffeepot and mugs. There were three windows in the room - two on the back wall and one next to the only door. The curtains were open. "This is a line shack," I commented.

"You're so far from town even God doesn't know where you are," Jesse said.

I thought about trusty old Matilda. "Where's my car?" I demanded, as much as a man with a shotgun pointed at him can.

"She's in the barn collecting dust. We thought it would make a good casket for you."

I felt better, at least Matilda and I would go out in a blaze of glory, and if my captors had been stupid, my suitcase with my trusty 9 m.m. in it was still in the car. If they were really stupid, they left the keys in the ignition. At least the thought gave me a ray of hope.

I could see the barn where Matilda was. Next to the barn were a rundown cattle pen and a loading chute filled with tumbleweeds. Not far from the house was an outhouse with no door. It was a four holer. An image of four, old, crusty cowboys sitting in the outhouse together entered my mind. It wasn't a picture that would be good on a greeting card.

Jesse started a fire in the wood stove, but he wasn't a happy cook, he didn't whistle while he cooked. After a while he set a cup of coffee down in front of me and a few minutes later a plate of fried spam.

I choked down a bite of Spam. I'd learned in the Army to eat whatever was in front of me, but, I would hate for my last meal in life to be fried Spam.

"You know, it was really a strange deal you hooking Barbara and all," Jesse said, sitting down. "Who would have thought some private detective would go fly-fishing and hook her that way. It was an accident we had to leave her there and an accident you hooked her."

I finished my Spam and sipped on my cup of coffee. "How much would it cost me for you to let me go if I promised I'd drive until I hit the ocean and never come back to Colorado?" I asked.

"Roosevelt, you don't have enough money for a down payment."

"How about $10,000?"

Jesse looked at me like a black jack dealer in Las Vegas who was pulling in my last bet for $10,000. I wanted to get Jesse into a conversation. He was so confident he might make a mistake and by some miracle I could break free so I said, "I don't think you killed Barbara," and gave him a look like I understood all the turmoil he had gone through.

"I didn't kill Barbara," Jesse said. "The day it happened I thought we were going to the river to make another movie."

"I know who the other person was who was in the movie," I said. "I also know who was taking the videos."

"I don't care what you know," Jesse said. "It's time to put you back to bed."

"Let's sit here and talk, I can't go anywhere, it's the least you can do for a condemned man."

"Don't beg," my Guardian Angel said looking at me like he was ashamed. "Go out in class."

"It's easy to be brave when you can't get killed," I told him.

"Are you insinuating I was a coward when I was alive?" he asked, slightly peeved.

"I have no doubt."

"Why not, we can talk," Jesse said, his cowboy sense of fair play overruling his smarts.

"Thanks," I said. I figured I should be polite to my captor, even though I would like to politely knock his brains out.

Jesse got a bottle of whiskey. "We might as well have a few snorts," he said. "It's better than what they do for men on death row."

"When you snort whiskey do you pour it up your nose?" my Guardian Angel asked.

Jesse poured a double shot in my coffee cup and sat down opposite me. He laid the shotgun on the table, pointing in my direction, and took a swallow of the whiskey right out of the bottle.

"Do you want to hear what I have figured out?" I asked Jesse.

Jesse took another swallow of the whiskey. "You bet I've always liked listening to stories."

"You have to understand that most of the things I discovered I didn't know what they meant at the time."

"That's life," Jesse said. The statement has never made any sense to me. If it is not life than what is it? Death. Go figure?

"Think about this," my Guardian Angel smiled. "I am dead, but I am not dead because I am an angel and an angel is an entity. So can I say with the same meaning, that's death, like if I said, that's life?"

I felt like I was back in the sixties after eating a tab of acid laced with speed "Right after I hooked Barbara I decided to search the area," I began. "I knew she hadn't been dead long since she wasn't overly stiff. I didn't find any blood in the area and no signs of a struggle. I found a bare footprint going into the pool but none coming out. Whoever shot Barbara shot her with a small caliber pistol while she was in the river and Barbara had to trust them. I found her clothes neatly folded not far from where I'd hooked her and a spot where it looked as though she had sunbathed. Back by the camping area I started to make a fire and there were still hot embers in the fire pit. I knew somebody had been there earlier. In the fire pit I found a few burnt bottle caps. I presume that right after the murder, somebody pulled into the camping area, the accident you mentioned. Instead of being able to haul the body off, you had to think quick and you and your accomplice weighted

Barbara down in the river, planning on coming back later to get her. But in your haste you forgot her clothes. And, to top it off, here comes good old me, intent on catching a trout, and I snag her - caboom, perfect murder plan ruined."

Jesse took another swig from the bottle. "Very good, Roosevelt," he said.

"What puzzled me at first was why there were no footprints in the area? You cut pine boughs and wiped them off and left them by the trail."

"That was my idea. I'd seen it done in an old John Wayne movie."

"At least John Wayne movies are worth something," I said, "when I was a kid I was more into Gene Autry and Roy Rogers and all that singing stuff."

"Figures," my Guardian Angel said. "That could be one reason you have never been able to accept reality."

"That night I stayed in my camp and the next morning, instead of going to town and reporting the crime, I went to Platoro, but before I went to Platoro I found a package of Lucky Strikes on the edge of the camping area with only two gone. I figure somebody tossed them out of the window by mistake. People do strange things when they're nervous, especially after killing somebody. At the bar I meet you and Willie and the Colbert boys. The fact there were only two trucks outside at the time didn't seem strange - now I know you hadn't been with them all the time. You rode your horse from your cabin to the camping area, and then rode into the mountains after the murder and met them at Red Lake."

"You're so smart it's going to get you killed," Jesse said.

"At the bar I noticed Willie smoked Lucky Strikes, right away he became a suspect. I also found out Ranger Fisher had been at the bar the day before. Later in the day, when I reported the crime to Sheriff Rogers, he also smoked Lucky Strikes, plus I'd seen him driving away from Platoro the day I drove in - he was also a suspect. The Sheriff and I, along with Highway Patrolmen Hayworth and Hoffman, went back and he and I pulled Barbara from the stream, discovering she was attached to two cinder blocks with a chain. Sheriff Rogers didn't take any photographs of the crime scene and it seemed he went out of his way to track up the area. Hayworth and Hoffman were shocked when they saw the body. Barbara had a gold chain around her middle, a diamond tennis bracelet and a diamond ring on so I knew robbery wasn't the motive. While the Sheriff and two cops were there, I saw a set of small boot prints and one large set of boot prints and I found a chewed on stick match - somebody had been at the camp while I was in town - it was you and Ann, but the stick match wasn't either one of yours - I had missed it earlier. You two had come to scout the area, planning, I presume, to get the body that night, but you found my camp. Of course I didn't know this at the time."

Jesse grinned, but his grin wasn't going to get him on Wheel of Fortune.

"That night you tried to fill me with buckshot, but by pure luck, I wasn't sleeping in my tent."

"It wasn't luck," my Guardian Angel said giving me a dirty look. "It was only because of me."

He's trying to get brownie points with God.

"After the shooting, when you drove away, you ground the gears to your truck so I knew it was a stick shift. Ann's Explorer also grinds gears but she couldn't have run away as fast as you did."

"You almost got me," Jesse grinned. He must think almost getting shot was funny. "Ann told me to dust you because we had no idea what you had found out."

"Why would Ann want him to pour dust on you?" my Guardian Angel asked.

"The next day, Sheriff Rogers and two detectives from Denver came to the camp and I showed them exactly what I'd done when I hooked Barbara. I figured they thought I might have done it and they didn't seem to give a hoot about somebody taking a pot shot at me."

"Go on," Jesse said, taking another shot of whiskey.

I hadn't touched my whiskey. "After the detectives left, I was still curious and searched the area again and found a piece of Wrigley Spearmint gum. When Ann invited me to stay at her house to try and solve the murder I discovered she chewed Wrigley's and also smoked Lucky Strikes that she lit with a stick match."

Jesse took another pull on the whiskey.

"By then I had four suspects, Ann, Sheriff Rogers, Willie, and Ranger Fisher. Ann told me Barbara had been sleeping with the two Highway Patrolmen, Ranger Fisher, and the Colbert boys. She said Patrolman Hayworth had given Barbara the gold chain for her belly and Fisher had given her the diamond tennis bracelet. I went to the Ranger Station and Ranger Reeves was about as helpful as the plague and had small feet. She got added to the suspect list. She seemed to want to protect Ranger Fisher. By now I was as confused as a bull in a pasture with 50 cows. Ranger Fisher confessed he'd slept with Barbara and that he'd given her the bracelet. Staying at Ann's you tried to kill me again, but once again I was lucky, I'd fallen over a table. The thing that confused me at the time was why did you try and shoot me through the window."

"I don't know if you ever noticed, but the bed in the bedroom you were in is exactly window high. I didn't have to see you to shoot you, but as I was about to shoot I saw the light come on in the kitchen, ran around the house and saw you through the curtain. You're one lucky guy," Jesse said, shaking his head. "I had you dead to rights."

"I heard somebody running down the road but no vehicle drive away. You shot at me and circled back around to your cabin with all the intentions of calling the cops."

"You have a good brain," Jesse said.

"You don't know him as well as I do," my Guardian Angel said.

"What surprised me the most was how quickly Sheriff Rogers got to Ann's house. At the time I figured he'd shot at me. So now Ann, Willie, Ranger Fisher, Sheriff Rogers, the Highway Patrol and the Colbert boys were all prime suspects."

"I bet your little brain was doing flips," Jesse said.

"Flips, how about double somersaults," I said. "I went back to the Sheriff and looked at the autopsy photographs again and noticed Barbara's ears were pierced three times. Being Willie was a suspect I broke into his trailer and found earrings, three sets, which I doubted he wore, and a 12-gauge shotgun."

"You still haven't told me who else is in on this," Jesse said, drinking more whiskey, which seemed to be fazing him about as much as if he was drinking iced tea.

"I have no doubt they will come out here. I want to tell them face to face," I said.

"Why will they come out?" Jesse asked.

"Because Ann wants you all here so she can kill all of you," I said truthfully.

"Go on with your story," Jesse told me, not believing Ann would kill him.

I continued. "I met Ann's neighbors and through them found out everybody involved in the case at one time or another had been at Ann's house. I then went to Ranger Reeves' house and saw her earring collection. But still, with everybody being a suspect, there really was no motive, but I know the motive now."

"Tell me," my Guardian Angel said.

"Later, I don't want to ruin the plot."

"What plot?"

"I found out Ann and Barbara are half-sisters and their father was Big Abe Maiden, a major gangster from Texas who owned topless bars. After going to your house and talking to you at first I didn't feel you had anything to do with it, even though you own a 12 gauge shotgun that had recently been fired and had buckshot on your table, and your truck ground into gear. I felt you were a good, dumb cowboy, and believed you when you told me you had never laid a hand on Barbara."

At first Jesse didn't know whether being, 'a good, dumb cowboy,' was a compliment or a put down, but he decided on a compliment, and smiled.

"But when I broke into your house and found the photographs of Barbara showing off all of her well-used charms I knew you were lying through your teeth. Ann must have told you about me going through your house because when I went to talk to you again, you brought up the photographs yourself to try and not be a suspect."

"It was then you must have known Ann was guilty," my Guardian Angel said.

"I think I was going through denial," I said. "Budding love has a way of messing up a person's mind."

"How can something so good be so bad?" he asked.

I didn't have an answer.

Jesse drank more whiskey.

"I went to Alamosa to look up Highway Patrolmen Hoffman and Hayworth to try and rattle their chain. I found out Hoffman had bought Barbara earrings...remember, Barbara's ears were pierced but she had no earrings on when she was found. I also found out it was true that Hayworth had given Barbara the gold chain. They admitted sleeping with her but said they never did a threesome."

"I then went and talked to old man Colbert. He told me about his boys falling for Barbara. A few days later, Frank and Ray told me they'd both been sleeping with her. Old man Colbert uses stick matches to light his smokes and owns a 12-gauge shotgun."

"Being a detective must be interesting," Jesse said. "Sitting around and figuring things out all the time."

"It's boring," my Guardian Angel said, "and most of the time highly confusing."

"An empty drawer at Ann's led me back to Rangers Reeves' house where I found a box full of skin flicks with everybody except three people in them."

"I have to hand it to you Roosevelt," Jesse said. "You've done a good job figuring it all out. But it seems to me you are a few days too late."

"Good timing to Roosevelt is about two days late," my Guardian Angel said.

"I promise if you let me go I'll take Matilda and never look back," I told Jesse again.

"You have tried begging, maybe crying will work," my Guardian Angel said.

"It's too late now, Roosevelt," Jesse said.

"Not yet, buckwheat," my Guardian Angel replied, but he wasn't the one handcuffed to a chair.

Jesse took another drink of whiskey. "I bet some of the people that come out here tonight will surprise you. You might not have everything as right as you think you do."

"I don't like surprises," I said. "But I bet you a hundred bucks, I do."

"I don't gamble," Jesse said. "And it's back to bed for you."

"I haven't finished my whiskey yet," I protested.

Jesse gulped down my whiskey, picked up the shotgun and pointed it at me while he unlocked the handcuffs and untied the rope. He prodded me with the shotgun back to the bedroom and locked me once again to the bed.

As he was walking out of the room I said, "You could call Ann and tell her I've changed my mind and if she wants to sleep with me I won't say no."

Jesse shut the door.

"I know one thing," my Guardian Angel said, while I pulled on the handcuffs to no avail.

"What?"

"You're no Houdini."

I sagged back on the pillow. "No," I said. "I'm one dead donkey, one cooked goose, one fried banana, one stuffed pig, one dead as a doornail, one up a creek without a paddle, one fried egg - in other words, my tripping ship has done hit the sand."

My Guardian Angel rubbed his chin and looked pensive. "Don't give up yet," he said. "And I have to tell you, your deductions about the murder are good."

"I haven't given up," I told him. "I'm just all messed up."

"I've always liked your humor, Roosevelt."

I shut my eyes.

When I woke up it was dark. I had the worst heartburn I've had in years, black coffee and Spam had done the trick, but I doubt Jesse will run to the store and buy me some antacid tablets. A soft light drifted in from underneath the door.

"It's time for dinner," I hollered.

Jesse came into the room with his ever-trusty sidekick, Mr. 12 gauge. He lit the lantern, uncuffed me and recuffed me to the chair, and tied me with a rope like he had earlier, leaving my right arm free.

"It's kind of nice out here with no electricity, no TV, no radio, just the stars," I said.

I noticed the curtains were still open.

"I'm no old hippie," Jesse said. "I hate natural. I get all the natural I want guiding city people up into the mountains. I want a house with shag carpet, a lot of windows, and I want to look out over a city filled with people. I also want a women that doesn't want to ride horses."

"How much money are you getting for all your dirty work?" I asked.

"50 big ones," Jesse said.

"You mean you'd sell your soul for $50,000?"

"I already have, Roosevelt."

Jesse's words chilled me. "You settled cheap," I managed to say.

"Not that cheap," my Guardian Angel said seemingly impressed.

In a few minutes Jesse put a plate of hot beans in front of me, a cup of coffee and two slices of white bread. "I hope we don't stay out here long," I said. "This kind of food would make a man want to die."

"You don't have to worry about seeing the dawn," Jesse said.

"It's been nice knowing you, Roosevelt," my Guardian Angel said, but he didn't sound sad.

Guardian Angels having already lived, understand the ups and downs of life.

CHAPTER FIFTEEN
SURPRISE – SURPRISE

With the odds highly in favor that I am going to die before the sun comes up, and the fact I was being served two slices of white bread and a plate full of hot beans for my last meal, the beans were going down my throat like large pieces of number two gravel.

Jesse was once again drinking whiskey - his trusty shotgun lying across his lap. My Guardian Angel was on his hot line to God trying his best to get assigned to a young and very sexy woman.

"The least you could do is go into town and get me a pizza for my last meal," I told Jesse.

Jesse looked at me like I was a roach and he was a can of Raid. "If I was going to die, I'd want a medium rare T-bone steak, a twice-baked potato, a whole wheat roll and a tossed salad with Caesar dressing," he said, adding, "and Cherries Jubilee for dessert."

"That does sound good," I said.

"Use your imagination and pretend," Jesse replied dryly.

I took a bite of T-bone beans and watched the flickering light from the Coleman lantern, wishing it was a candle and I was in an expensive restaurant with the woman I loved. She was telling me I was the best thing that had happened to her since run less pantyhose and she would pick up the check.

Jesse slurped down another shot of whiskey. "You know for some famous hotshot detective you sure got yourself in a wreck," he said.

There is something about people with little or no intelligence, who, when put in a position where they get a small amount of power they suddenly become jerks.

I ate my last bite of T-bone beans. "You will all get caught in time," I told Jesse.

"You must believe in karma," Jesse said. "What goes around comes around and all that garbage."

"It does," I said.

"Karma, smarma," Jesse said. "Rockefeller and Morgan stole millions of dollars and died in their 80's. I guess because they built libraries it changed their karma. Old Man Kennedy made a fortune smuggling booze on military airplanes and his family all became famous politicians. Jesse's argument had too much truth in it for me. Maybe karma is a good excuse for people who don't have enough clout to get even.

"Don't believe what you said," my Guardian Angel said like he really cared about my soul.

I was about to speak when Jesse and I heard a car approaching. He looked at me like a tick eyeballs a farm dog. I felt like a plucked chicken ready for the stew pot. The drone of the engine grew closer and closer until headlights swept across the front windows and the engine was cut off. I heard a door open on creaky hinges and the thud of boots as they hit the wooden porch.

"I guess there is no need to tell you this is more trouble," my Guardian Angel said.

The doorknob turned slowly and the door swung in. Old man Colbert, Mr. Leroy Colbert, walked into the room looking as mean as a biker who had been ordered to take a bath.

"I'll be the only tuna in a can of mackerel," my Guardian Angel gasped in surprise.

"Surprise, surprise," Leroy said to me.

"It's not my birthday," I replied, "and seeing you is no surprise."

"I didn't figure I'd outsmarted you," Mr. Colbert said.

Leroy walked over to the shelves and got a cup, poured a shot of whiskey in it, and sat at the table.

"You took most of the videos," I said to Leroy.

Leroy smiled like he was the only non-union cameraman in Hollywood.

"There were only three people I didn't see in the videos, you, Willie, and Sheriff Rogers," I said. "But I knew you took them. It was you who took the videos by the river the day Barbara was murdered."

"How do you know that?" Leroy asked.

"Yea, how do you know that?" my Guardian Angel asked.

"The stick match I found by the river was left by you. When Ann lights a cigarette with a match she doesn't chew on them. Sheriff Rogers chews on his, and you do, but the match I found matches what your matches look like."

"I'll be, it's a matching match deal," my Guardian Angel said.

"Problem with you son is you think too much," Leroy said, sipping his whiskey. He could care less about matching matches.

"In the box of videos I found at Ranger Reeves' house there was one blank one. I bet Ann had you erase the one by the river," I said.

"It's too bad because it was a good one. The lighting was perfect," Leroy said.

"How did you ever get involved?" I asked Leroy.

Leroy looked over at Jesse. Jesse shrugged his shoulders, "Tell him, he is about to become organic fertilizer anyway."

"All my life about all I've done is take care of cattle and horses. When Frank and Ray started seeing Barbara I didn't think anything about it. One day Frank and Ray told me we had all been invited over to Barbara's house for a barbecue. When we got there Barbara was running around with a pair of short pants on and a halter-top that wasn't big enough to cover an ant. Ann had on pants so tight they made paint look thick. One thing led to another, we were drinking and carrying on, and the next thing I knew Barbara and my boys were naked and Ann is taking videos. Before long Ann is naked and I'm taking the videos."

"Mr. Colbert, I'm ashamed for you," I said.

"You'll get over it," he said.

"I know you didn't kill Barbara," I said to Leroy.

My boys didn't kill her, either."

"Then why are you here?" I asked Leroy.

"I am here for money, denaro, grease, greenbacks, stash, poke, lettuce, whatever you want to call it. Ann told us she would give us $50,000 to keep our mouths shut."

""I bet you don't have the money yet?"

"Not yet."

"He is stupid, like you are, when it comes to money, "my Guardian Angel said.

"You have a ranch, a good life," I said to Leroy.

"Son, I lived my complete life on this ranch. I've worked from sunup to sundown. I've been cold, hot, and in-between and for all my years all I've got is a rusty truck, a couple of guns, and a sore body. I need money to die. I need money to pay doctors, money to get buried, money for an old folk's home if I have to go to a home."

"Your boys could have worked to help you out," I said.

"All my boys want to do is get out. They think there's a better world away from the ranch. They don't know the world is all messed up. It doesn't matter where you live, it's all the same. I love this ranch, but I'm too old."

"Give me a shot of that whiskey," I told Leroy.

Leroy got up and got a cup and half-filled it. I took a deep gulp of the liquid fire. It burnt, it tasted awful, it fit the moment.

"I guess the money god has us all," I said.

"He's got the whole world," Leroy said. "Ain't no freedom left son, no place to run, no place to hide, nothing to do but pay the man. It doesn't matter if you're a cowboy, cook, waiter, C.E.O. or Indian Chief, you still pay the man."

"I've told Jesse and I'll tell you also, Ann is going to kill you," I said to Leroy.

"When?" Leroy asked, trying to be funny.

"When your other co-conspirator shows up," I said. "She's twirled each of you around her little finger until all you can see is money. Your brains have turned into moans of pleasure. You both were hard-working men, cowboys, blessed with a life of the outdoors, blessed to be the last of a dying breed and you sold out, sold out to a big city woman."

"It could have been worse," Jesse said.

"You've watched too many movies," Leroy told me.

"For the cries of a doomed man it sounded good to me," my Guardian Angel said.

"When is Ann coming out?" I asked.

No sooner had 'Ann' left my mouth than the door banged open and Ann stepped into the room.

Jesse jumped up, fumbling for his shotgun. "Sit down you idiot," Ann ordered. "If I was a cop it would already be too late."

Jesse started to say something but changed his mind. Leroy sipped on his whiskey.

Ann had on a pair of black Levi's, a black sweater and black boots and over her shoulder hung a big black leather purse. She looked like what I imagine Dracula's mistress would look like. "Roosevelt, I like you all tied up," she said and gave me the raised right eyebrow look.

"Untie me and take off your clothes and pour Wesson oil all over your body and punish me," I said to Ann.

"I'll take the pictures," Leroy said.

"I'll watch," my Guardian Angel said but did not grin.

Ann sat at the table, setting the large leather purse by her feet. "You sure showed up at the wrong time," she told me.

Leroy took a Lucky Strike out of his pocket and lit it with a stick match. "Let me have one of those," Ann ordered more than asked.

Leroy gave her one and held a lit match out for her. Ann inhaled deeply.

"I know why you killed Barbara?" I said.

"It's too late now sailor boy," she said.

"You killed her because you had already set it up to have Big Abe killed and you would get most of the inheritance," I said.

"A dead man suddenly sees the light," Ann said. "I always hated my half-sister. She always got more than I did. Big Abe showered her with affection and everything I did was never enough."

"But he molested both of you," I said with an inquisitive look.

Ann's face was covered with hate as thick as chocolate syrup on an ice cream sundae. "He still liked her more than me. When she and I started doing movies, I started my plot to kill her. I only had to wait for the right time. She hired those underage girls that got us in trouble in Texas, but it really didn't matter. When the time was right, and both she and Big Abe were gone, I would be rich. Rich enough to go anywhere I wanted and start a new life - a life where nobody would know my past. I've got the body and the mind to be anybody I want to be now. When I leave this place, I'll start all over like a newborn baby with the brain of a 40-year-old."

"No," I said. "You made a big mistake."

"What?" Ann said.

"You involved too many people."

Ann gave me a look like I thought she was the dumbest person in the world. The Lucky Strike cigarette was hanging from her lips like she was a female Paul Newman in one of his first movies. I didn't notice her hands were underneath the table. When I did notice, it was too late, not too late for me, but for Jesse and Leroy. She jumped up from the table like a black cat jumping out of the way of a truck. The pistol she held in her two hands cracked twice. The first bullet hit Jesse dead square in the middle of his forehead. He didn't have time to say, "Pour me another one bartender," before he went head over heels out of his chair and the shotgun clanked to the floor. Leroy, old and slow, was only halfway out of his chair when the bullet went through his left eye. Ann calmly walked over to each man and nudged them with her boot. She then looked at me. "You were saying," she said, taking the Lucky Strike out of her mouth and butting it out.

"I was about to say how you planned your crime well," I said, adding, "That's the 22 pistol from your drawer isn't it."

"Of course."

"The same one you shot Barbara with."

"No, Barbara had a 22-pocket pistol. It's so far back in the woods it will never be found."

"I thought for a while there was a chance you might get out of this mess, but I think you can check in your boots," my Guardian Angel said, adding, "Ann is a good shot."

Ann picked up the shotgun and stood it in the corner and went through Jesse's pockets until she found the keys to my hand-cuffs, which she put in her pocket. She put the pistol on the table and dragged both men into the bedroom. There were only a few small blood spots on the floor as the 22 hadn't made an exit wound, but rattled around inside the men's brains like a hornet caught in a soda can.

"I told them you would kill them," I said.

"They should have listened to you."

"What are you going to do now?" I asked.

"Wait for another person and my lover."

Under different circumstances I would be happy that I know who they both were.

Ann put water on a rag and worked on the small blood spots on the floor. After she'd rubbed them for a while, she went outside and came back with a handful of dirt and sprinkled it on them and scuffed the dirt around with her boot. "Good as new," she said inspecting her work.

"I don't understand why she became little miss spic and span," my Guardian Angel said.

"It might be the out, out, damn spot, syndrome," I said.

Ann sat at the table and calmly at me. "At least this way I won't have to pay you," she said.

"You could pay me and let me go," I said. "I promise I'll never come back."

Ann didn't bother to laugh. "You know I've had sex with so many men it really doesn't mean much to me anymore, but I have to tell you Roosevelt, I respect you for not sleeping with me."

"I don't respect him," my Guardian Angel said frowning.

"You were planning on killing me from day one, weren't you?" I asked.

"The first day we met I knew I had seen you somewhere but it didn't ring a bell until you told me your name. Then I remembered the TV show you were on after solving that kidnapping case in Florida. The way things worked out having you at the house was the only way I could keep tabs on you. So, to answer your question, yes Roosevelt, you have been a dead man since I put my eyes on you. But you always knew in your heart of hearts I was guilty, you couldn't put it together, but you knew."

"If you remember, I told you not to tell her your real name when you met her in Platoro," my Guardian Angel scolded.

I'd like to slap him just once before I die.

"You'll get caught, Ann," I said, not admitting to her that she was right. I've always felt she was guilty. Dumb is dumb, but dumbest is a little too much to take on my deathbed.

"I'll take my chances," Ann said.

"At one time I thought I was falling in love with you," I said.

"I know," Ann smiled. "It was a mistake."

"Why is it women know everything?" my Guardian Angel asked.

I heard a vehicle approaching. "Your lover," I said.

"Not yet, one more victim," Ann said grimly.

When the door opened I wasn't surprised to see Ranger Fisher. "The cinder blocks gave you up," I told him.

"I didn't know she was going to kill Barbara," Fisher said. “I thought Jesse and Ann and I were going to make a movie with Barbara, and Leroy was going to do the filming. I was leaving when I heard the shot. Ann threatened to mail some of the videos to headquarters if I said anything. I'd lose my job. There was nothing else I could do."

"You drove to the camping area to make the video in a forest service truck that, by chance, still had cinder blocks in the back from working on a fire pit. After Ann shot Barbara, campers came into the area, but, you being a Ranger, you could haul the blocks and chain out of your truck and they wouldn't think a thing about it. You weighed Barbara down with the blocks and chain, planning on getting her later," I said.

"Why do you want me out here?” Ranger Fisher asked Ann, nervously.

It didn't take more than two seconds for him to get his answer from a 22 Smith and Wesson. One slug in the forehead and Ranger Fisher fell back against the wall and slid down it like a piece of wet spaghetti. This time Ann tossed a rag over his head so the blood wouldn't hit the floor before she dragged him to the other room with his other cohorts. When she sat back down at the table I wondered how Ranger Fisher's wife would move to Denver and marry a religious woman.

"You wanting to kill your sister I understand," I told Ann. "But having to involve all these other people and then kill them doesn't make any sense at all."

Ann took a Lucky Strike out of her purse and lit it with a stick match. "I hate these people. They're nothing but two-faced scum. When I first moved out here I really thought about going straight, no more skin flicks, work in the bar, maybe find me a nice cowboy, some ‘I love mom guy' who would treat me like a woman. I would cook, clean the house, have a few kids, teach the kids to ride horses, but all I met were men who were like all the city men. All they wanted to do was sleep with me, they thought because they were big and strong and owned a pickup that my pants would come off as easily as a saddle blanket. Nothing really started until Barbara came out, and before I knew it, we were making films again and all of the people we met were more than willing to take off their clothes. It made me sick. But it gave me the opportunity to get rid of Barbara and Big Abe. I used these hayseeds like they had wanted to use me. They believed everything I ever told them. In the end, all they wanted was the money. Everyone except Fisher, at first he really did love Barbara. He bought her that bracelet. You men make me sick," Ann snarled.

"You could have let Fisher slide he would never have told anybody."

"No loose ends, Roosevelt, you know that as well as I do."

"I know who killed Big Abe?" I said.

"I hate to say it, Roosevelt, but your detective skills really impress me at times," my Guardian Angel said.

"Flattery on my deathbed is not greatly appreciated," I said.

"Knowing who killed Big Abe won't get you a reprieve," Ann said.

"Is there anything that would?" I asked.

She shook her head.

"You always knew I was like a Black Widow," she smiled, once again raising her right eyebrow.

"You're the best Black Widow I've ever seen."

"Thank you," she replied. "I take that as a compliment."

"Negative stimulus too many people is as reinforcing as positive stimulus," my Guardian Angel said.

“Pea Brain, right now I don’t need a Guardian Angel who thinks he is a college professor,” I said. “I need one that can untie knots and shoot a gun.”

My Guardian Angel tried to look offended with about as much success as a frog trying to feel guilty after eating a fly.

"When your lover comes, what are you going to do with all the bodies?" I asked Ann.

"I am going to torch this place everything will be burnt to a crispy critter. There is no connection with me as to what went on here. After a month or so my lover and I will disappear into the sunset."

"It isn't a fairy tale ending," my Guardian Angel said, "and she wasted her time cleaning the blood off the floor if she is going to burn this place."

"It is a fairy tale ending," I said, "you wait and see."

"I can't go anywhere until you are on your way to meet your maker," he said.

In the dim Coleman light Ann no longer looked like Dracula's mistress, she looked like a witch. Her beautiful face and body was nothing more than an illusion, a spell spun on the beholder, underneath the facade was evil, evil caused by a demented father who molested her, but evil - evil unchecked. I had to find a way to destroy her. If I don't stop her she will go on killing.

"You need help, Ann," I said. "Your pain has turned you into something you should never have become. It's not your fault."

"Don't even try, Roosevelt," Ann said. "My pain has nothing to do with it. I like hurting people. It's what I thrive on. It's my essence in life. Darkness is my keeper."

"Roosevelt, too bad it's not three hundred years ago, I could have her burned at the stake," my Guardian Angel said.

CHAPTER SIXTEEN
FOOLED AGAIN

Ann was smoking another cigarette. "Have you ever been in love, Roosevelt?" she asked. The witch was in a reflective mood.

"I have been in love several times," I said. "But it never seems to work out."

"I can't picture you in love," she said.

"Most of the time I can't picture myself in love either, but I always search for it. In fact, I don't think I know what love is anymore. I think I feel it. But I can't tell you what it is."

"It's sad isn't it?" Ann said.

"More than sad," I said, wondering where feelings go.

"People in love don't need to watch skin flicks," Ann said. "Skin flicks make money because people are lonely."

"The people who make skin flicks are lonely," I said.

Ann lit another cigarette off of the stub of the one she was smoking. I glanced at my watch. It was fifteen minutes after midnight. Strangely, even though I am handcuffed to a chair and tied up, I still had not lost hope. Even with my fatalistic outlook on life I am still a dreamer. I figure everything will turn out badly, but I keep hoping I am wrong.

"So now that Barbara and Big Abe are dead, and you don't have to pay any of your cohorts, how much money do you think you will get from Big Abe's estate?" I asked Ann.

"I figure about three million," Ann answered, like three million dollars is pocket change.

My Guardian Angel whistled and I could swear I could see his mind trying to figure out an angle on how he could become Ann's guardian angel.

I was about to speak when we both heard the sound of an approaching vehicle. "Looks like it's about bye-bye time for me," I said.

"It's strange," Ann said. "I feel bad about killing you. It wasn't your fault you snagged Barbara with a fly. You were only trying to get away from the world."

"My luck," I said.

My Guardian Angel looked out the window, turned, looked at me and ran his finger across his throat.

The vehicle came to a stop and the lights were turned off. Once again I heard a door open, slam, and the thud of boots on the porch. The doorknob turned. My non-fearing callous heart felt numb, butterflies, although not large, fluttered in my stomach. The door swung open and in from the dark stepped Ranger Reeves.

"Hello lover," I said. "I've been expecting you."

"You knew all along," Ann said.

I didn't swell up with pride.

"At times you are amazing," my Guardian Angel said.

"Let's kill this jerk and get out of here," Ranger Reeves snapped.

"Can I have one last wish before I die?" I asked.

Reeves glared at me.

"One wish for our almost love," Ann said with a twisted smile.

"I'd like a shot of whiskey and a cigarette," I said.

"Smoking is bad for your health," Reeves said sarcastically.

“You got them, Roosevelt,” my Guardian Angel laughed. “You got two wishes.”

"Pea Brain, that's not funny," I told him.

"Just because you are going to die, don't lose your sense of humor," he told me.

Ann brought me a cup of whiskey and handed me a lit Lucky Strike.

"Ok, now I want a joint, a line of coke, two hits of mescaline, a gram of hash, and four peyote buttons," I said.

"If we gave you all that when we kill you, you won't even know you are dead," Reeves said.

I sipped on the whiskey and took a deep drag on the cigarette and thought about her reply and decided she was right.

The whiskey tasted bad and the cigarette worse, a fitting way to go, no glory, no honor, no flag, no medals, no life insurance, no estate, no nothing.

I took one last drag on the cigarette and finished off my whiskey.

"OK, the famous for fifteen minutes private detective has had his last wish, let's get rid of him," Reeves said.

"She doesn't like you," my Guardian Angel said.

"After all the beer we drank together," I said to Reeves. "And our long talks about nature and the environment. All you want to do is kill me."

Reeves thought for a moment and forced a smile. "I have to admit I did enjoy having a few beers with you and our conversations were nice."

"How quaint," my Guardian Angel smirked.

"Where are Jesse, Leroy, and Fisher?" Reeves asked Ann.

"I already took care of them," Ann said. "They're in the bedroom getting as stiff as cordwood."

The news didn't shake up Reeves one bit.

"She'll kill you too," I told Reeves.

"No I won't," Ann said. "She and I are going to move to San Francisco and get married."

"You'll fight over who gets to wear the pants," I commented dryly.

Reeves punched me in the face, cutting my lip slightly. "What do you know about love, Roosevelt? You straights make all the rules and expect everybody to live by them. If you hadn't shown up it would have all been over by now."

"Why did you try and protect Fisher whenever I asked you questions about him?" I asked Reeves, acting like her punch hadn't hurt, when in truth, it hurt like the dickens.

"To keep you running around in circles."

"You know, if you keep them talking," my Guardian Angel said, "They might die before they have a chance to kill you."

"When you killed Barbara why did you involve Fisher, Jesse, and Leroy Colbert?" I asked Ann.

"Jesse knew what was going to happen. All he ever thought about was money. I told him I would take him to the coast and make him a partner in the movie business. I wanted Fisher involved because he loved my sister and I hated him for it."

"Old man Colbert was supposed to take the body back to his ranch and dispose of it?" I said.

"You win a trip to hell," Reeves said.

"I know you killed Big Abe," I said to Reeves.

"I'll be," my Guardian Angel said looking astonished.

"You had three days off from work and you flew to Houston and killed him. When I came by your house on your second day off I saw a suitcase by your table, people around here don't pack a suitcase to go to the store."

Reeves smiled, like murder was something to be proud off. "It was easy," she said. "Ann called him and said a friend of hers was going through town and needed a place to stay. Jesse drove me to the airport and I flew into Houston in the morning, went to his house, shot him that night and cut his tongue out for how he treated Ann and flew back. I was only gone 24 hours."

"Somebody will be able to describe you," I said.

"Don't worry. I wore a wig, dressed like a woman, and bought my ticket through a travel agent for cash and I have a fake I.D."

I was impressed, but didn't tell her.

"I called dad from a pay phone," Ann added.

"Who took the earrings out of Barbara's ears after she had been killed?" I asked. "When I saw the photographs taken of her during the autopsy I noticed she had three holes in each ear, but no earrings."

"I took them," Ann said. "They were mine. She always used to wear my jewelry and it made me mad."

"Why didn't you take the gold chain from around her waist and the diamond tennis bracelet and the ring?" I asked.

Ann gave me a look of disdain. "They didn't seem to matter."

"Let's kill him," Reeves said. "Enough of this chit chat."

"I don't know why you don't like me," I said to Reeves.

"It's only business," she said. "I like you in a weird sort of way."

"A weird sort of way is the only way you can like, Roosevelt," my Guardian Angel said.

"Did you bring the gas?" Ann asked Reeves.

Reeves nodded.

They drug the bodies out of the bedroom and put Jesse in the corner. Old Man Colbert they put by the table and Ranger Fisher they sat up next to the door.

I felt like I was in an undertaker's office that wasn't good at organization. Finished with the body arranging, Reeves went outside and came back with my pistol.

Reeves held the pistol with both hands and raised it slowly until it was pointed straight at my head. She smiled a smile that was somewhere between wicked, naughty, and having fun.

"It's been good knowing you, Roosevelt," my Guardian Angel said. "We've had some good times together. But getting shot with your own pistol has to be embarrassing."

"Thanks for all you've done for me," I said.

"No big deal," he said. "I had to do it. It's my job."

My Guardian Angel turned his back to me and I shut my eyes.

The explosion made me jump, but there was no pain. No white light at the end of the tunnel. No seeing my complete messed up life flash before me in less than a second. But there was the sound of shattering glass. I opened my eyes and Reeves was looking bewilderingly at a large blood splattered hole in the middle of her chest. Her arms fell to her sides, my pistol clinked to the floor, and she tumbled face forward onto the picnic table.

Ann was reaching frantically for her pistol when the door crashed in and Sheriff Rogers stormed in with his pistol aimed into the room. Ann swung her pistol at him. "Stop," Rogers ordered.

Ann didn't stop. Sheriff Rogers fired two quick shots. The first one hit Ann in the shoulder, spinning her sideways. The second shot ripped her neck half in two. She was dead before she hit the floor.

My heart was pounding in my chest like a hummingbird on too much sugar water. My throat was as dry as a sick dog's nose. My eyes were as big around as a politician trying to tell the truth.

"I was almost free," my Guardian Angel lamented, but he winked at me.

Sheriff Rogers rolled Reeves over and checked her pulse. I presumed she was dead. There was no doubt Ann was dead. Sheriff Rogers put his pistol back in his holster and glanced at Fisher and Colbert and Jesse.

"They are trying to talk their way out of hell," I said.

Sheriff Rogers sat at the picnic table, took a deep breath, pushed his hat back on his head, and pulled on his moustache. "Son," he said. "This old hick cop, who you never trusted, in fact who you thought might have been involved in the murder of Barbara, has saved your worthless old hippie, Vietnam Veteran, not so good private detective, hide."

"Sheriff," I said. "I've never been a good judge of character."

"Do you think this will get me on TV?" Rogers asked like a little kid who was going to the circus.

"I hope this will get you an Oscar."

"Me too," he said.

"I don't want to sound ungrateful, but it would be nice if you got the keys to these handcuffs out of Ann's pocket and set me free."

Sheriff Rogers smiled at me like a little boy who had caught his sister and her boyfriend naked on the sofa while he unlocked the handcuffs and untied me.

Rubbing my sore wrist I stood up slowly. "How did you know?" I asked Sheriff Rogers.

"I'll tell you later, Roosevelt, first I have to call for help and get this mess all in order. You can do anything you want except leave."

I went outside and gazed at the stars. I went to the barn to check in on Matilda. I heard Sheriff Rogers talking on his radio and with a bounce in my step I headed back to the house.

"Life is wonderful," I told my Guardian Angel.

"Roosevelt," he said. "If I was alive you would give me ulcers."

I smiled.

"I'm glad you are not dead," he said.

"I know. It would be bad on your résumé."

CHAPTER SEVENTEEN
GOODBYE COLORADO

Sheriff Rogers was sitting behind his desk puffing on a Lucky Strike. The smoke drifted through the room like a high-class opium den in Hong Kong. He was leaning back in his chair and had his booted feet up on top of the desk. He was wearing his hat. I ignored his bad hat manners because I was going through a small paranoid attack thinking about second hand smoke, which is insane, because I don't seem to worry about car pollution, which kills more people than cigarettes, industrial pollution, pesticide residue, or the fact fish are full of mercury and our water tastes like a chemical bath.

Already one day had passed since my brush with death. Sheriff Rogers and I hadn't left the line shack until noon, by then the bodies had been photographed and shipped off to Denver, and every police officer in the state, except Hoffman and Hayworth, had stopped by for coffee and donuts. I had to explain everything that had gone on at least ten times. When we finally could leave, Sheriff Rogers went to Ann's house and picked up the box of skin flicks. I drove Matilda to the jail, took a shower and slept in a cell.

Rogers blew a large smoke ring and took his feet off his desk. "The first time we met, I had the feeling you thought I was a suspect. Don't get me wrong, it didn't make me angry, in fact, I got a chuckle out of it. But, what I couldn't figure out was why you would think such a thing?"

"The first day as I was driving to where I camped, I saw you driving off of the dirt road," I said.

"What's strange about that?" Rogers asked.

"Only that you were in the area. Then after I'd found the body, I searched the area and by accident found a pack of Lucky Strikes and a discarded stick match. It stood to reason whoever had killed Barbara had dropped them and the match. You smoke Lucky Strikes and sometimes light them with a match."

"That's a good reason for suspecting me," Sheriff Rogers agreed, "but I don't lose cigarettes. Cigarettes are too expensive."

"During both trips to the camping area, it seemed you went out of your way to destroy evidence, and the fact you didn't take any photographs of the area before the detectives came also aroused my suspicion."

"Investigating murders hasn't exactly been a major part of my work as a small town Sheriff," Rogers said, but I could tell he was slightly offended.

"It also seemed you really didn't want me to stay in the area."

"I had my reasons," he said, but he didn't tell me what they were.

"The second time I got shot at, you arrived on the scene way too fast for me to consider you might have been the shooter."

"I'd gone to Chama," Rogers said, "and happened to be driving back when the call came through."

"You told me that, but I thought you might have been lying. All I can say is, I was completely wrong about you and I want to thank you for saving me."

“You’re welcome,” Rogers said, which surprised me, an ex-marine saying, you're welcome, had to be hard to do.

"Roosevelt, when you by accident showed up in Platoro I was already investigating Ann," Rogers said. "I make it a habit of running checks on people who move into this area. Don't get me wrong, what a person did before they came here doesn't bother me, it's what they do while they're here. Everybody in life has made a mistake. But when I ran Ann and Barbara through N.C.I.C., their sheet was as long as the Antonito phone book. I called Texas and they told me about the skin flick business and that they were daughters of Big Abe Maiden, a well-to-do gangster. A few weeks later a federal boy came through town and informed me the Feds wanted me to keep a close eye on Ann and Barbara. There were rumors they might be getting into child pornography and the Feds thought she might have moved to this area to expand her operation. The best way I could figure out to learn anything was to get close to them - but not too close. This being a small town, it didn't take me long to find out that Fisher, Reeves, the Colbert boys, Barbara, and Ann, were making skin flicks. As I told you, I called the Feds but there is nothing illegal about skin flicks, first amendment rights and all that. After you caught Barbara with a fly, there was no doubt in my mind Ann was behind it. When you moved in with Ann, I figured you had to be one step dumber than a frog but there was no way I could tell you everything I knew because I didn't know if I could trust you. For all I knew, you would make a career move to being a porn star."

"His lead pencil is too short for the porn business," my Guardian Angel said holding his hand out with his thumb and forefinger about two inches apart.

"When you told me Big Abe was killed, I contacted the Feds," Rogers said. "They informed me a woman had been at his house and that was about all they knew. I thought it strange that Ann didn't really seem to care and also the fact she had never really been too concerned about Barbara's body or funeral arrangements. But, there was still no proof that Ann had been involved with Barbara's murder. The day you came by the office and said you were going to Denver I got a call from Texas. It seems Big Abe's phone was bugged and the number was traced to a pay phone here in town. Ann had called him and said a friend of hers was coming to town and could she stay at the house. I did some checking and the day of Big Abe's murder, the only people that couldn't be accounted for from the area were Reeves and Jesse. I figured Jesse might have driven Reeves to the airport and she might have flown to Houston, put a hole in Big Abe's brain, and flown back. Her name wasn't on any flight manifest but there was a Ms. Anna Roves who had flown to Houston on an early morning flight and returned on the red eye. I contacted airline personnel and the lady in question, according to the flight attendants, had worn a wig and fit the body size of Reeves."

"You used good crime solving skills," I said. "I figured Reeves did it only because I saw a suitcase."

Rogers scowled at me. I don't think he likes to be interrupted when he gets on a run.

Rogers continued, "I began sticking to Reeves like mud to a pig's belly. I saw you drive through town on your way back from Denver. It was only by accident that late the next evening I saw Jesse driving your car through town followed by Ann in her Explorer. At first I didn't think anything about it, but about an hour later, I saw Ann come back through town alone. I waited awhile, parked down the road from her house, and knew you weren't there. Something told me you were in trouble or already dead and trouble didn't matter anymore. I didn't think you would leave town and not say goodbye."

"Sheriff, you should move to a big city and become a private detective," I said, adding, "But why did you tell Ann I was going to Denver to see Chavez and Delong?"

"I thought it might make her nervous."

"You used me as bait?" I said in disbelief.

"Why not, you don't have any redeeming value to the world."

"No doubt about that," my Guardian Angel said.

"I have to have a small amount," I said.

Rogers shrugged his shoulders like who cares and continued. "I saw Old Man Colbert drive into town and then leave, and then not too long after that Ranger Fisher drove through town. I followed Fisher and watched him turn off of the highway onto a dirt road that I knew led to an old line shack on Colbert's ranch. I went back to town and when I saw Ann drive by I followed her and watched her also turn down the road. I waited awhile and followed her. About a mile from the house I hid my car in a gully. I was walking toward the house when I heard a vehicle approaching, I hid in a bush. It was Ranger Reeves. When I got to the house I saw Fisher's car and Colbert's truck. I went to the barn and found your car. I was standing by the shed trying to figure out what to do when Reeves came out and got your pistol out of your car. As soon as she was back in the line shack I snuck up to the window and saw you tied up like some two-bit rustler who couldn't even steal sheep. When Reeves pointed the pistol at you and started to squeeze the trigger I shot her. The rest is history," Rogers said.

"Life is all timing," I said.

"Great timing this time, one more second and you'd be talking with Saint Peter," my Guardian Angel said.

"Whatever happened to Hoffman and Hayworth?" I asked Rogers.

"They both have been dismissed without pay pending a review by the board over their conduct."

"Do you think the Colbert boys will sell the ranch?"

"As soon as they can and then they'll go blow their money in Denver and end up driving a truck for the rest of their lives."

"What will happen with Mrs. Fisher?"

Sheriff Rogers shrugged his shoulders.

I stood up, feeling no remorse for Mrs. Fisher, but I did feel bad for the child losing her father.

"I've got something for you," I told Rogers.

I went outside and came back in with my fly rod. "I want you to have this," I said. "I'm never going trout fishing again."

Rogers smiled like a kid who had gotten his first baseball glove.

"It's nice giving people something they like," my Guardian Angel said.

I shook hands with Sheriff Rogers. "I hope you make it to Hawaii and live out your dream," I said. "Tell Willie if he would shave he might find a good woman."

"Good luck, Roosevelt," Rogers said. "You are going to need it."

I turned to leave but turned back around. "I have to tell you this Sheriff," I said. "You should know it is impolite to wear your hat inside."

"I'm the Sheriff and I'll wear my hat wherever I want to," he replied gruffly, but took it off, smiled, and we shook hands again.

Matilda, lady that she is, started right up and I headed toward Denver. I was oblivious to the mountains and the other cars. I withdrew all my cash from the bank and stopped at a truck stop on the west side of town. Sitting at the counter drinking a cup of coffee I started thinking about all the highway cowboys - men strung out on caffeine and the never-ending vibration of their trucks, men who never stay in one place long enough to really know where they are. I felt like one of them but I want roots. I want a home. A home where I could hang my clothes in a closet, get used to the bed, fall in love with a nice lady.

I finished my coffee.

Standing by Matilda a new Lincoln with Arizona license plates went by.

"It's warm there in the winter. I've heard all the women wear short, short pants and tiny tank tops and have a tan all year long," my Guardian Angel said and licked his lips.

"My dad taught me how to play golf," I told him. "Before I went in the Army I was a pretty good stick."

"I don't think you could get into trouble on a golf course," my Guardian Angel said.

I started Matilda. I could see myself on the first tee of a golf course in Phoenix, wearing checkered short pants, a striped shirt, green golf shoes, and a straw hat.

"You might meet your soul mate in Phoenix. I doubt you'll find your purpose in life, but one out of two isn't bad," my Guardian Angel said.

"A good female friend would be nice," I said. "I might be too old for love."

"People are never too old for love," my Guardian Angel said.

"Most of the time I feel like a Bob Dylan song, slightly out of tune," I said.

"If you would listen to me you wouldn't get into so many jams," my Guardian said.

I pointed Matilda down the road towards Phoenix. I rolled the window down. The wind felt good blowing through my long hair. The sound of the tires on the highway relaxed me. The steady purr of Matilda's underpowered engine had a soothing quality to it. But no more than twenty minutes went by and I started worrying. I wondered if I still have a slice with my long irons and can't make a three-foot putt to save my soul.

"You know, Roosevelt," my Guardian Angel said with a wary tone to his voice. "On second thought, knowing you, I bet you can fall into a whole bunch of trouble on a golf course."

“Pea Brain,” I said. “Don’t rain on my parade.” But I smiled at him.

THE END

OTHER BOB ROOSEVELT MYSTERIES

DOULBE BOGEY MURDER – BOOK ONE
TROUT FISHING FOR BODIES – BOOK TWO
DOUBLE BOGEY MURDER – BOOK THREE
FROGS DON'T CROAK IN THE WINTER – BOOK FOUR

COMING SOON
BEACH BUM TANGO

For more of Robert K. Swisher Jr's many novels visit
http://www.swisherbooks.com/

www.ingramcontent.com/pod-product-compliance
Lightning Source LLC
Chambersburg PA
CBHW051922110726
47902CB00002B/386